EMPORIA PUBLIC LIBRARY

In Memory

Of

Evelyn Jernigan

One
Glorious
Ambition

Center Point
Large Print

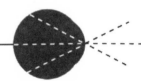

**This Large Print Book carries the
Seal of Approval of N.A.V.H.**

One Glorious Ambition

THE COMPASSIONATE CRUSADE OF DOROTHEA DIX

JANE KIRKPATRICK

CENTER POINT LARGE PRINT
THORNDIKE, MAINE

This Center Point Large Print edition is published in the year 2013 by arrangement with WaterBrook Press, an imprint of the Crown Publishing Group, a division of Random House, Inc., New York.

All Scripture quotations and paraphrases are taken from the King James Version.

This book is a work of historical fiction based closely on real people and real events. Details that cannot be historically verified are purely products of the author's imagination.

The text of this Large Print edition is unabridged. In other aspects, this book may vary from the original edition. Printed in the United States of America on permanent paper. Set in 16-point Times New Roman type.

ISBN: 978-1-61173-716-5

Library of Congress Cataloging-in-Publication Data

Kirkpatrick, Jane, 1946–
One glorious ambition : the compassionate crusade of Dorothea Dix / Jane Kirkpatrick. — Center Point Large Print edition.
pages cm
ISBN 978-1-61173-716-5 (Library binding : alk. paper)
1. Dix, Dorothea Lynde, 1802–1887—Fiction. 2. Large type books.
  I. Title.
PS3561.I712O54 2013
813′.54—dc23

2013002177

To Dr. Dean Brooks
and his compassionate daughters:
Ulista, India, and Dennie

Cast of Characters

Dorothea Dix	New England child of the 1800s
Charles and Joseph Dix	Dorothea's younger brothers
Madam Dix	Dorothea's grandmother
Joseph and Mary Dix	Dorothea's parents
Sarah and Mary Fiske	Dorothea's aunt and cousin
Anne Heath and the Fesser Family	Dorothea's friends
William Ellery Channing	pastor of Federal Street Church in Boston
Elizabeth Channing	Channing's wife, friend and supporter of Dorothea
Sarah Gibbs	Channing's sister-in-law, friend and supporter of Dorothea

George Emerson	educator and friend of Dorothea
Horace Mann	educator, legislator, supporter of Dorothea
Samuel Howe	director of the School for the Blind, legislator
Elizabeth and William Rathbone	Dorothea's English friends
Thaddeus Harris	Dorothea's uncle
Marianna Davenport Dix Cutter	Dorothea's cousin
Grace Cutter	Dorothea's cousin
John and Jane Bell	Tennessee senator and his wife
James and Sarah Polk	president and first lady
John Adams Dix	legislator during Dorothea's campaign

Abram Simmons	an incarcerated person relieved of his reason
Millard Fillmore	vice president and president of the United States, friend and supporter of Dorothea's work
Abigail and Abby Fillmore	first lady and daughter of Millard Fillmore
Cyrus Butler	industrialist and philanthropist
*Madeleine	a mentally ill woman cared for by her brother
*Charles	a child in need of mental health care in Scotland

*representative of patients Dorothea encountered

If I am cold, they are cold;
if I am weary, they are distressed;
if I am alone, they are abandoned.
DOROTHEA DIX

Give me one glorious ambition for my life
To know and follow hard after You
MARK ALTROGGE,
"ONE PURE AND HOLY PASSION"

As ye have done it unto one
of the least of these my brethren,
ye have done it unto me.
MATTHEW 25:40

PART
One

One

Like Orphans in the Chaos

1814

"I'm going to take care of us, so please don't cry." Dorothea thumbed the tears from her brother's blue-gray eyes, eyes the color of her own. "I'll make it better." He nodded, uncertain, she could tell.

The cold air, as stinging as finger slaps, bit at Dorothea's face as she waved one last time at her four-year-old brother, Charles, then pushed the door closed behind her and entered the Massachusetts dawn.

After two hours of walking, hoping the rain would stop, she shivered and her teeth chattered. Maybe this wasn't such a good plan. It was forty miles to Orange Court, their grandmother's house. A blast of wind rattled the elm trees and jerked late-clinging weeds from their branches, a few jabbing her already numb face. The snow-speckled grass proved better for walking, so she paralleled the muddy cart trail whenever she could. Eight miles passed before she came to a small village. No one asked about a child trudging along alone. No one noticed a shivery child. Not even the smith hammering at his forge raised his eyes as she halted briefly, warming her hands, smelling the hot metal as it singed and spattered in the water. People tended to their own lives, not worrying over wayward children.

She had eight more miles to go before reaching a stage that could take her the next thirty miles or so to Boston. She knew the way. She'd taken coins from her father while he slept, just enough to get her to the city. Her ankles ached, and her feet were as stiff as hammers. Outside the village, she slipped in the mud, her thin-soled shoes caked with greasy earth. She twisted to catch her balance and couldn't and landed hard on her bottom. The rain gained force and pelted down, turning to snow, the white flakes silent as death. Why should she get up? Would it be so bad to escape into the cold of nothingness, forget this challenge of being alive and rescuing her brother? The cold could simply rock her to sleep.

A crow *caw-cawed* above her. Charles loved to watch the crows. *For you, Charles. I'll keep going for you.* She dragged herself onward toward the goal, praying she walked the right path.

"What do you want?" The woman's eyes searched behind Dorothea, then back to her. "We've no need of rags to buy. And if we did, that would happen at the kitchen." She began to close the heavy mahogany door. Dusk hovered at the eaves. This was the second day of Dorothea's escape, and she had walked the last few miles in the snow beneath a pewter sky.

Dorothea thought she remembered the woman as the housekeeper, but it had been a few years since her last visit. "Please. I'd like to see Madam Dix."

"Madam Dix has no time for urchins."

"My name is Dorothea Dix. I'm her grand-daughter."

"What?" The woman squinted. Dorothea hoped she could see the same high forehead, the firm chin that her grandfather said she had gained from her grandmother. Perhaps her enunciation, clear and precise, would remind her of Madam Dix.

"Please. I've come all the way from Worcester. I've been here before, with my parents, Joseph and Mary Dix. I know where the library is, where the clock sits in the hall."

The woman frowned. "Clock's been moved."

"My chin. It's a Lynde chin, my grand-mother's." She touched her dirty gloves to her face. "See?"

The woman pressed her lips together and scowled. "Go around to the kitchen. I'll see if Madam Dix is willing to receive you."

Dorothea pulled her cloak around her neck and walked to the side of the brick mansion, across the snow-covered lawn, past the marble statues that marked the entrance to the garden that harbored the Dix pear tree, her grandfather's pride and joy. Before her grandfather's death, her family had come here when they had no food or lacked money for wood or had burned their last candles. They'd throw themselves on her grandfather's mercy, asking for assistance, insisting that this time would surely be the last. For a few days there would be comfort and hours in the library and warm food when one was hungry. But soon they'd be on their way to whatever temporary housing arrangement her grandparents could make for her father and his family.

Her father might have been successful once. He'd trained at Harvard. But he lacked "ambition," she heard her grandmother tell her father, Dorothea's face hot from hearing her father chastised. He'd even swapped land in Vermont for books. "Land," her grandmother said in disgust when she heard this, "is where wealth is." It was only because her parents had imposed themselves on friends in Worcester that she was close enough to get to her grandmother's. Then two evenings ago, when her parents failed to notice how the "friend" let his fat fingers linger hot on Dorothea's shoulder while he praised her "pretty face" or spoke of how "mature and graceful" she was for one merely twelve, his eyes like a wolf's, his smile a licked lip, she had made her decision.

The kitchen door opened and the cook, a smile on her face, introduced herself as "Mehetable Hathorne. Call me Cookie," and motioned her inside. Dorothea saw the back of the housekeeper and she said "thank you" loud enough for the departing woman to hear. At least she was inside. Whether she would be allowed to stay, whether she could convince her grandmother to send for her brother and parents, that would be up to Dorothea's persuasive ways. She was inside Orange Court! Half the battle won.

"Where are your parents?" Dorothea's grandmother stood before her, black cap tied beneath her chin, her hands over a hickory stick she used as a cane. She was not much taller than Dorothea. "And Charles?"

"In Worcester. With friends. It's . . . it's not good there, Grandmamma. Not good at home either. Papa's . . . consuming again, and Mother is . . . sleepy and when she wakes, she's . . . wild-eyed and unpredictable. Or she doesn't seem to know Charles and I are even there. I have to cook and clean the sheets and wash his clothes and—"

"Complaints are unbecoming." The older woman's jaw set hard like the flat irons on the shelf behind her. The scent of onions cooking at the kitchen hearth brought water to Dorothea's mouth. Cookie bent to her work as though she were alone in the room.

" 'Tis not a complaint, Grandmamma, but

bold truth. You always told me to tell the truth."

Her grandmother tapped her hand on the cane. "Take off that wet cloak and cap, Dorothea." The girl complied and pulled a knot of her thick chestnut hair behind her ear. "How did you get here, anyway?"

"I walked. And took the stage partway."

"Indeed. Well, what would you have me do then? I'm an old woman with limited resources. I can't take you all on."

"Take in Charles and me, then. We could bring in wood for you . . . and cook." She glanced at the cook's back. "I'd look after Charles. He's a bright boy, interested in many things." A knot worked in her throat as she thought of her parents and how quickly she had stopped pleading for them. "We'd be no trouble, really, we wouldn't. And you'd have . . . companionship." Her grandmother only snorted. "If you took us all in, maybe Papa could help fix the shutters and he could look after Mama—"

"Companionship you say? What need have I with the companionship of undisciplined children?"

"There'll be a third." Dorothea dropped her eyes as she spoke. "It's imperative that you help us now."

"Imperative!" the older woman grunted.

Dorothea wasn't sure if it was the idea that she had spoken indirectly of a pregnancy that

18

distressed her grandmother or if the thought of yet another mouth to worry over in her second son's life caused the woman to now purse her lips. It was Dorothea's strongest argument—the safe arrival of another Dix. They'd need the refuge of her grandmother's large home in Boston if they were all going to survive, especially a baby. Couldn't her grandmother see the logic in that?

Dorothea's emotions swirled like leaves in a whirlpool in the continuing silence. She heard her heart beat faster at her temples. Snow outside accumulated on the sills of the wavy glass windows.

"You're our only hope." Her voice broke. *I must not cry.* She stiffened her narrow shoulders. She stood as rigid as wrought iron. She knew one thing for certain: if anyone ever pleaded with her for help as she now beseeched her grandmother, she would find a way to meet the depth of the request. "We suffer," she said.

"Everyone suffers. Some more than others. There's nothing to be done for it. The suffering will always be with you. Scripture states it. Time you learned the lesson."

"The child will come right after Christmas, Grandmamma. Don't let it struggle too. And Charles. He's only a child!"

"Then your mother will need you much more than I will, Dorothea." The woman's voice softened into a sigh. "You must go back, girl. I simply can't take you all in again. I'm sorry. Your father has made his bed and he must lie in it. Which apparently he does quite often."

With that the woman turned away, the brim of her day cap fluttering with the brusqueness of the turn. As she pushed her wide hips through the narrow door she stopped.

She's changed her mind! Dorothea thought.

Instead, the woman leaned toward the cook and spoke quietly, then she moved into the safety of the mansion, a small dog that Dorothea hadn't noticed before following at her heels.

"It'll take them a bit to bring the carriage around." The cook turned to her. "You come warm yourself at this fire and have a bite to eat. I'll fix you a basket to take with you. For your little brother and your parents."

"Thank you, missus . . ." Dorothea dropped her eyes. She couldn't remember the name of the woman, the one person who was at least going to give her stomach comfort before she was sent back into chaos.

"Cookie." She motioned for Dorothea to sit at the table.

Dorothea removed her wet wrap to hang beside the hearth.

"Your shoes too, dearie. May as well get them a little drier while you sit."

Dorothea sank like a weary dog onto the chair, removed her soaked shoes, her ungloved fingers pulling at the wet leather laces and hooks while she watched Cookie gather a spatter of potatoes and onions from the hearth and a slice of dried beef from the larder. A butter round appeared with a loaf of bread.

"Eat now," she said.

Lifting the bread took all the strength Dorothea had. Cookie placed a piece of ham in a basket and added a round of cheese, and the girl saw her nestle dried pears in a small stone pot, then put a few more pieces of the fruit on the table for Dorothea.

"Don't be too hard on your grandmother." Cookie continued loading the basket with food, then tied the white cloth into a big bow of protection. "She's a good woman. Done much for this district ever since your grandfather's death. She's likely carried your parents across many a swollen stream."

Dorothea wiped her mouth with the back of her hand, breadcrumbs tumbling onto the bodice of her dress. "But we could assist her. I could."

"She might not say it, but I suspect she's proud you come to her for help. She just can't give it to you the way you're askin'. But that's what we're about, you know, we women. We find a way over troubled water, even if it has to be a boat bobbing in the currents rather than a bridge."

Dorothea ate slowly, savoring the food and warmth and taking in the wisdom of this ordinary woman. It was apparently all she would get from Orange Court. Who knew what trouble she would face when she was returned to Worcester. The outrage of her father for disappearing. Would her mother have noticed? She sighed. Her journey and her words had failed.

Two

The Arrival

Dorothea's newest brother, Joseph, screamed into the world during a January storm. Snow drifted near the eaves of the Vermont cabin Dorothea's grandmother had arranged for them to rent just after Christmas. Dorothea imagined the conversations held between her grandmother, aunts, and uncles as they decided what was to be done about her father and his growing family. This latest settlement was a farm where a drafty lean-to served as a workshop for her father's floundering printing business. Now, a year later, Joseph's squalls could be heard even in the small shed where Dorothea sat at the bookbinding table. With each cut of the cloth, each swipe of the glue on the board cover, Dorothea's mind said, *Pick up Joseph! Pick up that child!*

"I should help Mama." She set her bookbinding tools on the bench and stood.

"Your mother must tend to a few of her duties." Her father, tall and some would say handsome, ordered her to sit down. "Finish what you've started."

Charles sat across from her at the table, his small hands unable to do much except offer her the brush when she put her palm out for it. The smell of the glue appeared to make him sleepy. She picked up the paper punch and sewing needle. The crunch of the punch through the paper reminded her of the sound of summer beetles squished when she walked. She tried to distract herself from the feel and the sound by remembering her grandfather's library, books full of facts and sprinkled with pictures of plants and faraway places hidden beneath thin protective pages. She drew the needle and thread through the latest hole, pulling it tight to hold the document.

Joseph's crying continued.

This work was as tedious as shelling walnuts, a task that left her fingers stained black for days but with more sustenance to show for it at the end of the day. If they made books for paying clients, there'd at least be some hope of coins. Instead, her father *bought* loose sheets and wrote about his newfound religion. He bound the tracts and then sold them to support his family, but it was never enough to cover even the cost of the paper. At least he hadn't commissioned Dorothea or

Charles into selling the articles on street corners. Yet as soon as the snow melted, her father would head to the village in the late afternoons, tracts in hand to sell, and leave Dorothea to tend to her mother and brothers.

In the year they had been in Vermont, nothing much had changed except for Joseph's arrival. Dorothea's mother floated through the days often unaware that a child cried until Dorothea lifted Joseph, changed his napkin, and handed him to her mother for nursing. It was Dorothea who urged her mother to eat so she could nurture the baby, and it was Dorothea who reminded her that it was time they heated water for washing the family's undergarments and nightclothes. Dorothea let the sheets go some-times for a fortnight or more because the effort of heating and stirring the heavy cloth in hot water drained her, made her short of breath, and caused her to cough and feel sick. She could afford none of that. She had to be strong to care for the family.

But Dorothea also saw her mother gently hold her youngest, brushing his dark hair with her long fingers, repeating soft admonitions of "Shhh . . . shhh." She didn't know what it was, but a strange, pulling feeling rose up her spine when she watched this display of affection, felt herself grow small as she observed her mother's kindness in tenderly stroking Joseph's fine brown hair.

What was wrong with Dorothea that her mother could not give such warmth to Charles or her only daughter?

Still, one day when Dorothea complained about the binding work and her father's disappearance each afternoon, her mother defended him.

"You should be proud of your father. He works so hard to support us."

Didn't Grandmamma support them with her payment at the village store accounts and the rent for this farmhouse?

"But Papa has so little to show for his efforts." Dorothea set the steaming broth on the bedside table where her mother lay ailing, always ailing.

"This does not diminish his goodness. It's the work that matters and that his heart is in it."

Dorothea remembered the interchange as rare both for her mother's defense of her father and the kernel of wisdom that seeped out between her mother's sighs, her moments of wild-eyed rage, or endless sleepiness even when she was awake.

This past winter had been different because of heavy snows. Her father spent more time binding the books and less time selling. That kept him around the house more, and it meant even fewer pennies for candles or corn. He brewed the ale necessary in every household, teaching Dorothea the skill "that every wife needs to know."

"Dorothea!" Her father pounded the table with his fist as she worked in the bindery. "You've missed a length. Where's your mind? Stay with your task!"

"Yes, Papa." She'd been daydreaming more often, not certain why.

"And you!" He swiped Charles on the side of his head with the back of his hand. "Wake up! This is no time for sleep. Do that at night."

"We can't always." Dorothea raised her voice. "The baby—"

The switch stung across her knuckles. She hadn't even seen her father grab the willow he kept beneath his desk.

"Speak when you are spoken to, girl. You listen well to your betters. You hear me?"

She sat hunched over, shivering, awaiting the next blow.

"I spoke to you, girl!" She felt the wind of the switch slice the air. She shrank and waited. But it was Charles who wailed.

She opened her eyes. "Don't hurt him. I hear you, Papa. I hear."

"You're a curse. All of you." He stomped from the lean-to into the house where Joseph cried a hiccup cry, and she heard her father shout at her mother, "Pick up the brat."

Dorothea motioned to Charles. "Let me see your back."

Her brother stood and lifted his thin shirt, his spine as bony as a carcass forgotten on the forest floor. He shivered.

"I'll get salve. It didn't break the skin this time. Just very red."

"It stings." He shook.

"I know it does. I know. I'm sorry. I'm the one that upset Papa." She wrapped her arms around him, careful not to press against this latest wound. She looked into his blue-gray eyes. "Better now?" She must not daydream. She must concentrate. She must be the mother hen with Charles her chick. Joseph too. She prayed she would be forgiven for causing her brother to suffer.

On April 6, 1816, two days after Dorothea's forgotten fourteenth birthday, when the roads were clear and the spring melt ran in rivulets down the hillsides, a wagon arrived at the farmhouse. Orange Court's faded crest was printed on its side.

"Is there meat in there?" It had been months since Dorothea had tasted good meat. Her father was a poor hunter. So rabbit more often than venison filled the family's watery stews.

"Whatever does my mother want now?" Her father stood at the lean-to door, arms folded over his chest. He rubbed his back against the door. The milder weather with ferns spearing through the forest floor might have softened him. He hadn't struck either of his children this week. He'd begun making sales again. He'd even allowed Dorothea to feed a stray cat after she argued that the animal would keep the mice population down. Field mice wreaked havoc on paper and books.

"Maybe she's sent food."

He pushed Dorothea to the side. "Is she sending us even farther into the provinces to rid us from her sight?"

The driver smiled at Dorothea and tugged on his beard. "She sent letters ahead. Said you'd be ready."

"We've had no mail for weeks," her father said.

Dorothea pushed her way around and approached the wagon. She stood on tiptoes to look over the high sidepiece, her hands resting on the smooth wood. There were baskets inside! She could smell the smoked hams. Charles pushed against her skirts. She dropped her hand to his shoulder, holding him to her, patting him in comfort. "Grandmamma sent food."

"Yes, miss. She sent hams, potatoes. Sacks of wheat." He cleared his throat, glanced at her father, then said to Dorothea. "And you're to return with me."

"We are?" She smiled, squeezed Charles's shoulder. Her heart felt light as a feather.

"Just you, miss. Her granddaughter, she said."

"Just me?"

"Take her where?"

"To Worcester, sir. To your sister's, I should

think." He handed her father a letter sealed with Orange Court wax.

"My mother thinks she can get whatever she wants."

Would her father fight to keep her, insist that her work was essential for his success? Who would do the laundry? make the candles and soap? plant the vegetables in the garden this spring? Her mother wouldn't, couldn't. Her father removed something from the letter, folded it into his blouse, then read out loud beside the wagon. "You're to live with my sister, your aunt Sarah, and her dear doctor husband. You'll have a fine time of it." His lip curled and he spat.

"We're not going to Orange Court? But that's what I asked for."

"You're responsible for this?" He struck her, the slap like a tree branch, quick and stinging. "About time you learned the lesson that my mother serves her own master." He began to unload the wagon, tossing a sack of grain over his wiry shoulders and carrying it into the barn.

"May I . . . go?" She rubbed her cheek. What of Charles? Who would look after her mother and Joseph? Her thoughts bounced around like rocks in a wagon. Her letters had gotten through to her grandmother, but her pleas were only partially heeded. She wasn't going to be living at Orange Court. She would live with the Fiskes in Worcester. She barely remembered them. This wasn't what she had prayed for. She squeezed Charles's shoulder as he looked up at her, those blue-gray eyes they shared wearing confusion. If she went, she'd be saved from gluing the last headband onto a book board, saved from having to punch another hole. But as she looked into her brother's eyes, the reprieve was like the last note of a funeral dirge. The mournful song was over. She'd chosen: a future of loneliness without Charles and baby Joseph.

"Don't forget to feed the cat," Dorothea whispered to Charles as she pushed her satchel up to the driver. "It will keep Papa happy. And know that I'll send for you. I will. I just don't know when."

Charles nodded and lifted his slender hand. He was the only member of the family to wave good-bye.

Three

Relative Rule

The room that cousin Mary Fiske showed Dorothea to was larger than the farmhouse in Vermont. A fireplace invited sitting, with logs crackling as winter seemed destined to crush the

New England spring. The bed with four posts and a thick down comforter promised luxury Dorothea had known only as a small child at Orange Court. Even during her week with her grandmother before being sent here, she had slept beneath quilts, but nothing as splendid as the goose-down comfort of this room.

"The maid will help you unpack," Mary told her. Blond curls bounced from the cluster at the back of her head. Three years older than Dorothea, Mary moved like a fawn, light and graceful on her feet. She likely never took a spill into snow-laden mud.

"I have little to unpack." Dorothea lifted her carpet valise onto the smooth walnut bench at the foot of the bed. She became aware of the smell of candle wax, and Charles came to mind, causing her throat to close. They'd made candles together. "I'm sure I can do it myself." She opened her valise.

Mary shook her finger at her. "You must discover how to deal with maids and gardeners and such." She fluffed her hair in the mirror as she moved toward the door. "Best to begin now. Maids need to feel useful. Papa will join us for dinner, and then Mama and I will meet with you in the parlor and discuss the rules." Dorothea blinked at these last words. "Oh, they aren't odious. They're meant to get us married." She giggled. "There are any number of skills required, and Madam Dix wasn't certain which you had or lacked. We must assess that in order to properly prepare you."

"Will there be time to attend school?"

"Girls don't go to school. But there will be a tutor, as Papa is quite conciliatory toward girls. But marriage, dear cousin, is the goal of every young woman."

"Must it?" She pressed her fingers against her temples as though massaging a wound. How wonderful it would be to be so certain of one's future.

"Oh, quite." Mary picked up a porcelain vase and set it down by the washbowl and rearranged the roses. "I dried these myself. I'll teach you." She swirled back to Dorothea. "What would we do without husbands? Be forlorn and alone, living with Mama and Papa. I have every intention of making sure *that* does not happen. You should make sure of that too."

With that, Mary took her small, almost childlike frame through the door. She waved in the maid, who curtsied as Mary left.

"Will your trunks follow, miss?"

Dorothea opened her palms to her valise. "All my worldly goods."

"They will hardly fill the armoire, miss."

"You're right. And your name is?"

"Beatrice, miss."

"Well, Beatrice, the armoire is much larger than

I need. And I'm certain you have other things to tend to, so please, let me finish here." She curtsied to the maid and said, "It's a pleasure to make your acquaintance."

"Oh, miss, you must never defer to me. You haven't made my acquaintance. People like me never truly meet people like you."

"I suspect I'm more like you than the Fiskes."

"Oh, you mustn't say such things, Miss Dix. Madam Fiske will think us too familiar."

"Yet familiar is just what I'm looking for."

"It cannot be with me, miss."

Dorothea sighed and stepped back to allow Beatrice to unpack her things. She may be standing in the light of luxury, but she belonged in the shadows.

Dorothea splashed fresh water onto her tired face and made her way to the dining room, where she was introduced to her uncle, the physician, and where the soup was served in silence, the main course of lamb and fresh greens eaten with brief mentions of her uncle's day, and the dessert taken up with Mary's chatter about the ball they would be attending within the week. Then the three women retired to the parlor.

Dorothea scanned the room stuffed with fine furniture, needlework beneath the vases of flowers made of human hair, suggesting skill and patience. A small collection of books of Thomas

Gray's poetry lined the round table at the end of the divan. She would explore these books later, if allowed. Her cousin produced a basket with yarn and needles.

"Do you knit?" Mary asked.

Dorothea stared at the yarn mass as though it was a tangle of snakes. "I've never knitted. Only stitched, a little."

"I see." Her aunt Sarah started to rise but grabbed at her hip.

Seeing her discomfort, Dorothea said, "May I help you?"

Aunt Sarah sank back and patted the space next to her on the settee, and Dorothea carried the yarn basket and slipped in beside her. Her aunt placed her hands over Dorothea's as she showed her two stitches, knit and purl. Dorothea's fingers felt like stumps, but she liked the warmth of her aunt's touch. She could repair her brother's pants and stitch her own hems, but no one had shown her how to knit. She also couldn't remember the last time an adult had touched her with kindness. She felt her face grow warm and blinked back tears.

"I can assist with your needlework lessons," Mary said. "Until my marriage."

"Which hasn't been established as yet," her aunt reminded her. She patted Dorothea's hands and said, "We'll carry on this lesson later, and yes, Mary, you may also instruct. For now, let's discuss the household routines and how Dorothea might fit into them."

She enumerated the schedule of early morning readings of the Bible and other chosen works and time in the library. Needlework would follow, along with arranging flowers and conferring with the cook about the supplies needed, then a light lunch that her aunt assured her would be more than the graham porridge and potatoes Dorothea was accustomed to. Tutoring in French, calligraphy lessons, occasional outings to the stable for riding lessons, and preparation for evening gatherings would end the day. "I've placed paper and lead in your room so you may write letters to your grandmother and brothers and parents if you choose."

Not a single moment punching together her father's books. She had entered the gates of heaven.

Her aunt cleared her throat. "This is a transition, Dorothea. Or might we call you Dolly?"

Dorothea hadn't considered that name, but it was lighter, less formidable. "Dolly would be fine."

"Yes, well, your time here is a transition from your childhood to being an adult. Goodness knows you look like an adult. You're as tall as your uncle." Dorothea sloped her shoulders, hoping to lessen the effect of her five-foot-seven-inch frame. She pulled on the worn lace of her sleeves and revealed slender wrists and clothes not suited for her fourteen years.

"Sitting up straight is a womanly thing to do. I encourage it and wish I could, but my bones . . ." Sarah rubbed her hip. "Never mind my afflictions." She stared at Dorothea for a moment, then said, "You are quite beautiful, child. You have lovely skin, thick hair. And a melodious voice. Quite . . . engaging."

"Her exotic eyebrows should attract attention," Mary noted.

"Yes. Nicely arched brows that won't need painting—not that I would allow such a thing. Good body composition."

Dorothea squirmed on the divan. These were compliments, but she felt like a horse being auctioned.

"Your goal, Dolly, is to meet a man who will take you without dowry, as my brother has frittered away his inheritance. It will be the only way you can secure your future needs."

"Yes ma'am." Dorothea dropped her eyes, stared at the needles holding her fingers hostage. She would do all that was required, anticipating regular food, a warm bed, and access to the library and all the many books, medical and philosophical and botanical. As well as that poetry collection. How her brothers would prosper in such an environment! If only she could bring them too.

"Do you have any questions?"

She swallowed. "I wonder if my brothers might not be allowed the shelter you're offering me. Charles is sturdy and could help with the sheep and geese I saw on the lawn. Joseph . . . could teach me how to care for a child, something every woman must know. Is that not true?"

Only the wood in the fireplace cracked into the silence that followed. Finally her aunt said, "Girls must be wary of asking for more when they've been given much. Mothering will come to you when the time comes . . . and your brothers are not your responsibility. They're your father's."

Dorothea started to protest, but her aunt raised her hand for silence. "For now, you're the child my mother deems ready for proper training. She's sent help to your father, though whether he will appreciate it is questionable."

Dorothea shrank back as her aunt reached toward her cheek. The look of surprise on her aunt's face told Dorothea that no one had ever struck this woman. Perhaps here Dorothea wouldn't be struck either.

"I only wished to push that thick ringlet of hair behind your ear," she said. "So lustrous."

Dorothea pressed her hair behind her ear herself, her hands shaking. "I'll do my best to be of help here. I know I'll learn many things." She wanted to learn how to make a life where she could one day bring her brothers to be with her.

She would do her best to be a mouse in the corner, listening, obeying, doing what she was told, and hoping for a suitable mate who would allow her to have her family with her. And bridle her tongue. A girl must be careful not to ask for too much.

Dorothea spent the first night staring at the high ceiling of her bedroom in the Fiske home. The down comforter weighed on her chest. She was with family but so alone. What was Charles doing? Was her mother changing baby Joseph? He had just begun walking when Dorothea left. She stifled a racking cough, one that often came in the spring. She wondered what might happen if she became ill in this new place. Would they send her back? Did she want to go back? No, she must find a way to help her brothers—from here.

She rose, lit a candle, and began writing. The lead felt different. It must be the more expensive Faber brand from Germany, not the Thoreau pencils from New England that she was used to. She found the writing soothed her, and she poured out her sadness at being here alone. She wondered if her father or mother would even read her letters. She hoped they would so Charles and Joseph would know they were in her heart.

Returning to her bed, she prayed for her brothers and for herself, asking that she might find a way to use this time of strangeness and confusion for their good or someone's good, to be made stronger, turning her despair into healing others if not herself. Then she blew out the candle and let the sleep of exhaustion overtake her. Tomorrow would bring what it would.

Four

Instruction

Monsieur Brun arrived at the Fiske home without books but carrying lead and paper and instruction.

"*Brun* means a person with brown hair," he told Dorothea. "I should like to have been named Monsieur Chevalier, which means knight. But alas we live with what we are given, *oui* mademoiselle?"

"*Oui*," she said and curtsied, then caught herself, not certain if he was a servant like Beatrice or an elder to whom she should defer.

"None of that." He motioned her to stand. "Now then. I will only use the French for our lessons."

"But how will I know what you're saying?" A flutter of butterflies invaded her stomach.

Monsieur Brun said something in French and then pointed to the desk at which she sat, giving her a French word. The rest of the morning was filled with nouns. Dorothea smiled when he

39

returned to a candle or a desk or paper, and she easily remembered the words. This wasn't work at all! She loved the flow of the language, liked the strange sounds even when she didn't know what he was saying, and seemed able to repeat them with the proper inflection. At the close of the lesson he spoke again in English and wrote out several words and told her she must learn to write them before his next lesson in a week.

"You did very well, mademoiselle. A sure student with a lovely timbre to your voice." He clicked his heels and bent at the waist as he handed her a list of fifty words. "I shall tell Madam Fiske and will look forward to your progress. She will be pleased perhaps that one in her family takes easily to the languages."

"Thank you." She dropped her eyes at the compliments, as rare in her world as night-blooming cereus in a cold northern spring. "I may yet disappoint you as the lessons become more difficult." She often disappointed.

"I see it as a gift, your felicity with the language. It is not Miss Mary's gift." His blue eyes twinkled. "But I will do as you suggest and not make the comparison." He said the last word with his lilting French accent.

Throughout the day a bubble of joy rose up in Dorothea at the memory of Monsieur Brun's compliments. By evening's end, when she wrote to her brother, she tempered the joy. After all, he was in a miserable state, and she had no right to joy while he suffered and she was helpless to relieve him.

"Miss Dix. It is a pleasure to meet you." The tall man wore a collarless white shirt, black home-spun pants, and a tweed jacket. He tipped his hat to her. "It is my understanding you have never ridden a horse?"

Dorothea ran her hand along the withers of the large animal they stood beside in the stable of the Fiskes' neighbors, her palms flat against its flesh, the scent of the animal a blend of sweat and hay. Mary had already mounted and now rode in the distance, along with two friends.

"I've only made the acquaintance with cart horses."

"And a fine family line those old cart horses descend from."

Dorothea had not thought much about the lineage of horses, but she said, "Yes. Predictable, hardworking, and usually gentle with children."

He lifted a bushy eyebrow. "All attributes of a good wife."

Dorothea laughed. "Oh, Mr. Frank. What would your wife say to such a comparison?"

"I have no wife."

"Your boldness suggests why."

Her instructor laughed, his bearded mouth an O of delight. "I think we shall have a good time at your lessons, Miss Dix. Shall we begin?"

The mare chosen for her was named Mercy. She stood firm while Mr. Frank walked Dorothea around the animal, let her run her hands down the legs and gently pick up the hoof to show her how to check for small stones or wounds that might have been overlooked. He had Dorothea stand in front and breathe into the horse's nostrils and let Mercy breathe back at her.

"That's how she'll remember you," he told her as she stroked the mare's velvet nose.

When he thought she was ready, Mr. Frank assisted Dorothea into the saddle and straightened her skirts around the sidesaddle's hook.

Mr. Frank pointed out that Mercy kept her head straight, didn't brush back to nip at Dorothea's knee nor lay her ears back with the knowledge that a novice was in the saddle. Instead, the horse, led by Mr. Frank, walked straight into a small paddock area where Dorothea was led around until she recognized what Mr. Frank told her to be aware of: the subtle movement of the horse's ears, the shift in pace if Dorothea leaned forward or held the reins too tightly. She felt like a baby bird perched high in a nest, a bird that could be pushed off in a moment.

"A light hand is always best," her instructor told her when she pulled on the reins and the horse lifted her head and stopped. "Never pull too hard. You're charming her in a way, letting her gain confidence that you know what you're doing. Once that message is communicated, the two of you will form a bond not likely broken. Are you feeling secure enough to let me release my hand?"

Dorothea nodded though her heart pounded. She licked her lips and tightened her grip on the reins. She thought of nothing else except staying on.

Mr. Frank let loose his hand, and Mercy picked up her pace. Dorothea shifted slightly. She became aware of herself in the presence of power, the give and take of movement between rider and horse. She looked ahead at the trees outside the paddock, heard Mary and her friends laughing in the distance. She had no desire to join them. Riding Mercy was enough. Feeling the strength of the animal and knowing that her hands sent signals through the reins gave her comfort though she didn't know why.

She pulled back on the reins then, and the horse sidestepped and shook her big head, the bit rattling like loose chains against a steel door. Mercy halted, then danced around, pitching Dorothea forward. Her hands grew wet and she hoped she wasn't sending messages of fright to the horse that danced to the other side now, twisting her head at her rider. Dorothea tried to remember if she should let loose or hold tighter, then the horse leaped forward.

Dorothea chewed at her lip. She moved her knees, movement that seemed to confuse Mercy into a trot. Dorothea was off balance, grabbing at the mane with one hand. She held the reins tighter, both in one hand now instead of one rein in each.

"Lighten your hand!" Mr. Frank shouted. "You're giving her too many messages!"

Yes, a lighter touch. Against her instincts, Dorothea lowered her hands and loosened the reins. Immediately, Mercy slowed to a gentle walk, and Dorothea's heart stopped beating at its rushing rate.

"I'm so sorry, so sorry."

Mercy twisted her head around at the sound of her voice, and Dorothea saw the long lashes flutter before she turned back. The mare walked slowly. Dorothea caught her breath, then pulled a rein against Mercy's chestnut neck and rode the animal back to where Mr. Frank waited.

"I didn't mean to hurt her."

"You didn't hurt her. Just confused her. Horses communicate without words. It's the little things that send the message. People do that too. Not bad for a first time."

Mr. Frank reached for the bridle, and Dorothea leaned forward and patted Mercy's neck. She liked the smell of sweat and leather and the silky feel of the horse and the calm beating of her own heart.

"You'll get the hang of it. Now, if you've time, let's try that again. This time turn your alarm into courage. You're learning something new and so is Mercy. It's a dance, and you want both of you to enjoy it at the end."

Dorothea smiled. She had already enjoyed it, even the fear that rose up when she felt off balance in the saddle. She had managed it. She was in control.

As she and Mary rode back to the house in the carriage, Dorothea leaned her head against the leather carriage pad.

Mary said, "I love riding with my friends and catching up on the news. Soon you'll be able to ride along with us. It will be much more fun than simply riding by yourself in circles in the paddock."

"Riding by myself is perfect. It isn't being alone. I have the horse to be with."

"Quite. But being with people is what riding is about, Dolly."

Dorothea chose not to argue. Instead she marveled that during all that time of instruction she never once thought about Charles or her family.

Her cousin Mary showed her how to adorn her hair for the weekly galas, and now, several months into her life with the Fiskes, Dorothea looked in the mirror askance.

"It looks ridiculous." She fingered the beads wrapped into a high mound at the top of her head. She was already taller than many likely suitors. Why add three inches to her height?

"It's the fashion," Mary insisted. Dorothea found her cousin quite firm in her views of proper etiquette and much less interested in the meaning of Thomas Gray's poems. "We do it this way in Boston society. I don't know why you resist."

"But if the fashion is meant to attract, then why do something that makes me stand out for the wrong reasons?"

"It isn't wrong. It's the way we do it, so it's the right way. You want to blend in, demonstrate that you're aware of what's proper."

"I'm like milkweed in a poor pasture." Dorothea pulled the beads from her hair and unwound the chignon that had forced it into thick twists. "Being plain and simple shows elegance too. This will be better. It will."

She crossed her arms and caught her image in the mirror as that of a petulant Charles. She lowered her arms.

Mary pursed her lips. "Your hair with that tint of burgundy is a crowning gift. Women of our station must show an awareness of our gifts. I'll have Beatrice come in and salvage it for you. I need to dress. We don't want to be late for our guests. That nice young man you sat next to at the choral event is coming." Dorothea wrinkled her nose. "Quite. You must make the effort at least."

"Quite," Dorothea said to her cousin's departing back. Dorothea stared at herself in the mirror.

The beads and fluff in her hair made her look like an ostrich wearing a wig. Then words from Gray's "Ode to Adversity" came to her: "Teach me to love and to forgive, exact my own defects to scan."

"My own defects to scan," she said to the image and sighed. She had many defects. Her height. Her tendency to seriousness instead of assuming a welcoming smile. She could recognize Mary's generosity in teaching her. She ought to be more generous in her nature and thank her. She redid the beads on a shorter, powdered wig and reminded herself to thank Mary for her guidance. Then she wondered if Monsieur Brun would be present at this dinner. She enjoyed his company though he was old enough to be her father.

Before each fete, Aunt Sarah and Mary gave her instructions on proper conversations with guests. "You must not disagree with anything they say," Mary noted. "Nod your head, smile, and perhaps repeat with new words what they've just said so they realize you understand them and simply want them to know that." Dorothea stared. "That way they will continue to carry on a conversation with you and remember you as someone quite wise."

"But what if what they're saying isn't correct or needs an informed response?"

"Never point that out. It would be rude. We are there to prop up suitors." Mary patted Dorothea's hand. "Once married, when they are obligated to care for us, then we can express opinions, but even then we ought not to say things with the certainty you seem to like." She shook her finger at Dorothea. "Our thoughts and ideas are optional. Our task is to find ways to adapt to what is."

Mary proved an apt instructor in the realm of engaging young men in conversation, although Dorothea sometimes ached for her cousin who gushed and blushed over a compliment but later said, "I'd never want to be in a marriage boat with him. I'd be paddling alone most of the time."

"But you seem to encourage him." Dorothea removed the beads, fingering their coolness.

Mary shrugged. "He might be all I end up with. I don't want to be kept from the boat altogether."

Dorothea had no interest in such boats. She also had no real confidants, no one to whom she could safely say she found these parties more stressful than learning Latin from her uncle. Who could she tell of her preference to sit by the fire and read rather than chat with young men? Sometimes Mercy the mare heard her concerns, but when she was riding, she didn't think about the cotillions. Instead, she was consumed by the feel of the horse, the botanical surprises along the trails, or the sound of a phoebe's chirp. She inhaled the smells of rich earth or honeysuckle in the air. Perhaps if she had a horse of her own, she could ride every day, and she would tell the animal of her worries and hopes as she brushed and curried it.

So far, Dorothea had found no young man she imagined in her future as a husband, though the instructor at the stables—who was never invited to the fetes—could make her laugh. She thought that was a higher prerequisite in a potential mate than the entries in his banking ledger or the number of years he'd spent at Harvard.

Her father used to make her mother laugh. She had all but forgotten that.

The letters Dorothea now wrote to her brothers were mostly stories she thought would entertain them. She didn't dwell on how much she missed them and never mentioned the lavish parties or strengthening food she ate. (She'd even had to let out a few of her dresses. They now had curves instead of being as straight as cook's wooden spoons.) She didn't write of her riding or her French lessons or her acquaintances and how she found she could make the gentlemen laugh with a well-stated word or that she enjoyed being able to put another at ease without revealing much of herself. She signed her letters "Thea," the name Charles used for her.

She never received letters back.

Five

Purposeful Behavior

Dorothea wasn't sure how long her aunt and grandmamma would continue to support her efforts with the Fiskes if she didn't show progress toward a suitor. As the seasons passed at the Fiske household, it became clearer to Dorothea that she lacked the desire to do what was necessary to acquire a mate, at least while she was but fifteen. She easily assessed the interests of young men and could keep them talking. She did not mind being a listener, as she always learned new things about botany or science, writers and religions. She never had to expose a thing about herself. But she minded that it was expected that, as a girl, she had no thoughts worth sharing.

This had been made clear to her one evening when one of the divinity students invited her to hear a preacher at the college. She accepted and enjoyed the deeper thinking of the minister, his discussion of God's purpose much more interesting than the companionship of the confident young man who invited her. The suitor rattled on as they walked home, never once asking for her thoughts on the sermon, but rather expounding on his own. When she offered an opinion in a rare pause, he said, "Yes, but it's more likely . . ." and then went on his own conversational trail. Is this what marriage would be like?

At the stone steps of the Fiskes', he'd stopped talking long enough to plant a kiss on her cheek. She stepped back and stared.

"Thank you for a lovely evening," he said, then scurried away like a boy caught stealing a candy.

She touched her gloved fingers to her cheek. What an odd sensation. She didn't think she liked it and told no one about it. She vowed she would never accept any invitation from him in the future.

She needed a purpose, she decided, one not attached to finding a mate. In her prayers she asked for a way to feel useful, not a burden, and still bring her brothers into her care. If she found a purpose ordained by God, she would find a way to rescue her brothers and find happiness, perhaps even the family everyone wanted for her.

The idea that propelled her forward came a few days later while she was in the midst of preparing for Mary's wedding. She helped arrange dried flowers, wrote invitations at Mary's request ("Your penmanship is so much more elegant than mine"), and pored over recipes for dishes the cook would be asked to make on the grand day.

Still thinking of her brothers and children like them, she told her aunt, "I would like to open a school." They were in the sewing room, Mary too, stitching small sachets to be given away at the nuptials. Dorothea sewed her own dresses now with material her aunt purchased. Her needlework was much improved, although her cross-stitching was not yet worth framing, and her knitting still left gaps in her stockings a kitten could fall through. "So many children have no chance to advance themselves because they have no school-ing," Dorothea said. "Their parents cannot afford tutors to teach them the basics about reading or writing. We would all benefit if more children had those abilities, don't you agree, Aunt Sarah? Boys and girls."

"I agree children ought to be educated, but it is their parents' responsibility."

"But Grandmamma and you are helping me when my parents . . . couldn't. Those children might not have a kind aunt and uncle to hire tutors or offer wonderful libraries for their use." She continued on with her plan. "There are few people here during the day when I would have need of the library for students. They'd be gone by evening."

"Mama, you cannot let her bring street urchins into our home," Mary protested. "Not with my wedding plans."

Dorothea answered, "There are reform movements urging the education of girls as a benefit to the entire family. It could be a paying school for boys and girls and pay my way here." She did not add that she would be able to claim preparation for her classes as a way to avoid the invitations from young men who stole kisses. "I could buy linen on my own from school fees." If the school were successful, she could open a separate evening school for the children unable to pay, but she did not share that plan. Not yet. She would use a gentle hand here, just as her riding instructor always advised. Her riding instructions were appropriate for this negotiation.

Aunt Sarah remained silent. Should Dorothea have written out her proposal, given her aunt time to consider with a document to share with her husband?

"Every girl needs to earn her keep," Dorothea added.

"How do you propose to find your students?"

Dorothea described in detail how she would advertise among the church patrons. She'd offer grammar, some writing, biblical memorization to enhance both memory and virtue. "And manners, of course. You and Mary have taught me well."

"Have you ever been to school?" her aunt asked. She turned over a sampler Dorothea had worked on and evaluated the stitches. She nodded approval before setting it down.

"No. But I've read about many teachers. And you would be close by to consult with, wouldn't you?" She would not teach math or science, as she lacked the background in those. "I could even offer needlework. Mary, don't laugh!"

"Your needlework is quite fine," Sarah said and smiled.

"It would please the parents to know their daughters recorded various letterings and stitches, the finished products acting as a kind of encyclopedia they could refer back to as they worked on future textiles."

Music or art would cost more, as she would have to acquire special teachers if the parents wanted that. It didn't worry Dorothea that she had never had a teacher beside her. She had taught Charles to read. She understood what was required of teachers: they were to be moral leaders and transfer both knowledge and values. She was certain she could do that.

By running a school, Dorothea challenged no one's authority in the house, and her idea offered additional income for the Fiske family and lessened the burden for Dorothea's care. They had to agree.

"Would you forgo your French lessons so that money could be saved . . . or used to help cover your other expenses?"

Dorothea nodded yes.

"Mary reports some . . . familiarity with your riding instructor that perhaps should be inter-rupted."

Dorothea's heart skipped a beat. She loved

French. But give up time with Mercy, the one relationship where loneliness faded? Yes, for such a worthy purpose.

"If I could have one more French lesson and go once more to say good-bye to Mercy, then yes."

"I'll discuss the matter with my husband," Sarah said. "It's quite uncommon for a girl your age to do such a thing. But then we Dixes are an uncommon lot, don't you think?"

"Thank you, Aunt Sarah. It is all I could ask for."

"I shall miss your visits here, Miss Dix." Mr. Frank snapped the ropes to the halter on either side of Mercy's gentle head, then removed the saddle and blanket.

"Perhaps I'll have an income of my own one day so I can return and ride again for pleasure."

"You should find a husband who will allow you such a treat."

Dorothea's face warmed in spite of herself. "You're sounding like my aunt Sarah." She brushed Mercy's back where the saddle and blanket had matted the hair. "It's possible I will never marry. It's quite respectable not to do so. So long as one can stand alone without the support of kith or kin."

"If any should be so independent, it would be you, Miss Dix."

"I take that as a compliment, Mr. Frank, but wonder why you think so."

"You ride for the solitude, not for the camaraderie of friends chatting. You notice the apple trees ready to blossom. I see you stop and smell them. Choose a place to ride to and return. No meandering that I can see. You ride with a purpose."

"Yes, I suppose I do."

It was how she planned to undertake her school: with purpose. She could only hope it would help her ease the sadness she felt when she led Mercy into her stall and brushed her down for the last time.

Two weeks later, while Mary and her new husband sat at the marriage dinner, Dorothea mused about her school. She would be busy and not miss her brothers so much, nor Mary, whose absence she realized would make her sad. Still, her school gave her a ready excuse to avoid parties. Mary had met her purpose in finding a mate. Dorothea had succeeded too—making her case for something important, and she had won with a gentle hand. Onward! That would be her motto.

With the Fiskes' help, Dorothea had twelve students within a week of Mary's marriage. She arranged the library room, pushing chairs against the cherry table. She picked a bouquet of tulips newly bloomed in the Massachusetts spring. She would have good reason now to spend time in the forests and the ornamental garden. They would become classrooms soon. With early fees she purchased papers and Mason and Dixon lead pencils and a few slates for those who might forget to bring them. She laid the pencils out on the table, marking the space for each child.

The night before Dorothea's students arrived, she could barely sleep and rose to light a candle to go over the lessons she had prepared and the rules she needed to impress on the children the very first day. Once out of control, they would be like puppies in a litter pummeling each other, undisciplined. Hers must be an orderly classroom, safe and secure for everyone to be able to learn.

In the morning she welcomed parents as they entered with their children. Dorothea stood on the stone steps, greeting each with a nervous smile and a stern nod. There would be time to relax this pose when the children respected her as the one in control. But the youngest of the arrivals, girls with curls like sausages bouncing on either side of their faces, saying, "Good morning, dear teacher," caused her to open her face in a smile. How could she not? They were adorable, and she let her hand linger on their heads as she welcomed them up from their polite curtseys.

"Just sign here," she told a parent, handing him a contract. "Soon your son will be able to draft contracts and your daughter will be able to read them."

"Just teach her letters. So she'll write to her mother and me when she marries and moves away, as girls always do." How sweet that a father hoped to hear from his daughter when she was gone from the home. Dorothea bit her lip and thanked him for his signature.

The girls appeared to wear new dresses, the dyes leaving tiny rims of red or yellow on their necks. White lines on the boys' necks revealed fresh haircuts. Each child carried a slate. Nervous chatter followed her up the stairs to the library, and Dorothea couldn't keep the smile from her face. She imagined what their lives were like outside these walls and envied them, just a little, that at the end of the day they had someone to share their adventures with, someone to welcome them home with warm arms.

She hoped her aunt would ask how things had gone on her first day, but she didn't count on it. Beatrice the maid would listen, but it was Beatrice's job to defer to the conversations of the Fiske residents while she dusted or mopped.

"The most important rule," Dorothea told the faces staring at her on either side of the long table, "is to be orderly and disciplined and to follow my directions. That way you can hear the instruction, and the other students may take in the knowledge they need as well." She didn't want to sound too stern. Mr. Frank's words about "a light hand" rang in her ears.

A boy of maybe ten raised his hand. "Master Hamilton? What is it?"

"What happens if we don't be orderly and disciplined?"

"There will be consequences. And you don't need the word *be* in your question. It's enough to say, 'What happens if we are not orderly and disciplined?' "

"What be the consequences then, Miss Dix?"

"What are the consequences?" He nodded. She wasn't sure what she would do. "Perhaps you'll be the first to find out." He shrank in his seat. "Let's move on. This is the schedule I've prepared for today. I'll give you older students your assignments first so you may work on them while I then instruct the younger students."

She looked at the smaller children, blue and brown eyes intent on her face, anticipating the joy of newness. "As you finish your lessons, you may listen to the older students' instructions to see what your future holds if you work hard and learn much."

The boy again raised his hand. At least he was being polite and not barking out his questions.

"Yes, Master Hamilton?"

"Can we be . . . I mean, can I listen to the younger ones' lessons? They might be easier for me than what you give me to learn."

"*May* you listen to the younger students? Is that what you're asking?"

He nodded.

"Yes. But you must always strive to learn more than what you know already. If you do that, you will soon discover that listening to what you've already learned is a waste of time. There is always more to learn, Master Hamilton. The difference between *may* and *can* is but one of those lessons." She smiled at him then and walked closer. "Do you understand?"

"Yes ma'am. I mayn't not listen if it's what I already learnt."

She imagined him as Charles. She would encourage his willingness to ask questions, as much of learning involved a curious mind. She would work on his grammar independently.

Partway through the second week, Dorothea had assessed each child's strengths and weaknesses and planned her lessons accordingly. She was glad she had only twelve students. Twice that number would have been a trial, and the evening hours she spent preparing would leave few hours to sleep.

"Miss Otis, would you be kind enough to assist these younger girls? I've heard your reading and it's excellent."

"Yes, miss." The girl curtsied. She seemed happy to be able to stand and not sit for long hours at the table.

For lunches, the children remained at the table to eat what they brought from home. When the weather was agreeable, they would go for walks, two by two, and Dorothea would point out the bobolink's call or the name of an early fern.

As the days turned into weeks, Dorothea found the children's chatter and stories brought from home added pleasure to her days. She listened intently as they talked, and she wove their experiences into her lessons.

"Suzanne has a new brother at home. In our writing today let us imagine what having a new brother and sister would be like. Take out your slates and write one sentence of what is good about having a new brother or sister." She didn't criticize when she had them read their sentences aloud, even when one child wrote, "when they gets older you got someone to blame for eating the last piece of cake."

When someone told a story of a family visit to Cape Cod, Dorothea asked each child to write what they would pack in a basket that would serve a dozen family members on a summer day at the ocean. She had never been there, so she would learn from their writing. As part of the discussion, she read from Matthew about the miracle of the loaves and fishes and all the fragments of food left over.

"Each of us has something to contribute, and sharing tells everyone how big your heart is."

"My heart?" A child pressed a hand against her chest.

"Your heart will stretch when you use it to give to others." She hoped that was so.

After a time, she allowed the youngest girls to call her auntie and did not feel intruded upon when a child would ask what she did on Sunday afternoons.

As the months progressed, she drafted sessions that involved being outside to study but also found managing behavior in the gardens and orchards proved more challenging than when the children were confined to one room. They wanted to sprint ahead or linger, their heads bent over a slug making its way beneath the lilacs. She liked their curiosity but worried over the control of so many children, wanting to be certain no one was hurt. The parents would not appreciate her if a child returned home with a broken arm or a cut that brought on a fever.

Dorothea was surprised one day by the sound of giggling and turned to see two girls snickering and passing notes—and wasting paper—while she was instructing the younger children. She noticed the younger children's attention stray, their eyes casting curious glances between the rowdy girls and the teacher.

"There must be a consequence," Dorothea told the girls.

The two looked up but kept an amused look on their faces.

"Order and self-discipline is what's important,"

Dorothea said. *What if they defy me?* Her father's impatience as she bound his books came to her, the switch he used stinging in her memory. "I would be remiss if I allowed you to express your emotions inappropriately. Laughing and giggling when you're to be working does not demonstrate the qualities of fine young ladies." She allowed a bit of her father's seething quiet to infuse her words but heard her heart pounding in her ears, her face growing warm.

"What will you do?" One of the girls said, her eyes as big as biscuits. She was the daughter of a cotton exporter and well knew a life of ease.

"Switching ain't so bad," one of the boys said.

"Isn't so bad," Dorothea corrected without looking at him. "Except that it is." Dorothea knew one could endure switching, but the scars were constant reminders of both one's disobedience and one's confusion over grave disfavor living in the eyes of someone loved who could cause such pain.

"Will you switch us?" Color faded from both of the girls' faces. Dorothea blinked. In that moment, she saw fear and suffering in their eyes. It had come from her, from someone who cared about them, who only wanted the best for them. Obedience, self-control, and respect were all important. *So is compassion.*

Dorothea looked at her palms, rubbed them, and pushed them behind her. She remembered the humiliation of the switch. Shame was a terrible motivator. "No, Cora, I believe I will not switch you or Isabelle. Instead, if this happens again, where you are disrespectful of other children's learning time and fail to find a good use of your mind, you will make a placard. You will carry it around your neck through the remainder of the day. Then you will wear the placard home. As you walk through the streets of Worcester, the shopkeepers and deliverymen will see you for what you are and you will have to explain to your parents what brought on your new attire."

"What . . . what will the sign say?"

" 'I was a bad girl—or boy—today.' Your parents, not I, will administer the discipline when they see you have brought shame upon them. And making the sign will help you work on your lettering. We'll go to the woodshed after lunch and see what we can find. All of you. Each of you may as well find the wood for your own placard. You'll likely need it."

Satisfied that she had a plan, she turned back to the younger children and prayed she would not hear giggling. Cora and Isabelle now found great interest in their lessons.

A light hand. Remembering one's pains and making sure others do not suffer the same, surely that was as powerful a lesson as the pain of a switch.

Six

Why Are You Crying Now?

Dorothea gave every waking moment—except Sundays—to her school. She thought up new ways to engage her students. They took more trips into the woods and along streams, and if someone asked a question Dorothea didn't know how to answer, she would say, "We'll consider that tomorrow." At night she would pore through the books in the library, seeking the answer. Once or twice she asked the question at the dinner table, and if a guest was startled by her wondering where paper came from or what zinc was, the men seemed pleased to pontificate on the subject and did not seem at all offended.

She broached a local printer for the remains of paper discards and dried ink. She revived the ink with vinegar. She sought permission and received it from the Fiskes' cook to collect turkey quills and refine them into pens. She had the children write letters to her about their days, naming any questions they might have or telling what they liked or did not like about schooling. While she told herself it was to have them practice their writing, she found she looked forward to knowing how they thought.

I took Jessie's apple. Please forgive me, Auntie.

I'm sorry I fell asleep during needlework. My fingers got tired.

My little brother bit me and I bit him back.

You are the most beautiful, beautiful, beautiful, beautiful woman I ever seen. I'm sorry if I stare.

In the evenings, she wrote stories for the children much as she had done for Charles in years past. One day she received a letter from Charles. He was excited about the sea and wanted to become a merchant marine when he grew up. She didn't have the heart to tell him that he was destined for Harvard if her grandmamma was still alive to make that happen. Joseph also wrote now, but she could tell her father had spent little time working on his lettering. He was only five, but her five-year-old students wrote complete, though short, sentences already. Joseph wrote only his name and drew pictures.

At evening meals, she sat straighter at the Fiske table. Her payments to them might have resulted in the pork roast or the side of bacon they ate. She declined invitations from Mary's friends to parties, and while her aunt sometimes raised an eyebrow, Dorothea guessed the increased income overrode her finding a husband in Worcester.

"You'll come for supper?" a parent asked Dorothea one Friday at the close of the day. "Our

Suzanne has done so well under your tutelage. We would be pleased to have you join us."

"I'd . . . I'd be honored." Conversations with her students' parents proved far less stressful than those with potential suitors. The meals were lively with the children present, and the stories they told from their schooling gave Dorothea special recognition. She smiled so much her face was sore during the carriage ride home, and she breathed a prayer of gratitude. This was her destiny. To teach. To touch. She was so grateful to have found a love of her life, even if it wasn't the suitor for whom her grandmamma hoped.

Nearly five years into her time at Worcester, when Dorothea had grown to know the grounds by heart and love them, Aunt Sarah called her into the parlor.

Her aunt lowered herself with her cane onto the settee. She had aged, and her face powder highlighted the deep wrinkles around her mouth rather than hid them. Dorothea suspected that chronic pain brought on many of those lines. She and her aunt often talked in the parlor about small issues related to the school, so she assumed this was why they met.

"It seems we have failed you, Dolly."

"You've done nothing of the sort. You've been more than kind to me and allowed me to find the passion of my heart—teaching."

Her aunt sighed and shook her head. "Though you are now nineteen, you are no closer to finding a suitable mate than when you first arrived. We are well into the new decade, and yet you have no prospects for your future."

"The school has been a success. This is my future."

"It has been a fine service. But that was not your purpose in being sent here." The arthritic knuckles of Sarah's hands sat like white porcelain door-knobs on her cane. "I have enjoyed your presence, Dolly."

Her aunt's words warmed. "Thank you. I hope that my presence helps fill the empty days with Mary gone."

"I shall have to find another way, I fear," she sighed. "Your grandmother has called you to Orange Court."

"For a visit?"

"No. You're to live there permanently. My mother is getting older, and having you to assist her will be very useful. Especially now."

Dorothea felt pain like an ice chip stuck in her throat. She'd always said she wanted to return to be with Charles and Joseph, but now she had her students. "What do you mean by 'especially now'?"

Tears filled her aunt's eyes. "We've received word. Your father, my brother, has died. He was irresponsible and unpredictable, but I loved him." She wiped at her eyes with a handkerchief. "I didn't think it possible to love and be angry with someone at the same time."

That was a lesson Dorothea knew well.

"What . . . what did he die of?"

"Consumption, though it was likely hastened by his . . . consumption of liquor."

Emotion rattled like stones in her chest. "Your mother has been sent to live with relatives in New Hampshire. Mama is bringing your brothers—and you—to live with her now. To Orange Court. She has need of you, and I suspect she thinks she can be a better matchmaker than we have been."

"Charles and Joseph? They'll be at Orange Court?"

"They will indeed. And I suspect you may be asked to provide instruction for them. Mama's situation has changed. Your father left you nothing."

A bitterness came into her tone, and Dorothea wondered about all the money her grandmamma had given her father over the years—land he had sold, businesses he had begun and abandoned—resources no longer available to the other Dix descendants either.

"So you can assist your grandmamma now in her declining years as you are as yet unencumbered. And having seven- and eleven-year-old boys about will not be easy on her. You are needed there, Dolly. I will miss you." Her aunt's voice caught. She raised her head and announced, "You shall leave in the morning."

"But . . . my students!"

Sarah hesitated. "Yes. Something must be done for them." She tapped her fingers on her cane, reached for her handkerchief and dabbed at her nose. "I'll speak with their parents."

"They'll need other schools. Please, I need to tell them of my leaving."

"They'll adapt, Dolly. You're not the only person in their lives, you know."

They are the most important persons in mine. "It's unprofessional to simply quit. Your husband would never leave his patients without an alternative should he stop treating them, would he? It's a matter of . . . honor to do the right thing."

Her aunt sighed. "You're correct. I'll send word to Orange Court that you'll be ready in a week."

"Thank you. Thank you, Aunt Sarah." She rubbed her fingers at her temples, then asked, "My father . . . did he leave a letter . . . anything . . . for me?"

"Not that I'm aware."

"Will there be a funeral?"

"The Methodists took care of that. He's gone and buried."

"And my mother . . ." She had to ask, had to know if she had improved or still wandered in her mind.

"My mother did not say. Only that her relatives

70

were willing to take her in, just not the children. She was never . . . right, you know, Dorothea. There was always something that blocked her from thinking clearly, from doing what a mother needs to do. Unfortunate from the time my brother rescued her, for that's what it was really. A rescue. Just as your grandmamma is now rescuing your brothers and you from poverty and indistinction."

The rocks in Dorothea's heart continued to rattle as she made her way to her room. She'd soon be with Charles and Joseph, but she would have to say good-bye to her students. She'd be staying with her grandmother and brothers in the mansion of Orange Court. She'd have a family. But her father had died with no word for her, not a single thread to cling to that he had cared for her. Her mother was whisked away to be looked after by others.

Dorothea spent the evening writing a letter to each student that she would distribute in the morning. As she finished the last one, tears smeared the ink. She tore up that missive and began again, but not until she had wiped her eyes and splashed cold water from the porcelain basin onto her face.

"Why are you crying now?" she asked herself out loud. *Because those children filled your empty life, and now you're leaving them. Because your father has died.*

In the morning she handed out the letters after telling the students she would be closing the school.

"You have an eye for plants and flowers, Master Hamilton. That will enable you to bring forth food and beauty from your family garden and perhaps one day an orchard or a farm."

"Thank you, Miss Dix," the boy said. He was eleven now and tall for his age. "I'm sorry you have to go away."

"I am too," she told him. "You continue to study in these areas that you may be faithful for meeting the needs of your wife and children one day." She handed him the letter she had written. "My note to you describes your many attributes. I hope you'll save it, and when you are feeling low, reread it to know that you are a capable young man. Even your grammar is vastly improved."

"Did you say that in the letter?"

"Yes, yes, I did. Your father will be pleased."

"Miss Otis." She handed the cotton merchant's daughter her letter. "I have seen you encourage the younger children in their studies. You have the gift of compassion and perhaps teaching as well, though the latter requires a stern position at times. You must remember that, dear Isabelle. The placard is a gift for teaching discipline, as you well know." Only once had Isabelle worn her status around her neck.

Each child received her full attention. She saw

each as singular and unique, like jonquils that bloom in spring, and hoped her words made each child feel the same.

"You have been my family," she concluded, tears now seeping from her eyes. *I must not lose control.* "And I will miss you. I promise, if you write to me, I will write back. But I also know your lives will change and you will have a new teacher one day to help you make your way. You may find little time to write to Miss Dix. But I will not forget you. Not ever. Now, let us take out our slates and work on today's spelling words. I've made up a new list."

She turned her back as though reaching for the list, but instead she held herself steady against the sideboard until she felt strong enough to finish the day and let them go on without her.

Seven

Orange Court's Welcome

The ride to Orange Court took two days, the journey giving Dorothea time enough to imagine her homecoming. She would hug her grandmother the way her youngest students hugged her when they arrived in the classroom. She recalled the feel of their small arms around her neck, the scent of their morning toilet, the press of cheek to smooth cheek. As she adjusted to the bumps on the road and grabbed the coach side to straighten herself on the carriage seat, she thought it might be joy she had felt with the morning touches of her students. Happiness.

She hoped she would find joy inside Orange Court in the arms of her brothers and grand-mamma at long last. She imagined what Charles would look like, those intense blue-gray eyes they shared. Would he remember her at all? And Joseph. He had been a toddler when she had last seen him.

She wondered which relatives had taken in her mother. Why hadn't they come forward when help was so desperately needed when Joseph was small, when Charles was little, when Dorothea cowered to avoid her father's rage and her mother's absence as she sat before them, listlessly poking food with her fork.

She must not dwell on that. Aunt Sarah had said it was best to let her mother be in the care of "her people." Dorothea's disciplined mind must not permit despair over what had already been. She was going home to safety, to family. She had her brothers, and she would celebrate that, wrap her arms around them. They would stand like the circle of friends she sometimes witnessed among her students when they played outside.

The long driveway swept up the hill to the

mansion that wasn't quite as elegant as the other estates on Beacon Hill. Last year's leaves clustered at the base of the hedges, and the gate to the pear garden swung back and forth in the spring breeze. Either someone had forgotten to latch it or the latch was broken. What appeared to be a stray cat hovered near the corner lilac bush, then scattered like a windswept leaf when Dorothea stepped from the carriage.

The driver lowered her two trunks, leaving them on the driveway as he pulled the carriage away. This time there would be no Beatrice to help her unpack. Saying good-bye to her had been a tearful affair, one she was glad Mary was not around to witness. Her good-byes to her aunt and uncle had also surprised her with the size of the ache in her heart. She heard the *clop-clop* of the horses leaving across the cobblestones. She gazed up at the three-story building that would be her home at last.

Where were the boys? her grandmamma?

She lifted her skirts and climbed the steps. She opened the door. "Grandmamma? Charles? Joseph? I'm here. It's me, Thea."

Silence.

She called out again, then made her way through the long hallway, past the staircase, beyond the dining room on her right and the parlor on her left. She looked briefly inside each room. "Is anyone here?"

"Excuse me?" The voice startled her and she turned. The woman must have been upstairs when Dorothea entered. "May I ask who you are?"

"Dorothea Lynde Dix. I'm to live here." She faced a woman as tall as herself, with large hands she now wiped on a rag she had been cleaning with.

"Ah. The granddaughter. I'm Mrs. Hudson. I manage this boardinghouse."

"Boardinghouse? But my grandmother—"

"Has taken over the caretaker's cottage. Along with her cook. She pointed with her chin toward the small house to the east.

"My brothers?"

"Ah. The rascals. They live in the cottage as well." She motioned for Dorothea to move into the parlor and take a seat. Mrs. Hudson sat across from her, using the rag to wipe dust from the round table beside the divan.

"My trunks should be taken to the cottage then."

"I have a room set aside for you. I understand you've been operating a school in Worcester. That will be fine. Most of the boarders are gone during the day, and the extra income will serve us both well—along with your grandmother. The boys have need of schooling, I can assure you of that!"

"My grandmother . . . leased Orange Court to you?"

"Yes. It was of mutual benefit. I'm sure she'll explain." The woman squinted at Dorothea. *No, she just has narrow eyes.* She wore her hair in a braid knotted around the top of her head the way Hessians do. "I've forgotten my manners. You must be weary from your trip and the news of your father. I'll bring us tea if you'd like."

"Better I should visit my grandmother."

"I'll have Isaac bring your trunks in. That's my brother. He lives here too. You'll meet the other boarders at supper. Served at seven sharp. I'll show you to your room."

With that, Mrs. Hudson stood and called out to her brother. Then Dorothea followed her to the room in her family's home chosen for her by a stranger.

Dorothea removed her hat and gloves and laid them on the dresser, letting her fingers linger on the cool marble top. It was a well-furnished room with an armoire, writing desk, and small fireplace, along with a large four-post bed. Dorothea knew the room had once been her father's. Her grandfather had told her this when she was a small child, with free run of the mansion. But this was no longer her grandfather's mansion. She was a guest in someone else's boardinghouse.

Isaac brought up her trunks, and she began to unpack them by removing the Thomas Gray poetry book and holding it to her heart. Her aunt Sarah had gifted her with the complete collection. She set the book down. What was she doing here when Charles and Joseph and a reunion were just steps away?

She descended the steps, nearly skipping past the pear garden to the caretaker's cottage. The path was well worn with stones lining the walkway. She heard birdsong in the elms, and the afternoon sun felt hot against her head. She bent to smell an iris, then stood and brushed wrinkles from her skirt. She had never been inside the single-story cottage that boasted a thatch roof like those seen in English picture books. The fence had recently been painted, and the flower and herb gardens on either side of the steps were well tended.

Dorothea knocked, and after a pause the door flung open.

"Thea!" Charles bounded out and grabbed her, swinging her or attempting to, but he was still an inch or so shorter than she. "You've come at last!"

"I have. Let me look at you!" She held him at arm's length, then pulled him to her. "Oh, how I have missed you." She whispered in his ear, their cheeks together, the bones of his narrow shoulders like handles she could hold.

"And I you."

"You look . . . like a young man. So grown up."

"I am grown up."

"Where's Joseph?" she asked as the two separated, Dorothea dabbing at her eyes, gazing at her brother.

"Walking out back. He's a favorite of Grand-mamma."

"I'm sure you are as well."

Charles flicked his thick hair on either side of a center cut back behind his ears.

"I haven't seen Joseph since he was a baby."

"I'm no baby no more." Dorothea turned to the quiet voice. Joseph led his grandmother from around the side of the house.

"No, you aren't," Dorothea bent to be face to face with him. "You're a young man." A small dog waddled beside him.

"I see you made it at last. Come inside," Madam Dix directed. "You too, Benji." Strings from her black cap hung on either side of her wide jaw. "Charles should have brought you out back without my having to come get you. Take the eggs inside, Joseph. Charles, lend a hand."

Charles slipped beside his grandmamma. She leaned against the cane as much as against Charles. Joseph smiled over his shoulder at Dorothea as he handed her the egg basket. He patted his grandmother's waist with his little hand.

"Hello to you too, Grandmamma," Dorothea mumbled. A night breeze cooled her warm face as she followed her family, including Benji the dog, inside.

Eight
A Touch of Friendship

Over Cookie's hearty rabbit stew, Madam Dix informed Dorothea of the change in circumstances that led to the leasing of Orange Court.

"I'm well into my seventies, and my knees are not so good. Being in the cottage seemed better than climbing the stairs to bed each night. And Orange Court offers an income necessary to care for all of you."

Cookie placed fresh bread before the family in the small dining room, then she pulled up a chair and joined them. Butter from an iris mold was passed around.

"Papa died," Joseph said.

"Yes, he did, and that's very sad." Dorothea watched Joseph. He didn't appear to need comforting, and yet their father had died and Joseph was separated from his mother. He must feel sadness just as Dorothea had when she had been sent to Worcester.

Joseph stuffed his mouth as he spoke, and Madam Dix said nothing about his lack of manners. If it had been Dorothea making a mess as a child, her grandmother would have corrected her. Things were different with boys.

"So we came to live here," Charles added cheerfully. "We're closer to the wharfs. I love going there to watch the ships. They bring in blue porcelain from China and silks from I don't know where. I'm going to go to sea one day and find out."

"After Harvard," Dorothea told him.

Madam Dix raised her eyebrows to Dorothea. "That'll be our hope, at least."

So finances were more strained than she had realized if even Harvard wasn't a certainty.

Dorothea was about to say something more about her father's death and the promise of a future with him in heaven when her grandmamma said, "According to my daughter, your school was successful even if our hopes for your marriage were not." Dorothea nodded. "I've already conferred with Mrs. Hudson, and having a school here will be fine. We can advertise in the circulars. The income will be useful. We can hope you'll meet suitors at church and thus enter the Boston social scene."

"I did enjoy the children."

"Not necessary to enjoy what one must do to survive," Madam Dix said. She wiped her face with a napkin, beads of sweat having formed above her lip. *Is she ill?* "Mrs. Hudson has faithful boarders, many of them divinity students from Harvard. Thank you," she told Cookie after the cook had poured hot water into the tea caddy before rising to clear the soup bowls. "The others I believe are legislators and their wives. They are in Boston during the sessions."

"I've met Mrs. Hudson. She seems more than adequate to the task of running the house."

They finished the meal. Since it was already late, Dorothea said good night. She hugged Charles and shook Joseph's little hand when he put it out to her. Then she walked in a daze across the lawn to Orange Court. No one had said a word about their mother. Better that she forget she ever had a mother. This was the family she had now. A lonely hoot owl expressed her feelings exactly.

Dorothea took her meals with the boarders while Charles and Joseph took theirs with their grandmother at the cottage. The family attended church together since her grandmother had already paid the pew fees. Dorothea's request that the boys live in Orange Court and attend her school when she started it fell into her grandmother's brooding silence like a rock sinking to the bottom of a pond.

"They will be tutored at the cottage," she said. "Your school fees can pay for it."

Dorothea watched her brothers roll hoops on the cottage lawn and didn't attempt to join them. She knew her grandmother would find it unseemly. Instead, she worked on her school, hoping to recreate the same sense of goodwill she had managed in Worcester. Her students would be girls. She would add her brothers if her grandmother relented. Dorothea expanded the age range, including girls up to age seventeen so that she might use the older girls as assistants and thus extend the number of students she could teach.

Not two blocks away from Orange Court a bestselling author had begun an academy for young ladies, and everyone praised her efforts. Dorothea could do as well, couldn't she? Her school might receive a public distinction that would help her find acceptance in Boston society, if not for making a "fine marriage," for doing something to further the public good. "Doing public good" was a constant theme of the divinity students who boarded at Mrs. Hudson's table.

The school began within a few weeks of Dorothea's arrival in Boston. Her previous success opened the door to parents asking her opinion about managing a child's behavior or how they could encourage their children at home. A few parents invited her to supper as others had in Worcester. She had even discovered that her youngest student, Marianna Cutter, was a second cousin.

"How wonderful! We're family," she told Marianna's mother, Grace, after the young widow shared the news.

"It's quite down the line, you understand. I believe your grandmother is my grandmother's cousin."

"Close enough," Dorothea said. She stroked Marianna's chestnut hair as they talked. The girl carried herself with confidence although she was but five. She had the same Dix blue-gray eyes.

"I'd invite you to supper," Dorothea said, "but it's Mrs. Hudson who permits supper guests or not. I'll speak with her and hope you can join us at a later date."

"In time we'll invite you." A grayish pallor painted the young mother's skin. She was as thin as a knitting needle.

Dorothea kissed Marianna on the child's pug nose—definitely not a Dix nose—and Marianna took her seat, waving to her mother as the woman left. Dorothea had already found delight in the girl. Her quick mind and helpful spirit lit up the room. Now she paid even more attention: Marianna was family, right here in her school-room.

After a few months, Madam Dix permitted the boys to attend Dorothea's school. "Their tutor tires" was her only explanation. Dorothea smiled when Charles and Joseph came into the room the first time and plopped into their chairs, surrounded by girls who simply stared.

"These are my brothers," Dorothea said. She

wanted to dance at the news. They *were* together at last. She had told the boys not to call her Thea in the classroom, and they mostly complied. She would hold them to high academic and behavioral standards.

"You didn't finish your writing assignment, Charles. That must be completed before you eat your lunch."

"Ah, Thea . . . I mean, Miss Dix. My stomach growls." She raised her finger at him. "It's a rule, Charles. You must not defy me."

"You're not my mother," he mumbled but returned to his work.

She required Joseph to wear a placard after he pulled up a plant rather than study it when she took the class outside. It was the first time she had used the dreaded placard here, and she wished it hadn't been Joseph who introduced it to the other students. But at least they all knew she had no favorites.

"Grandmamma won't like it," Joseph told Dorothea as he tugged at the placard.

"You'll have to explain what you did then, and we'll see if she disapproves of the consequence."

"Be glad it's not Papa," Charles told him. "He used the switch on us."

She shivered at Charles's mention of the willow switch. At least she had found a means for order that did not require suffering.

"It is your failure that your students need to be

disciplined," her grandmother told her. She had come by the school after the other children had left. The faithful Benji panted at her feet. "Joseph does not need such a placard."

"He misbehaved. I cannot show favorites. What would you have me do?"

"Perhaps your lessons are too easy for him. He's not challenged. He's a bright boy. I think he doesn't need your lessons. I'll keep him at home."

She had failed with her own brother. Maybe others could teach all these children better. The truth of that tempered her accomplishment with the school and made her wonder when Charles would be pulled out as well.

Cousins Grace and Marianna lived in a modest home, and Grace's husband, once a sea captain, Dorothea learned, had left them a comfortable stipend after his death. Grace looked much the same, and her fingernails were chipped, her skin sallow. After a light supper of cod and fresh greens, Marianna showed Dorothea her room.

"See my picture?" The child handed her a pencil drawing of lilies in a common pond done on good paper.

"I had no idea you were an artist," Dorothea told her.

"Yes, Auntie. It's my favorite thing to do."

"Your writing is also excellent."

"Pictures make the time go so fast I forget to eat, Mummy says."

"When we find things we love, we do forget to eat and even sleep," Dorothea told her. The child's eyes lit up as they talked.

"Oh, I sleep lots. So does Mummy, but that's because she's sick."

"I'm not sick." Grace had followed them. She brushed wrinkles from a Dresden doll's dress holding court on Marianna's bed. "I'm just tired. Chasing after you, little one." She poked Marianna's tummy and the girl laughed.

Dorothea looked away, not wishing to intrude. But she ached for Marianna. It was hard to have a mother who was ill in body or in mind.

Dorothea began creating opportunities for Marianna and the other students to paint and draw. She even hired an art teacher. A few more children challenged her order, but she did not use the placard. Instead, she shamed them with words and later felt worse than if she had switched them. She worked harder to find interesting ways of teaching her subjects, hoping that discipline would be less troubling.

Before long, she returned the supper invitation, inviting Grace and Marianna to Mrs. Hudson's savory soup. Other boarders supped at the table as well, with the conversation bouncing from theology to politics to plants. A legislator sat at the head of the table, his wife with graying hair to his side. Marianna's large red bow tied up her curls, and she swung her feet beneath the table, her eyes watching the several guests. During a lull, Marianna's little girl voice said, "It's fun to be downstairs instead of upstairs in school."

Dorothea engaged her immediately. "What's so different?"

"Here Joseph doesn't tease me." She looked at her mother who shook her head.

"He bothers you?" Dorothea frowned. "Where do you see him?"

"When we're outside playing. He takes my basket and runs."

"You must stand up for yourself," Marianna's mother said. "Not complain. Every girl needs to do that." Grace's voice sounded breathless, as though she'd climbed stairs to an attic.

"He's jealous because I know the names of plants he doesn't." Marianna adjusted her bow, lifted her chin with a note of defiance.

"Girls need to defer to boys," a divinity student eating at the table said. He pointed with his fork. "It's only proper."

"I'm not certain I agree with you, Mr. Reynolds." Dorothea looked directly at the boarder. "No one person should be asked to downplay her intelligence simply not to embarrass one of another gender."

"Unless they do, they might never marry," he countered. "A terrible tragedy indeed."

Dorothea exchanged glances with a legislator's wife with raised eyebrows. Neither said a word, deciding not to add fuel to the fire. She clarified the value though: young girls in her charge would be encouraged to pursue the length and depth of wisdom, even if it bristled a young man down the road—including her little brother, whom she would watch more closely when the girls went outside.

"Thomas Nuttall, the botanist, will be speaking this afternoon," one of the boarders at Mrs. Hudson's table announced a few days after Marianna and Grace had visited.

"And who is he?" asked one of the legislators.

"He made the trek into the Louisiana Purchase with John Jacob Astor's party, going all the way to the Pacific in 1811. He recorded his observations and has dozens of drawings of various flora."

"Can anyone attend?" Dorothea asked.

"Of course."

That afternoon Dorothea donned her bonnet, gloves, and reticule and walked to the lecture hall. The summer day of 1822 was balmy, with sea gulls crying over the docks and a lingering scent of lilacs in the air. She took a seat next to a stately young woman dressed in fine fashion who nodded toward Dorothea as the lecture began. Lemon oil made the wooden seats shine and gave off a pleasant scent. Or perhaps it was the woman's perfume. Dorothea had seen the woman at church, but they had not spoken.

Dorothea settled in to listen, loving the man's stories. He spoke of places and plants she might never see. The idea of their existence pleased her. Perhaps it was the orderliness, how plants could be classified in such detail, created by a God who had so many larger things to contend with, and yet He remembered *Nymphaea odorata*, the lowly lily of the pond.

"Wasn't that grand?" her seatmate expressed after the final applause for the lecture died down and people stood, gathered their belongings.

"It was." Dorothea tugged on her gloves.

"I'm Anne Heath. I believe I've seen you at Mr. Channing's sermons." Her dark eyebrows lifted.

"Yes, Reverend Channing is quite brilliant."

"I love information for its own sake," Anne said. "Whether I *do* anything with the ideas and facts or not." She leaned into Dorothea. "I hope it's not a wasteful practice, listening to ideas, reading books on ancient civilizations or medical procedures or even the history of the making of paper, knowing those facts just rattle in my head until perhaps I can interject them into conversations. Nothing more."

Dorothea grinned. "I'm Dorothea Lynde Dix," she said. "My grandmother is Madam Dix."

"Of course. We don't see her much at Reverend Channing's sermons. I hope she's well?"

"She grows more feeble, I fear," Dorothea said. "She finds her Puritan roots to be more . . . uplifting of late."

"And you?"

"I attend Reverend Channing's lectures twice a week," Dorothea said. "He's . . . charming and inspiring."

"He's so short," Anne said.

"Or we're quite tall." They both laughed as they made their way to the back of the lecture hall and onto the street. They were of the same height, and Reverend Channing was barely five feet tall. Once outside, the smell of horse droppings over-powered any jasmine scent from the plants in the large pots beside the doors. A long line of carriages awaited the lecture's guests.

"My carriage is at the front," Anne said. "Would you care to come for tea? We can deliver you to Orange Court later if you'd like?"

"I'd be honored."

"We have quite the gatherings after church on Sundays. Just chatting and playing games. Sometimes we take boats out on the lake. A few scholars. My lovely younger sisters. Perhaps you'll join us?"

"I . . . yes. Perhaps in the future." Dorothea did not want to get caught up in the suitor circle again. Still, she enjoyed the company of this woman.

Maybe there were other young people she could spend time with without the weight of marriage on their minds. "My school takes up much of my time."

"Even teachers need recess." Anne Heath put her arm through Dorothea's as they walked toward the waiting carriage.

Dorothea felt the warmth of another person's touch and the possibility of a friendship. She did not shrink away.

Nine

Friends Sublime

Anne Heath had four younger sisters, a gregarious mother, a humorous father, and a home that others flocked to on Sunday afternoons like fox squirrels to bird feeders. Dorothea enjoyed the quiet tea with Anne, then found herself the next weekend with the Heath clan, as Mrs. Heath called her brood. The sweet aroma of kindness floated over the household, and Dorothea allowed herself to be wrapped within it.

Both Elizabeth and Mary, the youngest of the five Heath daughters, had leather-colored hair and blue eyes and were the instigators of the games they introduced before Dorothea had time to memorize the names of the other guests. They laughed over family stories. They primped each other's clothing, commented on their hairpieces and the stitching capabilities of each.

Seventeen-year-old Mary giggled easily as her sisters fluffed her curls. She was the only one to have natural waves in her hair. They exchanged stories of beaus, although Anne had none. Their parents expressed compliments both at the ideas articulated by their daughters and at their actions in caring for others. They sewed clothes for the poor and collected alms for those imprisoned. Like Dorothea, Anne deplored the practice of local jails charging for people to come and "view the imbeciles" often housed in debtors' jails.

"I don't think it at all Christian for people to gawk at others who are impaired through no means of their own," Dorothea said, thinking of her mother.

"But some are there because of their foolish choices," Anne said. "Consider the rum business and the sugar imports and what excesses do to families whose husbands grow crazy for drink."

"But those with epilepsy, flight of mind, mongoloid features; these are not there for reason of rum." Dorothea felt her skin prickle. She had not disagreed with Anne before.

"We need protection from them," Susan Heath ventured.

"Do we? I'm not so sure they do not need protection from us who are supposed to be more civilized. We charge coins to view them? Hardly civilized."

"No reason to argue, girls," Mr. Heath interrupted.

Silence filled the room before Mary told a story of losing her hat on the lake and the rush of boys who splashed into the water to be the first to retrieve it. Dorothea's heart steadied. Why was she so defensive of criticism for those relieved of their reason?

Meals with the Heaths were happy times with chatter and laughter. In each encounter with this family, Dorothea was brought inside, felt the warmth of the hearth fire not only on her skin but in her heart. She accepted compliments about the way she expressed an idea or how much Anne enjoyed reading the letters Dorothea had begun sending each week just to share the vagaries of her teaching days. Dorothea heard herself making observations that she saw pleased the Heath family, and she reveled in their pleasure. Here was a safe place where suffering did not intrude. She waded into the water of trusting a relationship.

"You're visiting with the Heaths I hear." Dorothea's grandmother spoke into the silence of a meal in the cottage house, where Dorothea occasionally ate with her family. Usually the quiet was broken only by the scrape of spoon against the soup bowl.

Dorothea often stayed afterward to read to her grandmother, whose eyes appeared to fail her.

"Yes. They're a fine family." She buttered one of Cookie's pan breads, handing it to her grandmother and asking Charles to pass the peas.

"You should keep their acquaintance. They will be able to bring you into Boston society. It won't hurt them to have a beautiful, articulate young Dix to add to their parties either."

A compliment from Grandmamma?

"I have been invited to a cotillion. Several legislators and artists and others will attend."

"Tell me the guest list, and I'll advise you who to ask to be seated beside."

"Grandmother, if I go, it will be to spend time with Anne and her sisters. They're much more interesting than the legislators. I converse with them at Mrs. Hudson's table, and I don't always find the conversation stimulating."

"You might if you knew of their ledger sheets."

"You might," Dorothea said. "It's of no interest to me."

Her brothers exchanged glances and poked at the salt pork slices.

"It must be!" Her grandmother nearly shouted each word. The spaniel Benji perked his ears at the thundered words, then cowered under the table. The two boys also jerked in their seats. "You are too much focused on the present without care for your future." The older woman's face held the expression that she had just stepped where the chickens pecked.

"I have the school," Dorothea said. "I can teach for a lifetime."

"Not all we do now will last."

"Then I'll trust that God has plans for me and will tend them better than I can . . . or even better than you can, Grandmamma."

"Don't be rude." She frumped her napkin beside her plate. "You won't teach your entire life. It's too much, and it will never prove to support you and your brothers. You need a husband, Dorothea. That is that!"

Dinners with the Heath family were so much more pleasant than those at the cottage. Dorothea listened to the fast-moving conversations around the dining room table and occasionally offered an opinion. The college students might be somber and professorial at times, but they always listened politely and did not seem to dismiss what she said simply because she was a female. The young men also nodded wisely to the offerings of the Heath girls, and their attention to Mrs. Heath's point of view seemed more than mere politeness. This, Dorothea imagined, was how men and women ought to be together, speaking frankly and with respect. She vowed to model this with her students so they would see what respect of others looked like.

One afternoon at the Heaths', plum pudding was being served in the garden overlooking the lake. The aroma made Dorothea salivate.

"We owe our fellow citizens ample opportunity to improve their lives," one student said. "It is our Christian duty. Duty to our fellow man, service that grows out of the journey of purpose. We must all find our purpose."

"I do believe Miss Dix has done so," Anne interjected. "Though I am still searching. Her school is quite successful. She's an observant and dedicated instructor."

"Ah, but what of others, students who cannot afford to attend her fine establishment?" This came from the Reverend William Ellery Channing, who with his wife and sister-in-law had joined the Heath group on this day. Dorothea still reeled from the power of the man's sermons and his persuasive voice. Hadn't he been a classmate of her father's at Harvard before her father dropped out? She'd have to ask her grandmother.

"At the last judgment," he concluded, "I believe Christ will say 'as ye have done it unto one of the least of these my brethren, ye have done it unto me.' What have you done?"

"Thea?" Anne asked. "Do you care to reply?"

"He's quite right. Those who cannot afford my school do deserve an education. But I don't know what to do about it."

"I have begun a ministry, Miss Dix, whereby I

visit the homes of the poor and destitute, the suffering. I find it untrue that most are people who deserve their fate or are people who have failed to lift themselves into proper society. They are instead mostly virtuous men and women who stepped out as best they could to rise above crushing poverty and found the path strewn with boulders too heavy for them to move alone. It is our duty to assist them, our Christian duty to respond regardless of the circumstances."

"Reverend Channing has taken it upon himself to raise funds to provide food, clothing, coal, whatever is needed for such people," Mary Heath noted.

The group had gathered under the gazebo in the Heaths' backyard, and the ice in the tea glasses clinked against the sides. From her tongue, Dorothea removed a tiny piece of sawdust left behind from the icehouse.

Mary's eyes glistened with admiration. "He is more than a sermonizer. He is a doer."

"As are you, Miss Mary," the cleric added. Polite applause followed as the pastor bowed enough to acknowledge their support.

When he raised his eyes, he held Dorothea's for a moment. She wanted to take action. Whether to achieve a small measure of his acclaim or to be able to respond to Christ's call, she was not yet certain.

Dorothea remained thoughtful as the carriage

ride back to Orange Court took her past the ice warehouses and cotton stores, past the buildings she knew were full of pineapples from the Sandwich Islands and blue porcelain imported from Britain. She had ridden the route a hundred times, but this time she noticed the children. Small, dirty, barely covered with threadbare clothing, they scrounged the wharves for droppings of food or bits of cotton baling they might stuff inside their clothes for warmth. Stray cats roamed the same wharves, and many looked healthier than the skinny children who ran among them.

She asked the driver to stop. "Please wait here."

Dusk hovered at the edges of the warehouses. The smell of the sea wafted to her, though not enough to cover the stench of the small child who stood before her, her hand out.

"Are you well, miss?" She thought the child before her was a girl.

"Aye. Just hungry. Do you have a coin for me?"

"I do." She removed the coin from her reticule. She hesitated. Perhaps the child would see she had more and reach for it, grab what she could. But the child accepted it and said, "This'll buy a soup bone for me mother. She's not well."

"And your father?"

"Mum says he ain't coming back. She works the mills to feed us."

"Your mother works when she's not ill?"

"She does, ma'am. Wants us to go to school, she says. Me brother and me, but we can't." The girl bit the coin.

"Yes, schooling is good."

"But not for now. She's sick, and me and my brother, we collect for her."

Dorothea gave the child another coin. "May your mother soon be well."

"I would like to use the barn," Dorothea told Madam Dix the next day. They sat in the kitchen of the cottage. Cookie served mashed yams with butter as the evening meal, but she had cleared the dishes and shooed Charles and Joseph out, leaving Dorothea and her grandmamma alone. Benji the spaniel lay at the old woman's feet.

"The barn? Whatever for?"

"To make it a school for children who cannot afford to pay."

"Wasteful of your time." She tugged at the strings of her black cap.

"I have nothing but time, Grandmamma. And I believe this is what God has called me to do: to teach. Did our Lord not say words that meant that as we do for the least of these we do for Him? I do this class for Him, for those He spent His time with, the sinners and tax collectors." Dorothea warmed to her subject and her reasoning. Even she could hear the increased confidence in her voice.

Madam Dix grunted, and the dog perked up his head. "However will you engage them? They're hungry and won't be able to think. Worse, they'll scamper around the estate doing who knows what. I do not think this a worthy cause."

"But you will not forbid me?"

"And if I do, would you defy me?"

"I will remind you that you have leased the 'estate' except for the cottage to the Hudsons, and if Mrs. Hudson agrees to let me use the barn, I will proceed." She swallowed. "It is a courtesy that I ask you before speaking to Mrs. Hudson." The woman squinted at Dorothea, who now heard her voice quiver. "The barn is not being used now, and the children might even be able to improve its value as they help prepare it for their own school."

Madam Dix sat silently for a moment and then said, "Use the carriage house at least. I don't want them jabbering that Orange Court offered nothing but a barn. And while we are on the subject of schooling, I may as well tell you that I have enrolled Charles in the Boston Latin School. It's time he had proper instruction."

The sudden jolt to Dorothea's stomach felt like a mule kick. "He won't be in my classes?"

"He can visit you when he comes home on weekends."

"And Joseph?"

"He'll continue with my teaching."

"Was Charles not progressing as you'd hoped?"

"It's better he has a male instructor. It will prepare him for Harvard. Living with other boys will be good for him too." She added, "I think I'll forgo your readings this evening, Dorothea," and hobbled out of the room.

Benji started after the woman, then returned, lifting his paws onto Dorothea's lap. She looked into his watery eyes and scratched his chin. He panted happily in response. "At least you offer a little comfort to me," she said.

"Benji! Come!" the old woman called, and the dog scooted away.

Dorothea dove into the new school project, pressing against the tightness in her chest when she thought of Charles's being gone and Joseph as distant as if he were too. Charles was ready for the Latin school, but she missed him and his sea stories. The latter made her nervous as she imagined him on a ship during a raging Atlantic storm. Still, she knew that her influence over him waned and would more so now.

Dorothea wrote daily to Anne, telling her of her project and her visits to the wharves and the business sections of the city. Wherever she encountered a small girl, she handed her a coin and asked if she might like to come to school so that one day she could earn more coins to support herself and her family. She never found the child she had spoken with on her first visit, but a dozen others were there to take her place.

"The school will only be in the late afternoons and early evenings," she assured the parents when prospective students took her to their homes.

"Why would you do this?"

Because it is my duty. "I have the ability and the gift given me to teach, and it is my desire to share that gift. It is your duty to receive it."

"Ain't had many gifts given me, so don't have much practice in recepting them," one father said. He pressed his hand on his daughter's head. Were those lice moving through her hair?

She would have to bathe them all. Dorothea cleared her throat. It would be something to manage in the charity school, head lice and even ticks perhaps.

"Give me to know that but one human being has been made better by my precepts, more virtuous by my example, and I shall possess a treasure that the world can never take from me," she wrote to Anne after the first week of her carriage house class.

Anne replied, "You are doing the Lord's work with these children. They will remember not only their education but the woman who made it possible, a woman who could have spent her evenings bowling on the lawn or reading the *Sunday Scholar's Magazine* instead of your charity. I am so proud of you, my sister. So very proud. Reverend Channing will be too."

Anne's words filled Dorothea, made her realize how important friendships were and how much she had missed having someone she could share her deepest thoughts with but who also showed her how to encourage others.

"I have a request," Dorothea told Anne one Saturday. They had come to the stables where the Heaths kept several riding horses. They had left the clan at home and now rode side by side, sunlight flickering through the trees. "Don't save my letters."

"Why ever not?"

"What if someone saw how deeply I express my emotions. My worries over Charles, my struggle with purpose, my wish that I had a child of my own. I've even shared with you Madam Dix's interruption in my guidance of my brothers, how deeply she hurt me. Those ought not to be read by others."

"I've written personal thoughts to you. Do you destroy my letters?" Anne asked.

"I do. But only after I've read them a dozen times."

Anne grinned. "When I broke the porcelain you gave me, I thought I had chipped a part of my heart away. I'm sure I wrote that."

"You did. And I treasure the words but keep them in here." She patted her chest.

"I do not have your fabulous memory," Anne

said. "I think you remember everything you read, word for word."

"Nearly."

"I wrap your letters in packets tied with ribbon and keep them in a wooden box in the attic trunk. No one will see them." Anne resettled her riding crop.

"Do you?"

"You're like one of my sisters. Letters are a part of who you are. It would be like ripping away a portion of my skin, my bones, to toss them away."

Dorothea leaned across her horse and reached for the bridle of Anne's horse to stop them both. She pecked her friend on the cheek and felt her face grow hot. "Thank you for that. You are my only . . . friend."

Anne touched her cheek. "Only because you do not share yourself with others as you do with me. My sisters adore you. Mary especially."

"Do they?"

"More would find your intellect fascinating and your heart as the fire in the hearth. You simply do not allow others to know you, Thea."

"If they did, they would soon find fault. I worry over that with you too."

"Nonsense. I find no fault in you except you do not laugh enough and you take yourself too seriously. You're a young woman, successful and full of generosity. But you should also have time for rest or you will become sick. I have seen this happen in men and women who work too hard in the care of others. With both schools operating, I fear you'll fall ill."

"I'll work harder at laughing," Dorothea said.

Anne laughed. "Somehow I knew you'd make a task of it." She leaned forward and put her horse into a canter. Dorothea followed closely behind.

Ten

That Little Stability

Dorothea's days were filled with her school at Orange Court, her evenings at the carriage house school, and Sundays with the Heaths, and in between she wrote. She wrote to Anne, to her former Worcester students, and to Charles and Joseph, giving them instruction for living. She wondered how long she could maintain this grueling pace. And it was grueling. She arose at 4:00 a.m., donned enough petticoats to ward off winter drafts, dressed in a simple black linen dress with a white lace collar, fixed tea, and wrote. She wrote down ideas, stories, and even hymns she intended to use in her school. A kind of frenzy drove her days, and she heard herself be short with her students when they seemed unable to grasp a concept a mere day after she had taught them. At least cold weather halted the head lice in the carriage house schoolchildren, and in November she temporarily closed that school as the children all had coughs.

She worried about Marianna and Grace. The child often missed class, and the last time she had seen Grace, the woman had a racking cough. She could help if only Grace would agree.

"Marianna needs to live with me." Grace's lips shook and her fisted knuckles at the side of her gray linen dress were white as bone.

"But you could rest more," Dorothea said. "I can tell you're ailing. Your cough grows worse. Marianna knows it. She worries about you." It was the end of the school year and the children had left the library, allowing Dorothea to have time with Grace.

"You are welcome to visit her during this break," Grace said. "I have appreciated all you've done to advance her lessons. She adores you, but no. I need her to be with me."

"But what does Marianna need?"

"She needs a loving mother, which I am." Grace's voice seethed.

"I know. I know. That's right. I'm so sorry." Dorothea's mouth felt dry. "I don't know what I was thinking." She reached for Grace who pulled back like a magnet against an opposite force. "Of course. She needs to be with a mother who meets her needs." Her heart pounded in her head. How foolish! She must never try to separate a child from a parent. She hoped Grace would not keep Marianna from the school in the summer term. "I only proposed it to give you some relief. I . . . if I can do that ever, even for a day, I'd be happy to have Marianna with me."

Grace's shoulders drooped, and she sank onto a high-back chair. "I can't seem to fight off the fatigue. Nor the cough for any length of time."

"What do the doctors say?"

"They don't know." She cleared her throat. "But yes, perhaps a few days this summer Marianna could be with you. I'll send a note of invitation. I know you only want the best for her."

"I do. Absolutely. And for you. You're family." She'd have to be careful. Families could so easily be separated.

A boarder who had recently been in Philadelphia talked of the Asylum for the Relief of Persons Deprived of the Use of Their Reason. Like an academic, he raised the issue of whether treatment for such people was possible. Could suffering be relieved or was such misery the result of the new industrial efforts, long hours worked in dark factories, farm girls brought in from the country with too much freedom and lack of discipline causing them to lose their ability to think? Boarders had opinions, and Dorothea listened.

"All people are worthy of opportunity to change their ways," she finally offered.

One of the boarders wiped at his mouth with a linen napkin. "The asylum is more for the relief of the rest of us." There were chuckles around the table, but Dorothea did not join in.

"Isn't the asylum a scriptural response to such people in need?" These were divinity students much more deeply immersed in Scripture. Dorothea was probably stepping into deep waters with these well-trained scholars; she didn't know how to swim. "They can't all be there because of excessive drinking."

"There might be a few innocents among them. Children, perhaps," said the student who had begun the discussion.

"Doesn't Luke 13:4–5 tell us that misfortunes are not necessarily the result of sin?"

"She has you there," said a scholar with a bulbous nose and glasses too small for his face. "The asylum is privately funded, so what are we to say about it anyway?"

"I don't believe it is privately funded," a physician-student commented, wiping his pencil-thin mustache with his napkin. "What alienist would put his money into such a venture? Surely a private medical hospital would be a better investment than a private asylum."

The conversation wandered into other kinds of investments, and Dorothea found herself lagging behind, her thoughts on her mother, the walnut-haired woman who had once joined them on Sundays, held up by her and her father whenever they entered the Methodist meeting hall. Her mother's head would loll from side to side. Although her clear skin and thick hair made her seem ageless, her eyes were often melted holes in snow-white skin. Was her mother a patient for an asylum? Would placing her in such a place keep her from offending her family and neighbors?

Dorothea often wondered how her mother was faring in New Hampshire. *Maybe I should visit.* No, visiting would do no good, but only agitate her mother at seeing her daughter after all these years. Maybe by now she had forgotten she had a daughter. Still, maybe her mother could be treated as though her state of mind was a disease. Maybe new apothecary salts and potions could induce a cure. Few considered the mentally ill curable. Aunt Sarah had suggested that Mary Bigelow Dix had never been right, never able to carry out her motherly duties. *Unavailable.*

The supper discussion ended. If Dorothea could help prevent mind deterioration by giving children reasoning tools, she could perhaps keep them from sinking into a world of too much freedom, a cause of mental disease that many agreed on. That was her task then as a teacher. Prevention. Her mother must have had no one teaching her when she was a child.

• • •

She had been sending sections of a book she was writing to Anne, and the two often discussed her progress on Saturday afternoons as they wandered through the Heath gardens or strolled beside the harbor. Dorothea wasn't sure if it was the conversations she enjoyed most or if just being with Anne lightened her days. This woman supported her and genuinely cared for her; the knowledge inspired Dorothea and gave her energy for teaching.

"You really think the book is interesting?" She'd thought her words a bit stiff, but if Anne approved . . .

Anne was as tall as Dorothea, and people nodded and stepped aside as the pair walked arm in arm through the streets of Boston, parasols sheltering them from the summer sun.

"The work is fabulous. You must get it published."

Dorothea wrote the book as a conversation between a mother and a daughter. The child would ask: Why, Mother, did you spend so much time in the factory the other day? I saw the spindles whirl till I was tired; do tell me why you looked so long at that great pile called machinery.

The mother would respond: I will tell you, my dear; I wished to understand the principle upon which the spools and spindle were set in motion; the action of the looms; and closely to observe every part of what you thought so uninteresting.

"It's a lovely way to share information, and it models respectful communication between mothers and daughters. Papa might have a publisher friend he could put you in touch with."

"That would be . . . that would be wonderful. Thank you. I'm nearly finished."

"You do so much more with your time than I," Anne said. They stopped at a clock shop and looked in the window. "I don't even need a clock. I don't really have to be anywhere on time. Except church, of course. But my sisters keep me apprised of my appointments."

"I'm not sure what I would do with my time if I didn't have these projects."

"I suppose that's why we're supposed to marry and have children. So we're always occupied and never wondering what else we're supposed to be doing. Yet marriage eludes us, it seems." Anne's hat brim brushed Dorothea's.

"Anne, has anyone ever proposed to you?" It was a daring question to ask. So private.

Anne began walking again, this time with both hands on her parasol. "I did have a proposal long ago." She hesitated. "I even accepted."

"Did you? What happened? If I'm not prying."

"He . . . felt pressured, I suspect. To make an arrangement before he went to Europe to school. And then he never returned. Papa received condolences from his family, apologizing for their son's behavior, but I never heard from him.

He married an Italian countess or something."

"I didn't mean to lance an old wound," Dorothea said. She wanted to reach out and comfort Anne, place a hand on her shoulder, but she didn't.

"Oh, it's a wound well scarred over. After that, I wanted only friends, not the ache of caring deeply for someone only to have him spurn my love. Not even care enough to tell me directly. I suppose that's the greatest humiliation. His parents told my parents. I felt like damaged goods being returned when I was as I had always been."

"Perfect," Dorothea said. "You are perfect. His is a terrible loss that he will never know."

Anne smiled. "Thank you." They paused next in front of a silver shop with Paul Revere pieces for sale. People dressed in finery walked behind them. Yellow and pink parasols reflected in the window. "And you?"

"Me? No. No marriage proposals. Not even an interest, really. A frightened kiss by a divinity student, however." Anne raised her eyebrows. "Nothing, really. I adored my French tutor and my riding instructor, but of course one must keep one's feelings controlled when it comes to the employed classes." Dorothea laughed. "Now I am in the employed class with parents hiring me to teach their students."

"You're a businesswoman. Very different," Anne told her.

"Still. I've found no one to give my heart to

except my brothers. And you, my friend. You are my best friend." Her palms felt clammy inside her gloves. Her chest hurt from exposing her care so openly.

"There's Marianna," Anne said.

"Yes," Dorothea whispered. "She is family and I adore her." She hesitated. "But it's you who mean so much. I should die if ever I did or said something that turned you from me."

Anne pulled her arm through Dorothea's and patted her hand. The brims of their hats touched once again. Dorothea smelled Anne's minty breath. "You should never worry over such impossibilities as that. Besides, families work through such things."

Dorothea looked away, felt tears burn at her nose.

That night Dorothea apologized in a letter to Anne. She had not meant to put such a weight on her friend by asking about proposals or burdening her with fears that Anne might one day find another dear friend. "I have never had a friend such as you, never. If I pass the boundaries of those lines of which I know nothing, please forgive me. You are the stake beside me that keeps me sturdy in a buffeting wind." She read and reread the lines, then sealed the letter with wax before she added more.

Boston publisher Munroe and Francis agreed to print and sell Dorothea's first book. They titled it

Conversations on Common Things, or Guide to Knowledge, with Questions. A subtitle *For the Use of Schools* was added. "You ought to add 'for use in families' as well," Edmund Monroe noted.

"Oh, I'm hardly one to speak of how a family ought to be. Too presumptuous."

Munroe shrugged. "And your name will go below that."

"My name?" Her heart began to pound and her breath threatened to catch in her throat. "Oh. No. That would be unseemly for a proper woman. No, just say 'By a Teacher.' "

Munroe wiggled his pursed lips, then shrugged.

Madam Dix would be appalled if Dorothea's name were to be associated with something as mundane as book publishing. It was not the proper pursuit of a Boston woman. For some reason, what the woman thought of Dorothea still mattered.

"Oh, that's silly," Anne told her later when Dorothea visited to thank Mr. Heath for referring her to Munroe and Francis and to share with her best friend this wonderful news. "Why not have a little public recognition for your work?"

"I have my students' and their parents' recognition. That's enough." She looked away, then said, "I would share this with you, and only you, Anne. I do not want the world's applause, but I would so like to be a fitting companion of the Virtuous Great."

"It's a glorious ambition to wish to receive 'well done, good and faithful servant' from God Himself," Anne told her and clasped her hand.

"I want that so much, with an intentness that threatens to annihilate the little stability that now sustains me."

Anne raised an eyebrow. "What a strange thing for you to say, Thea. You seem quite the stable woman to me. More so than many I could name."

Dorothea gave a choked laugh. "Of course." She pulled her hands from Anne's, fluttered them, dismissive. "I'm not sure what I was thinking. God, through your friendship, has given me all I've needed to be on solid footing for my life. I am forever grateful. Forget what I said about my annihilation. I . . . was being dramatic, something I rarely am. It must be the vapors coming on."

That evening alone in her room, she wrote to Grace and Marianna, asking if the child might be able to go to a concert with her at the Harvard campus. She had received no note of invitation from Grace, so she took the initiative with courage. She told Grace of her publishing contract too. Sharing a good thing with family was acceptable, wasn't it? The letter sealed, she fixed herself hot water with lemon and honey to fend off a sore throat and cough. Why did her cough seem to follow on the heels of consternation?

The thought of her name attached to the book had upset her. She wondered if Grace's cough might be related to the same kind of thing, a bodily response to an emotional turn of events. Nonsense. Grace had seen doctors. She thought Grace might suffer from consumption, and hoped it wasn't. Dorothea's cough was simply from the fall foliage making her throat feel as rough as poor paper. She blew out the candle, but sleep came late, riding on the recycling of her day.

Marianna wrote in reply, her tiny script saying she could not attend the concert but could Miss Dix please come to tea. *Miss Dix—no longer Auntie.*

The next day Dorothea walked to the small brownstone where Marianna and Grace lived. River mist her companion. Marianna was sweeping the brick steps of wet leaves as she approached.

"Hello, Aunt—Miss Dix." She curtsied, then dropped the broom and ran to her, hugging Dorothea's black skirts. "I'm so glad you came. Can we draw?"

"Whatever you like. But I thought I came for tea."

"Mummy is fixing tea, but I'd rather draw."

"Fancy that. I happen to have brought a set of paints with me. Would you like to try your hand at that?"

"Oh yes! Come! I'll tell Mummy and she can watch."

Dorothea did not gasp when she saw Grace

was as slender as a cap ribbon and just as limp. "Grace. You're . . . may I help . . . you're so . . . frail."

"I am. I am. But Marianna wanted you to come. And so did I. Please, sit."

Dorothea removed the reticule from her wrist and placed the carpetbag with the paints and small easel at her feet. Grace poured the tea, and the steam and the scent of mint lifted from the cups.

Dorothea glanced at Grace, then moved her eyes to the tea and added cream and sugar. She searched for words. Grace was so much worse.

Marianna pressed herself into Dorothea's side. "Mummy's been sicker."

"No. I haven't. Just more tired." The defense brought on a cough. "Why don't you go to your room and draw for a bit. Let Miss Dix and me talk."

"She brought paints."

"I did." Dorothea opened the carpetbag. "Here they are." Marianna smelled the pigments. "Why not take them to your room, as your mother suggested. We'll join you in a moment."

Grace nodded approval and the child skipped off.

"I asked you to come because—"

"You want me to take her." Dorothea was breathless, pressed her hands over Grace's. "I understand. It would be so much easier for you both. I'll take very good care of her, I will. She is an adorable child, and my looking after her will give you the chance to truly get better."

Grace leaned back in her chair. "No! No! Nothing like that. I asked you to come to tell you that Marianna may attend only two days now at your school. I need her here."

"I . . . Of course." Dorothea's face warmed. "I'm sorry. I didn't mean to upset you. I only want to help. You suffer so."

"I haven't forgotten your . . . offer, Miss Dix. But, for now, your being her teacher is what I need, just not as many days."

"She'll be missed." *I'll miss her so much.*

"Then enjoy her today as much as you can."

Eleven

Tumbling Down

Dorothea's first book came out in the spring of 1824. The publisher held a small party for her that summer. The Heath girls attended, along with some of the Harvard students. Mary charmed the room; her dimples and tinkling laughter were a magnet for the men. Dorothea wore a sable-colored linen dress with a feather-like bustle and matching collar, as dressed-up as she ever was. She allowed herself a moment of pleasure looking in the mirror before entering the room where all turned and applauded. Sales were rapid. Parents as well as teachers purchased it. As a result, an educational reformer approached Dorothea to teach at the Female Monitorial School in Boston. She would lead an afternoon session of needle-work for seventy girls—if she accepted.

"Quite the sugar in your tea," Anne said when Dorothea shared the news.

"Madam Dix said I was a novice for professor-level work."

"So will you do it? It means your days will be totally filled."

Dorothea wondered if she should. She would teach Orange Court classes in the morning, the monitorial classes in the afternoon until supper—if she took the position—and then her carriage house classes in the evening. She wanted to resume the latter. On Saturday mornings she helped Cookie wash the laundry at the cottage, and maybe, if Grace consented, she might tutor Marianna in the afternoon. She'd have Sundays for church services and visits with the Heaths. Not to mention she was already working on another book, writing in the early morning. Full days would relieve her soul of loneliness.

George Emerson led the school. He was a fatherly man with white hair, oozing wisdom and soft words. His new approach for instruction used schedules and activities as a way to prevent student disruption and restlessness. Assistants drilled small groups of younger students, moving quickly from one drill to another. In this way, Dorothea could manage seventy girls at a time while she supervised numerous assistants. She would be training future teachers and thus expanding the moral influence of education. She decided to accept.

In her own school, Dorothea noticed the older girls achieved more success with the students than she did. She found herself relying on the placard for discipline, and she was sharper with her words. "When you work with the girls, they seem more . . . attentive," Dorothea whispered to an assistant at the Orange Court school. They were eating goat cheese and Mrs. Hudson's fresh bread in the corner of the library. "You've never brought out the placard, have you?"

"I have not."

"Why is that?" The girl hesitated. "You don't have to be afraid. Just tell me what you think."

"They see you as playing favorites, Miss Dix. I'm careful not to do so."

"Favorites? I don't think so."

"Marianna." She whispered the name so the child wouldn't hear. "You let her skip assignments and seem blind to her . . . giggling and distractions. You never have any corrections for her even when she shows a need for additional guidance."

"Her mother is ill." Dorothea licked her finger, dabbed at a crumb on her bodice.

"Many have ill mothers or circumstances that affect their concentration, Miss Dix." She dropped her eyes.

"Favorites . . . I hadn't been aware."

The assistant, emboldened, said: "If I might add, you've been short of late. Impatient with the older students, which only adds to the disorder when the younger children hear your sharp tone and worry over upsetting you but not knowing why."

Dorothea wanted to snap back that if her assistant had any idea of how much time and work it took to teach three schools, meet with parents, confer with publishers, write letters, read to her grandmother, do the laundry for her and her brothers, and darn her own socks, she would understand why a woman sometimes lost her temper. Dorothea felt her face grow warm. "Best we get back to our duties."

She needed to find ways to save time and decided to wear only her black linen dress each day, easily brushed every evening. She would eat porridge for breakfast and work on her book projects while she ate, finishing with prayers and Scripture readings. She would forgo Sunday afternoons at the Heaths and use the time to visit the parents of the carriage house students, perhaps offer a class for them on Saturday afternoons. Their children would learn better if the parents also had increased education. Sunday messages by Reverend Channing were a must. Dorothea's sore throat came and went, but if she napped Sunday evenings, perhaps she could nurse it away.

"Your friends, the Heaths, express concern for you, Miss Dix," Reverend Channing told her one Sunday as she was leaving church, Anne having stepped out in front of her. "They fear you overdo with your many hours of service to so many."

"Is that not what we are called to do, Reverend?"

"Even the Lord went away by Himself at times to rest."

"I'll take that under advisement."

She chatted briefly with Anne, declining her usual invitation. She rode home with Reverend Channing's words ringing in her ears. Was he telling her to stop her services to others? Was he chastising her? Or did he want her to know that she was worried over? She liked imagining that this fatherly soul cared for her personal well-being. But it was his inspiration, his passion for service, that sent her on this task. Maybe he was telling her something else? But she wasn't sure of the message.

"You have to come," Anne insisted. "It's the Marquis de Lafayette's opening fete on Beacon

Hill. All the desirables will be there. And you, as a published author, famous teacher, child of a Dix—you have to attend. Besides, I've heard this rumor that 'Miss Dix is engaged to her former French teacher.' You must come dressed with your elegant shoulders bare and your hair coiled to the sky and flirt with every available man there so as to dispel the rumors."

"I haven't seen my French tutor for years," she squinted at Anne. "You're making that up."

"Not about the party for the Marquis." Anne drew closer. "You've always said you admired him and the help he gave our country. You wished your father held such bravery." Dorothea rubbed her temples with her fingers. "The president is attending! Papa got us all invitations. You deserve a party."

She did admire the Marquis. Had she shared her comparison with her father with Anne? It might be pleasant to say she had seen the president of the United States. Maybe her grandmother would be pleased. "I might not know how to talk with him if he should speak to me." She laughed and added, "Maybe I should just wait outside and jump into his carriage when he arrives and kiss his hand."

"I would love to see such spontaneity from you!"

"It isn't likely." Why had she said such a thing? "But I will come. I'll even let my students out early in honor of the great man's visit."

"It's been so long since we've had any time together." Anne pressed her head toward Dorothea's. "It'll be fun to do something grand. I'll loan you a dress, if you would like."

"If I'm to bare my shoulders, you'll have to," Dorothea laughed. "I wonder if we could get an invitation for Marianna. What a thrill that would be for the child." *And I would have a real purpose for being there, exposing her to such greatness.*

Anne stepped back. "You are pouring your heart into that girl and I worry for you, Thea. Besides, Marianna and her mother can hear of the great man from you. I think that should be close enough, don't you?"

She didn't know if that would be "close enough." Threads of worry for the child and her mother and a wish for herself kept entangling, never pulling closer to be sewn into something predictable and firm.

On the appointed day the ballroom was alight with hundreds of candles. Fresh bouquets of mums had been garnered from numerous Boston gardens to decorate and scent the room. Women fanned themselves in the August heat as they caught glimpses of their pearls and jewels in the many mirrors set around the room to reflect the candlelight. Dorothea watched as the great man met the eyes of everyone to whom he was introduced, bowing from his waist. Each person wanted to be blessed by his smile, his eyes, and he appeared to know it, meeting everyone's expectations. He caused even older matrons to giggle with silliness when he kissed their hands. Or had he kissed them? No, Dorothea decided, he merely brushed his lips at the air above the women's hands, which is what he did to Dorothea when she was introduced and properly curtsied to the Frenchman. Her heart pounded. Such a silly, girlish feeling. She wished she'd asked Marianna; she could move the girl forward between them, let the child have the attention.

His hair was combed forward, perhaps covering a balding spot, accentuating his long, sharp nose, his small mouth, and a deep dimple in his chin. He was portly and utterly charming. Although he spoke excellent English, Dorothea chose to address him in French when he stopped in front of her. She stumbled with her words, and her face turned as hot as a farrier's forge.

"Your French is exquisite, mademoiselle." She lowered herself into a curtsy. He lifted her chin as he spoke in English and took her hand. Her body reveled in alien sensation. *He touched me!*

"*Merci.*" His eyes were like marbles. They glowed. "I . . . I have long admired you, sir. For what you did for our country." *My corset! It will be the death of my breath.* The general's aide beside him whispered in his ear.

"Am I to understand that you are the famous young author and teacher?"

She regained her voice. "What I do is small in comparison to what you did to save the states."

"I only helped your compatriots forge your nation. Teachers do the work to keep the flames of democracy burning that it might be forever shaped in the fashion of the people, *oui*?"

"*Oui.*"

"Your voice with its cello charm would be a joy to listen to each day. I envy your students." The general released her hand with a single pat, sent a dazzling smile, then greeted the woman next to her with a silent nod. Dorothea felt moisture beneath her corset. How extraordinary! To be included in such an entourage. Her, a simple woman without a dowry. She fanned herself and caught Anne's eye. Her friend was smiling.

Alone, Dorothea remembered the evening and the Marquis's words, and her hands shook as she heated honey for her sore throat. Tears came to her eyes.

She wrote to Anne, "I was early taught by sorrow to shed tears and now when sudden joy lights up I find it difficult to repress the full and swelling tide of feeling. At least I did not embarrass myself or you by tears on the Marquis's strong hands."

The tea steeped, she wiped her eyes. Her hands shook as she sipped. She would be afraid to visit

Lafayette again when he returned in September. She would gush and make a fool of herself. What was the matter with her? A proper Boston woman simply did not bare her emotions to the world as though they were shoulders, inviting attention. Becoming giddy, almost tearful, when meeting a war hero suggested that she was childish, pedestrian, or worse—not in control of her reason. She swallowed a gasp. *Is that it? Do I fear becoming my mother in those moments?*

She slipped beneath the sheets and stared at the open window. She needed to be busier, take on new tasks, forgo any party invitations, leave no moments unscheduled, no time to ponder the origin of tears and giddiness. She would tutor Marianna on the days she could not be in school. They would roam the woods together. She would help the girl write little poems. She would work with the Fragment Society, the group from church who took knitted baby clothes to the tenement houses of the textile mill workers. Like the boy who gave his fish and bread for the feeding of the five thousand, she would give all she had to give. Perhaps there would be fragments left over to serve others. If not fish and bread, then books and time to tutor children. Yes, keeping busy. That's what mattered.

In the weeks that followed Lafayette's visit, Dorothea pressed herself further, rushed in where she might have rested. "Please, Mrs. Hudson. Could you leave the porridge out so that I might get it by four o'clock tomorrow morning? It took me more time than I can spare to have my breakfast."

"Of course. I'm sorry, I—"

"No, I'm sorry. I ought not to speak so sharply."

"You're very thin, Miss Dix, if I may say so. Your collar could reach twice around your neck."

Dorothea grabbed at her throat. She swept back toward her room. There was no need to chastise Mrs. Hudson. The woman did her work well. Why was not being able to find the porridge to heat this morning so upsetting? And it was where it usually was anyway. Dorothea overlooked it. Was she getting thin? She stared into a mirror.

Later, at the monitorial school, an assistant approached her, lightly touching her hand. She startled. "Miss Dix? Mistress Billings asked a question."

"Did she? I'm sorry. My mind wandered. Not a good thing for a teacher, now is it?" She patted her assistant's shoulder, then asked the girl to repeat her question. She ignored the curious look on her assistant's face. Was she becoming like her mother?

When word came via messenger that the book was going into a third printing, she let Anne know first. Her royalties were growing and she would send some now to her mother's family, for her care. The publisher would add "and Families" on the front piece so people would know *Conversations* was not for teachers only. And Munroe added Dorothea's name, her discovery of the fact too late to protest. She wasn't sure she wanted to object anyway.

"I so do not know what a family truly is," Dorothea told Anne. "Except for my time with yours. I fear the name is misleading, that I should be so bold as to instruct families."

"I always said you had talent," Anne told her. They walked arm in arm along the cobbled streets of Beacon Hill. They admired the window boxes of flowers, stopped to name the varieties, and heard birds twittering in the verdant trees. Blue sky was an umbrella over their heads. "Talent is a currency," Anne said, "and you spend it wisely. I'm glad your name is at last on that book."

"Is it sinful to appreciate recognition?"

"Of course not, though it would make an interesting discussion over our Sunday table— should you ever find time to join us. But I doubt that sharing one's talents could be called sinful, even if there is recognition for it. Are you still glowing in the Marquis's words?"

"No. I've rethought my tears alone in my room. There was no real recognition. His aide simply told him who I was."

"But he said kindly things about your teaching. And your voice."

They watched as a carthorse made its way along the street. It looked tired and hot.

"There ought to be fountains for the horses," Dorothea noted.

"You're changing the subject."

"Yes. To suggest that I understand families . . . this is misleading, I think. You are my only family, Anne. The only family who gives me what I so desperately need." Her voice caught and she turned away. *And Marianna, whom I would claim as my own if allowed.*

Anne pulled her arm around Dorothea's shoulder. "You are always welcome in our home."

Dorothea nodded and wiped at pesky tears. She prayed the promise would never be revoked. She wasn't sure she could survive if it was.

Dorothea picked up Marianna on a fall day, and they went to the stables, where she and Anne often rode. She was making time for pleasure. Anne said she needed respite, and Dr. Channing concurred. Time with Marianna gave her that. Orange, red, and brown leaves drifted from trees into fall-like colors on Marianna's paint pallet. Horses raced along the fences, then turned and stopped, full of play, then started again, tails raised, manes flowing.

"They're so big." Marianna, though now nearly eight years old, was a slight child. The tiny blue veins in the back of her hands were like etchings on fine silver. Her curls flowed beneath her brown straw hat wrapped in white gossamer. Two satin ribbons like a waterfall flowed down her back as she stepped in front of Dorothea.

"They are. But you're strong enough to handle a gentle horse. We'll find the perfect animal to introduce you to."

The girl stepped onto the bottom rail of the corral, white ruffles from her dress cascading over her heels. *Is she washing her own clothes?* She hung over the top with her elbows. "That one! The pretty red one."

"Chestnut, that's the correct name for the color."

"Could I ride that chestnut, Auntie? The one that's looking at me? Oh," she squealed. "He's coming right toward me!"

"I think it's a she, but it does look like she's picked you out." The mare lowered her head to Marianna's face, soft brown eyes watching the child. Marianna's hat ribbons fluttered in the wind, but the sudden movement did not bother the horse. *She'll be steady for the girl.* Marianna touched the nose of the mare, and the animal wiggled its whiskers. Marianna laughed. "Let's see what we can do to further your introduction."

They walked to the barn, the child's hand like soft butter in her palm. The horse trotted along the fence beside them. It was a great day. Dorothea hadn't said where they were going and perhaps she should have. But Grace hadn't asked. They'd be fine. Nothing would happen. This was a good stable, and all they'd do today is walk Marianna around on the back of the mare.

"Can we do it again, Auntie?" Marianna had taken a dozen turns around the corral, stepped down, and patted the horse's nose. A lovely, uneventful day.

"Let's take her to the water trough." Dorothea checked her chain watch. "We should return soon so your mother won't worry."

Marianna petted the horse and said, "Mummy's dying."

Dorothea stopped and looked at the girl. "Oh. No. She's just very ill."

Marianna shook her head. "She's dying. Mummy told me. I'll be all alone."

Why would she say such a thing to a child? "I'm sure you misunderstood. Cholera has been in the city, but your mother doesn't have that dreaded disease. She's just . . . frail. Come, let's take one more ride and then off to home we go."

In the carriage the child fell asleep against Dorothea's side. She pulled her closer. *A child of my own.* It was not to be. *But if Grace is truly dying . . .*

At Grace's, Dorothea apologized. "I hope you don't mind that I took her riding. I should have consulted you."

Marianna chattered like a squirrel about her

day. "And the horse came right over to me. It chose me, Mummy."

"No. I'm sure it was a nice"—Grace took a deep breath—"surprise for her." Marianna sat beside her mother as she lay on the daybed. The child adjusted the quilt across her mother's legs. The girl curled up beside her, laid her head on her mother's chest, her small hand patting her in comfort. "I'm glad you had a nice time."

"I told her, Mummy."

"Told her what?"

"I told her you were dying."

"Hush," Dorothea said. She swallowed.

Grace pushed herself up on the daybed, moving Marianna. "All our days are numbered, you know. I'm having a good day today. So it'll be awhile."

"I know my numbers, Mummy." She began counting.

Her mother patted her shoulder. "Show Miss Dix your latest drawing."

The girl slipped off the daybed. She stopped to hug Dorothea, the blend of horse and child scents causing an ache in Dorothea's heart. Marianna scampered off.

"I was just preparing her." Grace coughed, holding a handkerchief she pulled from her sleeve over her mouth.

Was that blood? Dorothea's heart pounded, and the words came out before she could stop them.

"Why don't you . . . let me adopt Marianna. While you're still . . . with us. It would reassure her that if something were to happen to you, she would have a place to be, a home to go to." There. She'd said it out loud, the desire of her heart.

Grace wouldn't look at her. "I have relatives."

"Oh, I'm certain. But your relatives likely have other children to care for, and it might strain them. I have my work, my royalties to support us, and she would be with family, and I'd have a fam—"

"I understand that you only wish to help, Miss Dix. But—"

"Please. Dorothea." She reached for Grace's hand. "She could remain with you of course until you . . . well . . . but there would be certainty then. For you both." *And for me.*

"Be grateful I share her." She pulled her hands from beneath Dorothea's.

Marianna halted in the doorway, confusion on her face as she looked from her mother to Dorothea.

"Now, I think it's time for you to go," Grace said. "And best if you don't return."

She couldn't argue in front of the child so Dorothea left, her heart eclipsed. How had she failed at being generous, doing what she thought was right? Trying to fix things. So much for an uneventful day.

Twelve

Except in Fond Review

The Heaths were not in church that December morning. Dorothea had prepared her presents and brought them with her so she could join them later for hot cider and crumpets. Anne had sent the invitation. Dorothea packed small sachets for Caroline, Elizabeth, Susan, and pleasant Mary and a fruitcake begun in early November with fine rum for the elder Heaths, along with a packet of tobacco. Charles had told her of one of the shops where she could get the plant imported from the southern states. Her brother had come to Orange Court for the holidays, and she had reveled in his maturity. He was a nice young man. For Anne, she had purchased a second porcelain of an English lady to match one she had given her for her September birthday.

A chill in the sanctuary soon eased with the arrival of cloaked communicants with smiles to match the Advent season. The clunk of boots on boards, purses hitting the backs of pews, as women moved to leave the outside seat for fathers and husbands, were comforting sounds. Dorothea placed the basket at her feet, unsettled since she sat in the Heath pew alone. Maybe too much snow kept them? She looked around, nodded greetings. She hoped nothing had happened.

Reverend Channing's words inspired, helped her focus on the Christ child and the gift of grace God gave through such a vulnerable baby. Her thoughts turned to Grace and Marianna. She had sent notes but had heard nothing since the October day when she and Marianna had gone riding.

The Heaths never arrived. Should she still keep their invitation? What was socially acceptable? After the services she chatted with a young pastor whom Anne had pushed Dorothea toward. She had met him at a party with Ralph Waldo Emerson during the summer, and Anne had later commented on what a fine catch he would be. Dorothea found him bright and interesting, full of ideas, though none seemed to encourage the role of women as teachers, nor girls as students.

"I wonder where the Heaths are this fine morning," she asked Mr. Gannet.

"Oh." His eyes grew immediately soft. He picked up Dorothea's gloved hand. "There's been a death."

"At the Heaths?" He nodded. Her throat constricted. "Not Anne!"

"No." He looked down. "Mary. The youngest. A sudden illness and she is gone. Barely twenty." He lifted his head, sounded stalwart. "They think cholera. The family grieves, of course."

"Oh, yes. Oh."

She needed to be with them, to comfort them in their suffering. She was family. *They* were family. She raced down the stone steps, hailed a cab, and gave the address. How awful for them. Mary—gone. But why hadn't they sent word to her? Why hadn't she been told?

At Brookline, she climbed the steps to the Heath estate. Black mourning bunting already draped the massive door.

"The Heaths are taking no callers today due to the death of Miss Mary," the maid intoned.

"But they'll want to see me."

"Oh, Miss Dix, only family is being permitted in."

"Could you, that is, might you ask Anne, Miss Anne, advise her that her friend Thea is here to comfort her?"

The maid hesitated, then invited Dorothea in, asking her to wait in the foyer as she closed the door against the cold. In a moment, Anne came down the steps, her eyes red, her long face puffed.

"Anne, Anne, I am so sorry." Dorothea dropped the basket, opened her arms to encompass her friend. "I would have come earlier, but I didn't know."

Anne allowed Dorothea to hold her for a moment, then pushed away, her handkerchief pressed against a new rash of tears.

"She's gone," Anne said. "Mary's gone. I

can't . . . Thea. I . . . We . . ." She sobbed, then turned and ran back up the stairs.

Dorothea stared after her friend's back. Why did she not invite her to join the family in their grief? Didn't she belong here to help relieve their suffering? The maid came from a side room, opened the door. A blast of cold air hit Dorothea. The maid motioned her out. "I . . . the funeral?"

The maid shook her head, handed her the basket of gifts. Dorothea would have to ask Reverend Channing about arrangements. Maybe Anne would write to let her know. Yes. Anne would write.

Dorothea attended the funeral, though she was ushered to a guest pew and not to the family pew where she had so often sat with the Heaths. Relatives from out of town, cousins, aunts, uncles, all filled the space; the women's black bonnets and dresses unbroken by white lace. Psalm 27 rang in her ears, the fourteenth verse granting the words that stayed with her: "Wait on the LORD: be of good courage, and he shall strengthen thine heart: wait, I say, on the LORD."

Wait. The family grieved. They would invite her back.

Afterward, Anne, Caroline, and Elizabeth received people. Though lost in an unraveling of bonds, Dorothea joined the line like dozens of other mourners to pay their respects. "May I help you?" Dorothea asked. "Please. I can stop by later—"

"We'll be at the cemetery and then with family at the house. I'll write," Anne said. "I . . . I am too grieved to speak." Anne took the hand of the next mourner, pushing Dorothea along.

Still reeling from confusion and grief, Dorothea attended the graveside service. The headstones of Boston's finest marched like gray soldiers. Nothing protected mourners from the stirred ashes left from the heavy fires set to melt the frozen ground so the diggers could do their work. December was a bleak time to die. Even the ground resisted the transition from this life to the next.

It was Dorothea's first funeral, and at the sight of her friend, she moved into the family circle, moved beside Anne and leaned on her, sobbing her sorrow. Anne startled, pulled away, Dorothea's arms dangled at her side.

A divinity student approached and pulled Dorothea away from the distraught Anne.

Dorothea said, perhaps too loudly she thought later, "I need to be with their family, to help them! They suffer so!"

He held her back and she watched the Heath family close in on itself, arms around each other, circled in their loss, gaining sustenance from each other—their backs to Dorothea. Elizabeth Heath cast a glance at her, turned away. They acted like she was a scavenger rooting through private things in which she had no part.

The family did not open their doors during the Christmas season, nor through Epiphany. Dorothea looked for them each Sunday, still sitting in the Heath pew although she had paid the fees for her own and for Charles and Joseph if they chose to attend. Days passed like snails. Even her students did not distract. She wrote too many letters to Anne that went unanswered. Lent arrived. Surely on Easter the Heaths would attend to celebrate new life.

But they did not.

Wait.

Then, after weeks of longing, Dorothea received a short note from Anne. She pressed the letter to her heart before opening. *Wait. Yes, the psalm had told her to wait.* She opened it. No mention of the silence or absence but an expression of still profound sorrow. Dorothea paced the room. She must relieve her friend's torment. She wrote back, reminding Anne of what joys still awaited her with her other sisters and with her friends. She implored her to think of others. At the end of the letter, she asked her to think of her. "Mary's death, your mother's deep grieving, your own sorrow all tug at my own loneliness as I am kept from you." Couldn't Anne see that she still had sisters, still had loving parents? Dorothea was an iceberg alone in a cold, cold sea.

Two days later Dorothea grabbed at Anne's return letter, then sat and frowned. It was a short note, saying their wounds were deep and Dorothea needed to understand that she needed time to grieve with her family. "I am not family," Dorothea said out loud, the slice of the realization like cold snow on her face. But she couldn't give in, she couldn't.

"I am alone," Dorothea wrote. "You are all I have." Charles and Joseph had Madam Dix. Marianna had her mother. Dorothea had no one. "Don't take that from me. The living have their claims. Common charity would not allow you to forsake me."

Anne's notes became fewer, the salutation now to Miss Dix, not Thea. Dorothea knew she erred, was causing rather than diminishing the suffering of another. But like the apostle Paul, she was doing what she didn't want to do and what she wanted to do escaped her.

"We've decided to suspend Bertha from your school. She's doing well with her needlework and lettering, and with the spring snows, it's just difficult getting her here."

"I understand." This was the fourth parent who had told her this in the past month. The carriage house school had already closed with winter's onset. Even before that, a few of the carriage house students told her they were needed at home, so they wouldn't be attending for a while.

Her assistants at the Orange Court school didn't make eye contact with her, and one even suggested she needed more rest. Rest? When would she do that? She still had the monitorial position, but even there she found less enthusiasm for teaching than she had ever known. If this was her purpose, God's calling for her life, then why were her students leaving her like icicles melting in spring from the eaves?

Dorothea's chest felt thick as snow. She reread Thomas Gray's words, seeking solace. "Elegy Written in a Country Church-Yard" she'd read many times. One stanza stood out.

Beneath those rugged elms, that yew-tree's shade,
Where heaves the turf in many a mouldering heap,
Each in his narrow cell for ever laid,
The rude forefathers of the hamlet sleep.

Mary Heath forever lay in that narrow cell. Dorothea felt as though she lived beneath a moldering heap. The poem went on, line after line, and she wept with each stanza that crystallized loss as though it were a shard slicing her soul. She reread the line about the deceased: "He gained from Heaven ('twas all he wished) a friend."

That's all she had ever hoped for: a friend, a sister. Her own family. She wrote to her aunt Sarah but shared nothing of her struggle. Her cousin Mary's life was filled with children now, leaving little time to correspond. Despite all her wishes to do otherwise, she had pushed her closest family away. First Marianna. Now Anne. Was she never to find friendship until heaven?

Malaise settled over her. Students at the monitorial school became indistinct. The boarders irritated her with their talk of worldly things. She spent more time in her room, working on her stories, writing in her diary. She rarely read to her grandmother now. Charles and Joseph were thin threads in the fabric of her life. An orphan. That's what she was and would always be.

Anne's invitation to her for a weekend at Brookline speared her day with joy like a firecracker exploding high in an evening sky. Dorothea prayed that she would find a way not to push, not to jump ahead of where her friend might be. She prayed she could keep the pain of her own wounds to herself, not add to the misery of her friend. *Let compassion, not self-service, be my gift.*

She fluttered in preparation, changing collars, ironing a day cap, wearing a small straw hat instead. She brought with her the Christmas items she had never been able to present. She set the basket on the marble-top table in the parlor, but

144

Anne did not approach it, nor did she offer up any gift she might have made for Dorothea, a gift that Mary's death had interrupted, a gift to tell Dorothea she still had a place in Anne's heart. Dorothea asked after the health of Anne's parents.

"They're doing as well as can be expected when one outlives a child," Anne said.

"And you, my friend? Do you find respite in the Scriptures? In the promise of spring?"

Anne nodded, her eyes pooling before she turned away. "To have all my sisters live to adulthood and then this."

"Too much sadness." Dorothea was about to add something when the maid interrupted and said the other guests had arrived. She was just one of the guests? Yes, as the afternoon progressed, she might have been a swan on a lake, floating indistinct from many others. She hovered at the edges; remained after the others left. She read to Anne while she knitted. Then the two reversed roles, but the old closeness had disappeared, a wedge of sorrow in its place.

As the fire waned, Anne looked at the clock in its gold frame. "I tire," she said.

"Of course. It's been a long day. Thank you for including me." She started to say how much she missed her, how grateful she was to be invited back, and ask could she come next week. But she stopped herself. A prayer answered. She gathered her things, pulled on her cloak.

"Farewell, Dorothea." *Not Thea now.* Anne did not add, "Come back soon."

Dorothea longed for the shade of Gray's yew tree, but what she took with her instead was the image of the moldering heap.

They still corresponded. Dorothea kept her letters light, but Anne's responses—when she replied—were full of petty criticisms. Dorothea's use of poor-grade pencils rather than ink. She chastised Dorothea for changing a few words in the hymns she compiled. She suggested her children's stories lacked luster. "Children need adventure in a story, not just moral tomes."

Anne addressed her letters, not to Thea, but to Miss Dix. When the Heaths returned to the church on Federal Street, there were new guests, the Peabody sisters, sitting in the pews with them. Dorothea had heard of them, bright and wealthy and part of the circle containing the Emersons and Thoreaus.

Dorothea slipped into her own pew, well behind the Heaths'. She could barely sing the words to the hymns, her throat so closed with tears.

In June, at the event celebrating the final days of the Marquis de Lafayette's American tour, Dorothea joined the fete, this one more open to the public. She did not need the Heaths' invitation. She hoped she and Anne might share a fond memory of the earlier event. But Anne and her sisters stood with the Peabody sisters arm in arm this time. Elizabeth Peabody, in her exuberance, jumped into Lafayette's carriage when the door opened and kissed his hand, much to everyone's delight. Anne laughed. Dorothea was a moon eclipsed.

Dorothea's cough returned. She sent a note to Anne in poetic form, thinking it might well be her last.

> And mark how much one little year can do
> How much of Friendship that seemed made
>   to last,
> Unwearied love, affection firm and true,
> Are now beheld no more except in fond
>   review.

It wasn't Thomas Gray, but she hoped it would tell her friend how much she meant to her.

Anne did not reply.

With the warmth of summer, Dorothea closed her school, as she often did, looking forward to reading and perhaps even writing again; healing the wounds of a friendship lost. But her grandmother deemed to fill Dorothea's social void and her malaise by sending her off to her pastor uncle Thaddeus Harris in Worcester. There he and his wife were to bring potential suitors into Dorothea's world. Her grandmother still worried over Dorothea's single state, at twenty-three, and while she resisted, she allowed herself to be persuaded. Perhaps it would take her mind from the dissonance with the Heaths and from her own uncertainty now of what her purpose was meant to be in life.

But she became ill at the Harris household. Its quiet, sparse, Puritan focus suited her need for rest, and she believed her uncle relieved not to have to find her potential suitors. She recovered from the cough and weakness as soon as she returned to Orange Court, ready, she hoped, to start anew with her school and her life. Her three-month sentence, as she thought of it, completed. She vowed to focus more attention on Charles and Joseph and her grandmother, blood being the best bond for enduring relationships. Once again, she erred in her understanding.

"Charles has gone to sea? You let him do that? What about Harvard?"

"He showed little flair for academics," her grandmamma said. "Joseph is much better with mathematics. Aren't you, dear?"

Joseph nodded. He'd been in the Latin school for the past year, and Dorothea had seen even less of him than she had seen of Charles. Charles had left without her being able to tell him good-bye.

"I will attempt a soiree on your behalf," her grandmother told her, "since you slept away your time at the Harris household."

"I was ill."

Her grandmother harrumphed. "Joseph, too, could enjoy meeting eligible young women. Do not sabotage these events, Dorothea."

"I do as you ask."

"You do as you please."

They were in Dorothea's room after a dinner with invited guests, and she had begun pulling her chestnut hair from the braided loops as she sat before her mirror. Her grandmother stood behind her, cane in hand. "You chase them away, Dorothea."

"I do not chase men away." She sighed. "They depart from me. I will not be false nor pretend to be something I'm not."

"You could learn to love. I did with your grandfather." Dorothea looked at her grandmother in the mirror. Gray hair curved out from her black cap. She supposed it was a kindness that her grandmother planned the dinner. She wanted her grandchildren to be secure. She started to thank her, but Madam Dix interrupted.

"You are a disappointment, Dorothea."

Her face burned. "And I shall always be for you. I cannot apologize for being who I am."

"I don't know what to tell you."

Dorothea sneezed at the powder puff she enclosed in the glass case. "I should rid you of such worries," Dorothea said. The older woman shook her head in lament.

God willing, she would do just that.

Within the week, she had closed her school and packed her trunk. At the porch she took a deep breath, and said good-bye to her grandmother. The old woman's face was as still as a statue in the garden. "I can make it on my own, Grandmamma." She reached to pat the woman's wrinkled hands, the skin as thin as vellum.

"I suspect you'll be back and have to be nursed to health." The woman removed her fingers from Dorothea's touch, fluffed at her day cap. "You'll wish you had listened to your old grandmother and accepted the offer of a young man I might find for you. It will be harder as you grow older, you know, all alone."

"I'll prove to you that I am the strong Dix you always wanted, capable on my own. You can stop worrying over my future. Look after Joseph's."

Dorothea shook Joseph's hand then. "Be good to her."

"As I always am," he said. "You might take note as to how it's done."

Dorothea realized the only beating heart she would miss was Benji's and maybe the cook's. And as the carriage rolled down the drive past the elms and rosebushes, she gained hope, like the first day she had ridden Mercy outside the corral: anything could happen on a new trail through the woods—even something good.

PART
Two

Thirteen

On Her Own

Dorothea's move to Madam Canda's boarding-house on Chestnut Street told Boston society that this Dix was on her own. She had a small income from book royalties, and she renewed her position in the monitorial school. She was optimistic if not refreshed. She knew there were risks in keeping a delicate balance between being an acceptable society woman focused on her family and raising children, serving the needy and ill, and becoming too worldly, a woman going beyond her benevolent role, the only role acceptable for a single woman in New England. She had to be careful or she would come under attack from gossipers. She knew several women authors who wrote under men's names to avoid public scandal. She'd kept her name on her subsequent books, took pride in seeing it there, remembering Anne's encourage-ment.

She still believed her route to achieving her lifelong purpose was to be a moral teacher who prepared young women to teach others. Yet, if that was her purpose, why had she lost students? Why was she supervising students who taught needlework rather than science or math or poetry?

When invited along with another female author and fellow boarder to edit a new children's magazine, Dorothea seriously considered the offer. Perhaps writing, not teaching, was to be her ambition. But she developed a cold that fall as she deliberated, then declined the suggestion, claiming fragile health and a focus on her students.

Reverend Channing from the Federal Street Church invited her to lead a Sunday school class. While she felt flattered with the great man's attention, she declined. "I have my students and my compromised health. Besides, I am in need of spiritual development myself."

"I didn't realize you weren't well again." At least he didn't chastise her for not attending church. She couldn't go where Anne would be sitting each Sunday with the Peabody sisters and hadn't found another pastor to stir her soul. "You must take care, Dorothea. The Lord has need of your talents."

If that were true, why couldn't she find a satisfying path?

He began to check on her weekly, a kindness a father might convey, asking after her health, expressing concern that she not isolate herself from the larger world of service. After a few weeks of his gentle persuasion, she did agree to teach a Sunday school class for young women at the monitorial school, thinking that would best combine both worlds.

"Excellent," Channing told her. He clapped his hands as he looked up at her. *"He is so short; we are so tall."* Anne and she had spoken of Channing that way when they first met. "Come to my classes on Friday evening, where other teachers discuss problems, theological and discipline. It's a small group. You would fit in well."

"I resist being out in the Boston cold in the winter evenings."

He had frowned but kept the invitation open.

If she were honest, she would have admitted that she worried about embarrassing herself by gushing over Channing in a small group. She had to bend nearly a foot to listen to his quiet words, and his five-foot stature made her conscious of her height. His words moved her in ways only Scripture and Gray's poems had before. She had constantly wiped her eyes during his sermons. Even telling him how much his words comforted and informed made her fight back tears. If she lost control in one of his classes, she would disappear like a rock dropped in a murky pond.

Another book was published, a novel of a fictional family that read the Bible together. She wrote to Grace Cutter and asked if she might bring a copy by and visit with Marianna and her. Grace replied that she was too ill now to see anyone, but she thanked Dorothea for thinking of them and asked her to send the book. Dorothea signed it to Marianna.

She heard nothing back.

Within a week of sending the book off, Dorothea's throat hurt. She had a fever. The boardinghouse mistress called a doctor, although Dorothea protested. He told her she needed rest. Much rest. She sent word to Channing that she could no longer teach the class. She told George Emerson she must take a leave from the monitorial school. She had no care to eat. Her heart raced, then settled like a small child running, then resting for a time. She could barely lift her pen, and eating strained what energy she assumed from her rest. Her jaw ached. She coughed until her insides threatened to leave her body. A fever developed. She perspired. She thought she might die.

She wondered that she should leave this earth now, when God had not yet set upon her heart that specific cause that should be her one glorious ambition. Had she impeded God's way, blown out the candle meant to guide her path? Perhaps she had met whatever purpose there had been, and at the ripe old age of twenty-four, she would depart this world.

Her fever deepened.

Then Anne came.

"Only the pastors are allowed." Dorothea's face felt hot, and she knew her arms looked like chicken bones extended from her nightdress sleeves. The room smelled of antiseptic, vinegar, and the unemptied chamber pot beneath her bed. Dorothea scratched at the linen aimlessly until she heard the sound and stopped.

"I came when I heard. You must get better. No more writing, Miss D—"

"Please." She coughed and reached for a sip of water. "Dorothea, at least."

"Dorothea." Anne pulled a chair closer to the bed and helped her with the glass. "We all wish you a full recovery."

"I covet your prayers."

"And you shall have them." She started to pat Dorothea's hand but stopped herself. "The doctors . . ."

Dorothea coughed, then pulled the handkerchief from her face. She checked. *No blood.* "Yes, they think it might be tubercular. I would not want you ill."

She wanted to pour out her anguish, the great emptiness at not having seen Anne for so long, to ask again what had happened to their friendship, to whisper what was life about. But she had no strength. It was enough that Anne came to see her before she died. She would accept that perhaps she had accomplished what she had been sent to this earth to do: to teach, to write a bit, to pray for others, to wait.

"I will pray you get better, Dorothea."

Anne's scent lingered long after she left Dorothea. Friendships brought such joy and yet fractured easily. She had assumed too much; given too much. Expected too much from a single human being. Her strength must not come from the love of others but from God. But she knew little of that love, she decided. Perhaps she knew nothing of any kind of love at all. She cried into her pillow; but for Anne's visit and promised prayers, she would have prayed to die.

Then, without knowing why or how, in the following weeks, instead of succumbing to the end, Dorothea began to feel stronger. Perhaps it was spring and the presence of lilacs that graced the bedside table. Perhaps it was having Anne visit, though she had come only that once. Maybe prayers were answered, because she had not died. There must be more for her to do. She began to sit up on her own. She wrote letters describing her improved health to her grand-mamma and aunts and Grace Cutter. Marianna sent her a picture of a horse with a small child on its back.

Then new respite arrived, as welcome as spring water. "Since you have no teaching position, I invite you to join my family as a tutor for Mary and Willy while we summer at Rhode Island at my sister-in-law's Oakland estate." Reverend Channing spoke the words in a formal way as Dorothea received the small man in the dining room of the boardinghouse. She was able to be up now for an hour or so at a time.

"Quite a lovely setting, on the sea. Lovely old rambling house. Miss Gibbs, my wife's sister, is a natural healer of invalid young women, and you will find the scenery and ocean shores invigorating. You will be a member of our family."

"I would be . . . honored."

"Good then. I'll alert my wife and her sister that you'll be joining us. We leave in June."

Her work was more as governess than tutor, as the Channings had hired a local woman to teach languages and literature. Rather than feel slighted, Dorothea was grateful. She could walk and talk with the children, using the sea and the shore as her books. She could be a family friend, disciplining as needed but only to keep Willy and Mary safe. She loved the smell of the sea. Tiny birds quick-hopped their way as though chasing tides. The sun's warmth on her face awakened her like Washington Irving's Rip Van Winkle after a long sleep.

The squeals of the Channings' two children got her up and dressed, ready for the day's adventures. Channing led morning services, then disappeared into his library. Since she did not need to teach, she could engage the children in picking up shells or racing with kites along the wet sand.

The light here was different than over the wharfs in Boston, which was as close to the ocean as she had been. She thought of painting the seascape, though she had never tried such a thing. Instead, she sat on the dunes and wrote while the children were with their tutor. Then she waved to them, just two years apart in age, as they scrambled over the dunes to join her.

Willy reminded her of Charles at that age, full of curiosity and a love for the sea. Mary was a red-cheeked child of wonder.

In the evenings, after their readings, Dorothea took the smooth wooden darner from her bag and mended socks pleasantly, listening more than talking. Pleasing Reverend Channing mattered much like pleasing her father and her grand-mamma with a difference: she had hope Channing might actually express appreciation for her work, whereas she knew she would never hear praise from Madam Dix.

"Come with me to Philadelphia this winter," Sarah Gibbs said. "It's not as cold as Boston. You can stay with a pastor friend."

Sarah wore a white shawl, her signature, as she reigned over her Oakland estate. She and her sister, Channing's wife, were best friends, and Dorothea was honored to be included in this little cluster of family. The summer waning, new plans needed to be made. Dorothea was now one of those single women that others had to find a place for since she had no home of her own.

"I'll have a letter of introduction sent. I'm sure you can remain with them through the winter, and the two of us can visit back and forth."

"I've never been out of New England."

"Then it's time."

Dorothea wrote two books while in Philadelphia. She visited a new school for the deaf but avoided the Asylum for the Relief of Persons Deprived of Their Reason. She wasn't sure why.

A compilation of poems and descriptions of flowers and plants she called *The Garland of Flora* was published by a new publisher. It was out for two months when she read the first reviews. They were not kind.

"I shall not attempt another book that might inflict such disgust upon the literary scene," she told her publisher when she returned to Boston.

"Ignore the critics. The books are selling," he told her.

"There is too much of me in those works. I ought only to write things on behalf of others. A proper woman does not put herself into the fray, no matter how popular the cause." Could she be anonymous again? "I don't want to be unknown. But to be known sets me apart in ways unacceptable to a proper woman's place."

Her publisher reminded her that her royalties

helped support her until such time as she would marry. "Write until that time."

She bristled. "There is something more I am to do in my life," she told him. "I have yet to have it revealed to me. Until I do, no more books will be forthcoming." She wished Anne were again her close friend, who could help her through this time of negative reviews and uncertain purpose. Sarah Gibbs told her to ignore the reviewers. "Most are jealous they haven't written a book themselves." Dorothea wasn't so sure. Their words had the tinge of truth, that her words lacked passion.

Dorothea returned to Boston and took the bold move of renting a house on her own. If she was not to write, then she must go back to being a teacher. She hired a cook and a laundress. She wrote to Charles, telling him he had a place to return to when he came home from sea, and she invited Joseph to consider the house his home as well.

Fourteen-year-old Joseph responded that he might come to her house if he could find employment in that area of the city. "I seek a business career," he told her. Which is what Joseph then did, securing a post that would take him to Asia. He came once for dinner at Dorothea's home, nodding as he surveyed her parlor, saying she had "furnished it well."

She opened yet another school, taking only girls this time and naming it The Hope. She charged eighty dollars for a twelve-week course, a fee much higher than the ladies' academy and four times the charge of the Female Monitorial School. Higher fees were necessary, she decided, because the students would lodge at the house, have their laundry done, have clothing mended, have church seats and transportation costs to and from the school covered. She poured herself into this singular business allowing the school to consume her. Teaching must be her ambition, she decided. She nursed ill students to health, took them with her to her pew, and was humbled when parents told her their daughters had learned of Christ through her, for which they were grateful. This must be how she was to spend her life.

Yet one winter, Dorothea accepted with gratitude for the interruption an invitation to again travel with the Channings, this time to the sultry island of St. Croix. While poverty surrounded them like the silent slaves that waited on them at the large estate where they stayed, it was the ravishing of the land that Dorothea wrote about to Sarah Gibbs, who had stayed behind.

She complained of the cane plantation's devastation to what must have been a jewel on the crown of creation. But of the condition of the slaves she said little, only commenting that the "workers were well cared for" and she saw no need to speak of radical legislation that would doom the economy of such islands or the South. Even Channing thought the abolitionists overstated their case, after being in St. Croix.

Back in Boston, Dorothea's days and nights were filled with activity: serving, preparing lessons, writing letters, sewing her clothes, mending her students'. She helped a new friend, Mrs. Torrey, the wife of a wealthy industrialist, channel money into a new infant school for children eighteen months to six years old and found the experience gratifying. She was in service. She fell exhausted into bed every night, waking tired but more certain she was following her destined path.

She still thought about Marianna, now sixteen. She had not heard of her mother's passing. Perhaps she had recovered. She would not ask.

Then, just when she thought she was in a rhythm she could sustain, she fell ill again. The fever was high, her chest as tight as a too-small corset. Five years had passed since her recovery in Rhode Island, walking the sand dunes and listening to the rhythm of the sea. Healthy for five years. Then this. If teaching were her glorious ambition, why did her weak and unpredictable body fail her? A racking cough proved her only answer.

Fourteen
No Paper, No Pens

Dorothea lay wrapped in a blanket on a deck chair aboard *The Virginian*, a ship that steamed to Liverpool. When Mrs. Torrey spread the word of her illness, the Fessers, parents of a quiet and favorite student named Joaquina, had arrived at Dorothea's home.

"You want me to go to Europe with you?"

"Liverpool initially," Joaquina said. As Dorothea had been, the girl was tall for her age. She had freckles across a small nose that she powdered to no avail. She seemed loved but lonely. "You nursed me to health, and now we'll do the same for you. Won't we, Mother?"

Mrs. Fesser smiled. She had a large overbite, so two white stubs like picket fences settled on plump lips. "We don't mean to be intrusive, but perhaps you could be Joaquina's governess on the trip."

"A journey will do you well," Mr. Fesser affirmed. "You've extended yourself beyond good reason. Even Reverend Channing expressed concern for you."

"Did he?" It had been some time since she had been to church. "I . . . It's most kind of you to invite me, but should I relapse . . . I'm just able to sit up for a few hours at a time, and I'd hate to burden—"

"We'll pack your trunks," Mrs. Fesser said. "They have doctors on board ship. You'll be well in no time, and Joaquina's studies will be advanced."

Days later Joaquina acted as her cane when Dorothea walked up the gangplank, huffing by the time they made it to the deck chair. Dorothea pulled her shawl against the cool air but breathed it in deeply.

"I'll get a robe, and after you've rested, we'll find our cabin. You and I are to share one. I hope that's all right." The girl's freckles looked like fairy footprints on her face.

"It's lovely." Dorothea took in another deep breath, hacked enough she thought she might lose what little breakfast she had taken before boarding. Sea gulls swirled overhead, and she could smell the steam building up. She licked her lips of the salt. "Could you reach my handkerchief?"

"Oh, Auntie, here." She handed her the cloth. "I'm so sorry you're sick. I truly am. Maybe we'd better get you to the cabin now, out of the air."

"No. I want to be here when we leave the dock. It's an adventure you've brought me on, Joaquina. I'll be forever grateful your family wished to include me."

She settled her on the deck chair. "I'm sorry. I just noticed that . . . young man over there. He's motioning for me."

"Best you be wary about young strangers." The girl's eyes fell. "Oh, go on. I'll watch you from here." Dorothea pulled the lap robe up around her neck and leaned back. She was going to Liverpool to get well. Well, why not? She closed her eyes, let her body sink into the wood chair, the sea breeze caress her face.

"Dorothea? Is that you?"

Dorothea opened her eyes. She had dozed and now heard Anne's voice. Could it be? She sat up. "Anne. How did you . . . ? Why did you . . . ?"

"Reverend Channing told me. I . . . I know it's been ages since we've spoken. And my letters have been so sporadic. It's all been a jumble these past years since Mary's passing. But I didn't want you to go without my saying good-bye."

"I know you miss Mary so." *Could you miss her as much as I've missed you?* Her words must be cautious. Like walking on lily pads.

People began gathering at the railing, waving to those on shore, gloved hands like white flags waved against a blue sky. Stewards carried trays with tall glasses. Joaquina waved to Dorothea, then turned back as her parents joined her and the young man she had been talking with.

Anne pulled up a nearby chair and sat. "I . . . never intended to exclude you, Dorothea. My grief set me on a path that kept me from reaching back to hold your hand and pull you toward me."

"We all do things differently when we face a terrible loss." She thought of her mother, wondered how she fared. She'd heard no word even though she sent royalty checks each year for her care. She'd barely shed a tear at her father's death.

"This will be a wonderful trip for you," Anne said. "Oh, here." She took a packet from her reticule. "Reverend Channing sent letters of introduction for schools on the Continent or any fine people he felt you should meet."

"He's so very kind."

Anne nodded. "And so very short."

"And we're so very tall." She had a twinkle in her eye. Both women laughed at the early memory of their meeting. "Thank you for coming, Anne." Dorothea risked taking her friend's hand. "It means so much to me."

"It should have been sooner." Anne patted her hand.

"What is, is. And I'm grateful."

"Our friendship may never be what it was," Anne said.

"Mary's absence will always be an emptiness we cannot bridge."

A whistle blew and men in uniform walked the decks to announce that visitors must leave in five minutes. They were getting underway.

Anne leaned and kissed Dorothea's cheek. "Get well first," she whispered in her ear. "Then enjoy this time. Come back and marvel us with tales as only you can do."

Dorothea's coughing episode when she boarded had been her last harsh one. Since then, her health had improved significantly. The ship's doctor prepared potions for her that cleared her lungs, and the food gave her vitality. Between the stewards and the Fessers, her every need was addressed. She even found strength to help a young mother by looking after her children, giving her and her husband time to walk the deck together. Joaquina's lessons resumed in earnest but without strain.

"You are a delight," the captain told her the evening the Fessers and Dorothea dined at his table. "Such knowledge for a woman so beautiful."

"And young," Mr. Fesser added.

"I'm surprised your husband lets you travel without him."

"I have no husband."

He had a mock look of chagrin. "What's wrong with my countrymen to let one as you go unclaimed?"

"She's an independent woman," Joaquina chirped.

"Your countrymen may know how difficult it is

to manage such a female," Dorothea said. "They may be wiser than you think."

Mr. Fesser removed the pencils from Dorothea's fingers. "You're to rest in between the tasks you set for yourself. No pens, no paper."

"I'm well enough to look after others while on board, so surely a little writing won't derail my recovery."

"Now, now," Mr. Fesser told her. "I've been given instructions by the Channings to be certain you do not extend yourself."

"They gave you instructions?"

"Indeed. Reverend Channing described you as a spinning top that eventually must stop and fall over. We're to make sure you slowly stop your spinning so you do not crash."

"But even a spinning top always has one point where it is truly centered."

Mr. Fesser grunted. "Nevertheless, reading I'll allow, but writing no. We want no relapse."

Sadly, Fesser's concern bore fruit. When they landed in Liverpool, Dorothea's cough and fever returned. Was it the heavy air? Anxiety of the unknown? Mrs. Fesser and Joaquina nursed Dorothea, ill in her hotel room, as best they could. But when the business needs of the Fessers required they move on to London, there was a decision of what to do. Dorothea hated being a burden. Hated it.

"I'm sure that with a good fire and the hotel staff bringing me broth, I'll soon be well." She stifled a cough. "You go do what you need to do. Please. You've been so kind." She swallowed. Her chest was a tight fist.

Mrs. Fesser blotted sweat from Dorothea's brow. "We can't leave you here. And we can't remain."

Dorothea roused herself on her elbows. "Please. Don't fret over me. There must be rooms I can rent as I improve. Perhaps I can rejoin you later. If you'll help me pack and move my trunks, I'll be fine. I'm used to being on my own."

"I know no other alternative," Mrs. Fesser said. She twisted a handkerchief in her hands. "Edward, find her a room."

It was a cool May, and the rainy cold seeped into Dorothea's bones in the small room the Fessers had found for her. The cough grew worse. She lost track of time in between her dozing and the honey and lemon the landlady brought for her tea. She was alone. She knew no one. She eyed the letters of introduction from the Channings that lay useless in their folder.

Maybe they are of use. She plodded her way across the room, the effort like climbing a mountain. Only one letter wasn't for a school director. It was addressed to William Rathbone.

"Do you know this man?" Dorothea asked her landlady when the woman came to check on her.

"Aye, quite well known he is. A philanthropist from an old Liverpool family. Quakers, I believe. The top of the respect ladder."

"Will you write a note for me? I'll send this letter along." She dictated, mentioning that she was recovering from an illness and her traveling party had other obligations, so they had arranged for her to remain in Liverpool. Could he suggest a lung doctor? She sent the letter off, then waited. Always, life demanded that she wait.

She prayed as she had not for many days, that her suffering might be over, somehow, soon. Her mind was fuzzy and thick as a lamb's coat. Her head throbbed. She could smell the perspiration, but she lacked the strength to wash herself. Could there be anything worse than to suffer alone? What was the psalm? *Be of good courage, and he shall strengthen thine heart: wait, I say, on the LORD.*

Fifteen

Servants of Greenbank

Was she real? This woman who leaned over her, smelling of lavender? Grains of sand scratched Dorothea's eyes as though she walked on a windy day along a Rhode Island beach. Awake. Sleep.

"Coughs without production," as the doctor had said, though they produced chest pain and weighed as though andirons crushed her chest. *Is this what it's like, drifting into heaven?* Sleep. Awake. *Need to wipe the tears.* Sleep. Awake.

"Miss Dix? I'm Elizabeth Rathbone." The lavender-scented woman pressed a cool cloth to Dorothea's head. "My husband and I are here to take you home with us."

She moved like a hummingbird as she fluffed a pillow behind Dorothea's head, treating her neck as though it were fine porcelain, her touch light and without pain. She sat next to Dorothea on the bed. "William is a great admirer of Reverend Channing. His family has stayed at Greenbank. That's where you'll go as soon as the doctor says you're well enough."

"I haven't . . . called a doctor."

"We did. Here, take this." She spooned something foul tasting through Dorothea's lips.

She swallowed. "I'm not sure . . . It might not stay down." The room spun.

Elizabeth put a bowl beneath Dorothea's mouth. "Whatever you need to do. I'm here now. I'll stay." Her British-accented words lilted with warmth.

Sleep. Awake.

Evening descended. Kerosene lamps lit the room, the smell causing Dorothea to reach for the bowl.

"It's right here," Elizabeth laid down her book and quickly stood to place the bowl where Dorothea could reach it. The woman wore tiny glasses and had a single white doily over the rolls of glistening black hair at the top of her head. "Pant like a dog. My mother taught me that. It can keep you from spewing."

Dorothea did as she was told, and the nauseous feeling passed.

"What time is it?"

Elizabeth looked at her lapel watch. "Nearly midnight. Are you feeling better?"

"A little." Dorothea blinked. At least her eyes had the sand out of them.

Elizabeth brought cool water to her lips. "You must have fluids. Once I hiked on a hot day and didn't drink water or tea and found myself confused and turned around like a falling top. The doctor said it was lack of hydration." She wiped Dorothea's brow again, touched her cheeks like a butterfly. "Do your eyes hurt?" Dorothea nodded. "Let's put a cucumber slice on them. Another gift from the Hindu country." She placed the pungent-smelling slices on her eyelids. "They'll draw out the pain."

Her eyes restful beneath the cucumbers, Dorothea slept again, but she did not dream.

When she awoke in the morning, she removed the warm cucumbers. Elizabeth's chin rested on her chest, her hands draped over a book of poems by Thomas Gray. If she hadn't already saved her life, Dorothea knew that she would adore Elizabeth Rathbone if only for her choice of poets.

William Rathbone arrived shortly after Dorothea ate a piece of toast, the first real food she had eaten in days. It stayed down and did not bring on a cough. "As soon as you're ready, we'll pack up your things. We can nurse you better at Greenbank."

"I'm so sorry to be a burden."

"It's a privilege to help another in need. You give to us when you let us." Elizabeth smiled and added, "Do you have just the one trunk?"

The estate—Greenbank they called it—rose over a mound of green that rolled like a carpet to the lake beyond. Elizabeth hovered over Dorothea as William and a steward who came out through the porticos helped lift her from the carriage. She was an awkward colt, all arms and legs. She could not remember ever being carried by anyone in her life, let alone strangers, let alone as an adult. The men were tender, and Elizabeth covered her legs with a blanket as they entered the cool of the mansion.

"We'll put you here on the first floor." Elizabeth opened a double door. The bed was massive, and two armoires reached to the tall ceilings. A coal stove warmed the room. A bucket beside it was filled to the brim. The men placed her on a deep chair with a hassock pulled up for her legs.

"This room is beautiful." She recognized Joshua Shaw's haunting painting of the burning of Savannah, the pink and gold of his fiery scene from the Revolutionary War reflected in the coverlet on the pillows and bed.

"It's a hand-colored aquatint," Elizabeth said when she noticed Dorothea's gaze. "A reminder of the ravages of war, however noble the cause. Peace is our morning prayer, and this painting turns our heart to that."

"This is . . . your room?"

"It's the most convenient, that we might care for you. There are a dozen other bedrooms on the second floor. When you're well enough, we'll move you into one of those. But for now, please consider Greenbank your home and this room your refuge."

The periods of sleep and wakefulness changed their patterns. Over the next few weeks Dorothea was warmed by a small black-and-white dog that often curled its back to Dorothea's and let her pet his soft fur when she was awake. Strength slowly returned, though the ache in her chest continued to worry the doctors the Rathbones brought in for counsel.

Elizabeth brought her breakfast daily, acting like a servant when she commanded a dozen. Sounds from the rooms beyond—of people chatting, the scrape of a chair, a door closed—

gave comfort. Outside this room were those willing to care for her as she had never been tended in her life. It was as though she were a child with a mother able to love and care.

Elizabeth administered the potions herself. She refilled Dorothea's toilet water from her own supply. Elizabeth's help when Dorothea needed the chamber pot was given without annoyance. This must be what it's like in a loving family, where people give their best for another.

Sleep. Awake. Sleep. Awake.

Elizabeth and William Rathbone often read to her from the classics. On an evening she might hear music coming from the piano room. Elizabeth apparently played. One afternoon they asked her permission to invite in some guests "who would not disturb you."

"It's your home," Dorothea said. "I surely have no say in whom you invite."

"We might make noise with our conversations. We're quite passionate and have been known to include heretics at our dinner parties." She grinned; her black eyes twinkled. "Our editor friend Charles Dickens is passing through. He's quite distressed by the lack of laws protecting children, their need for education, and of course reforms for those who have lost their reason. My dear William is an overseer of the lunatic asylum in Liverpool, and we often get into debates about the best treatments. We don't want you to be dismayed if our voices are raised."

"You argue about treatments?"

"Indeed. We believe many of the mad can be cured, but at the very least they must be treated with dignity and respect. Dr. Tuke refers to it as moral treatment, treating the insane as though they were more normal than not, instead of tying them up or putting them in almshouses to be forgotten like animals. Worse than animals." Color rose on her cheeks as she spoke.

"When I am able, I hope to be included on the guest list."

"Oh, you will. Many are eager to hear of your teaching practices and the carriage house school you opened for indigent children."

"Yes, when I was in service."

"You will be again." Elizabeth's warm fingers moved a wisp of hair at Dorothea's temple.

Voices came from the rooms beyond. Laughter. Joy. Intense speeches. Something to look forward to. She returned to her sleep.

She joined them for a supper in the large dining room. It had been nearly three months since her arrival, and the guests stood and applauded when she ambled with a cane to the table.

"It is I who applaud you for bringing me to health." That glorious evening she was introduced to Elizabeth Fry, an educator passionate about schooling for girls, and a Quaker prison reformer who spoke with intensity over roast duckling and fresh greens. William Tuke, proprietor of the York Retreat for the mentally disordered, and a champion of moral treatment, sent his grandson to tell stories of renewed lives for any number of residents in the quiet, homelike setting.

"Even those lost of their reason respond to the softness of flowers, the placidness of lakes, the chirping of birds. It inspires them, seeing how God is so good to even the least, and they begin to see that they are valued too," said the grandson. "Being treated as a human being restores sanity. They sit at table to eat, are expected to bathe. All normal."

One of Dorothea's physicians joined the meal as well, making points with his fork poked in the air, a smile toward Dorothea when she offered an opinion.

That evening she wrote to her grandmother that the course of her disease had been part of the debate. "Here I am quite pampered and petted."

She basked in these new friendships, seeing great stimulation in conversations with passionate people wanting to serve the "least of these." Ducks floated on the lake, which she could see better now from her upstairs bedroom. She had insisted the Rathbones retake their boudoir, a sign that her health had truly improved.

"Perhaps you have imposed too long on the Rathbones," Madam Dix wrote. "It's time you returned to Boston. I have need of you. Mehetable tires easily. A young woman should lend us a hand."

Dorothea responded, saying she was still not well, which was what her doctors argued over: the cause and the treatments. Perhaps hiring a nurse would help Cookie. Dorothea would send money.

Madam Dix replied that she had hired a young woman Dorothea's age, but she had become ill as well. "It's time for you to come home and help your family."

Dorothea sighed and lay the letter down. Her own Latin studies reminded her that the word family came from the Latin *famulus* meaning servant. She had a servant's heart, didn't she? Servants did what was required. Yet the thought of returning . . . She pulled her shawl tighter around her shoulders.

The people hovering around the central fires at Greenbank were interested in the world around them and active in their pursuit of ministry without being demanding of others. They paced themselves in their work and thus had much to draw on for the care of others. They gave their time, their strengths, as well as their money. God's love, that's what should burn the fire in the hearth of a home. As Dorothea accepted the hot tea Elizabeth brought to her room, she told herself, *This is what love looks like. This is what a family feels like.*

Spring growth pushed its way through the dried grass on the Greenbank lawns. "My grandmamma's caretaker has taken ill," Dorothea told Elizabeth after her latest missive from Madam Dix. She held the knitting skein as the older woman wound the yarn taken from sheep on the estate. "And I sit here not able to tend anyone, a failure of my duty."

"Your time is yet to be," Elizabeth reminded her. "I feel certain of it. You must simply wait upon the Lord. He has a plan for you. Someday you will say as we Quakers are known to, 'If it is to be, it is up to thee.' Something will call to you, and through it the Lord will have you toss away your cane and peel away the crust of uncertainty that stifles you. You will go places you have never imagined."

"Do you really believe that's so, for me?"

"I know it. I pray for it. I trust it will come, and we will all be the better for it."

Dorothea found a peace here despite the rule of no paper, no pens for at least an hour a day. "If God is to speak to your heart," Elizabeth told her, "you must put away distractions so you can hear His voice."

This was new to her. At Greenbank, she yielded. Not certain of her direction, she let others move into the stream of life around her, hoping that soon she would follow. It was a route through suffering she had not before allowed. She was grateful.

Sleep now. And then awake.

Sixteen

An Orphan's Tale

Dear Auntie. You are now my only real mother. My own dear mummy is at rest. She is past all trouble and pain and in the home of the blessed. Please come to be my mummy." Marianna Davenport Cutter signed the letter that reached Dorothea in the spring of her second year at Greenbank. Her hands flew in her packing. Elizabeth helped.

"Are you certain you're well enough for travel?"

"I have to go. This is what I've wanted my entire life. This child. She's a cousin, and I wanted to adopt her before her mother passed, but I did not press my case well. I ought to have persisted. But now it has come, this door to a child, my child." She clasped a dark skirt to her chin. "I have sent a letter, but they take so long. I hope she knows I am coming."

Elizabeth handed Dorothea the book of Gray's poetry to pack. "I wish we had time to visit Thomas Gray's grave. It's not far from here."

"Next time I come. I'll bring Marianna with me." Dorothea embraced her friend. "It is an answer to a prayer. As are you."

As she boarded the carriage for the ship leaving Liverpool, she stuffed into her valise a letter that Elizabeth handed her. Postmarked from America. She would read it while she listened to the horses clop down the winding driveway taking her from Greenbank home to Marianna. She waved good-bye, leaned her head back against the leather pad; a smile on her lips.

Dorothea waited until on board the ship before opening the latest letter, anticipating another note from Marianna. Instead, it was from her grandmother's solicitor telling her that Madam Dix had died of influenza. The solicitor provided a few details Dorothea read through her shroud of guilt for not returning at her grandmother's request. Her grandmother had wanted her back not because she missed her but so that Dorothea could do her duty, a duty in which Dorothea had failed. She sighed and continued to read while the steamship swooshed across the Atlantic. Orange Court would be divided between Dorothea, her brothers, and Dorothea's uncle Thaddeus Harris, husband to Madam Dix's daughter—the summer aunt and uncle, where she had taken ill instead of finding a proper suitor. The other uncles and aunts were apparently settled, and her grandmother had provided for her two children who had the least resources for caring for their families: Dorothea's father and the woman married to that poor minister, Thaddeus Harris. But she hadn't left the estate to her daughter, but to her daughter's husband, Thaddeus, instead. Dorothea wondered that her grandmother didn't leave Dorothea out of the will, left the other half to her brothers. She supposed it was because she was single. If she'd married, her husband would have been named in the will. Dorothea would have a home with some surveillance by her uncle, as she was still a single woman, but there would be a place for her and Charles and Joseph and now Marianna as well. God does look after each of us, Dorothea decided.

She set aside the shards of guilt and thought instead of joining Marianna at last. Anticipation brushed Dorothea's face like the ocean breezes as she took her daily walks around the ship. She bundled up tightly, already aware of the coming fall and the cold of Boston's winters. But she would be warmed this winter in her home at Orange Court. She was stronger than she had ever been. She would have a child of her own, one who would never leave her, and she would educate her, prepare her for a life of service and compassion. They would sit by the fire and read together. She would sew dresses for the young lady, brush her hair. They would try new mouth soaps to whiten their teeth, and in the spring they would take picnics. She would bring her to Greenbank! Yes, she would share this healing place.

Dorothea made lists in her diary of things to do to brighten up the mansion, trying to decide whether to continue it as a boardinghouse or make it a real family home. Surely her aunt and uncle would not want to move into the house, as her uncle had a life and ministry in Worcester. She made lists of shopping she would do with Marianna, though she hoped Marianna wasn't overly impressed with fashion. She would help her grieve the loss of her mother. She imagined pouring out bushel baskets of love onto the child, all that Dorothea had stored to give away. To continue her good health, the first she had ever really known, Dorothea kept an hour each morning on board ship without pen and paper, where she simply tried to discern God's intention for the day. Being well was her fervent prayer so that she might be the mother Marianna truly deserved.

"But—"

"It has been arranged, Miss Dix."

"But she's asked for me, claims me as her only mother." Dorothea sat in the paneled room of Grace's solicitor. Potted ferns drooped near the floor-to-ceiling windows and reflected Dorothea's emotional state after her long journey. Distant cousins sat across from her, three of them en mass. Marianna was not present though.

"She's not yet betrothed," the cousin said. His

starched collar was too small for his thick neck, and he pulled at it as he spoke. "Marianna had to go somewhere, and we, her cousins, have taken her in. After all, you were in England and not well."

"Your grandmother told us you were on death's door. What were we to do?" the cousin's wife whined.

Another cousin, a sister, unmarried as Dorothea was, knotted her handkerchief in her hands. "She's been with us for more than two months. It would be criminal to move her now."

"Yes. Criminal," her male cousin agreed.

"Only in that I imagine it would force you to give up that portion of the Cutter estate that came with her," Dorothea charged. "That would be the crime, I suspect."

"Oh, now, now," her cousin blustered. "You've no right to impugn our motives. What of your own?"

What would move them? The graciousness of the Rathbones? Was there a way for her to influence them? to change their minds?

She softened her voice. "It was good of you to be there for her. I know Grace would be grateful. I would take her without the estate attached to her."

"So would we!" the maiden cousin shouted. Her brother shushed her.

"You can keep the resources for the care you've already provided," Dorothea said.

"And as soon as we agreed to that, you'd call the solicitor to demand the money for her dowry."

"I wouldn't. I have no need. It would be my pleasure to provide for Marianna." Her voice broke. "I have a place for her. I have means. I don't need the Cutter share. I simply want what's best for Marianna."

The solicitor cleared his throat. "Have you as yet met with Madam Dix's executor? He is a member of our firm. I know you're just recently arrived."

"No, I haven't met with him." The solicitor's interruption was like a bee buzzing at her ear. She had taken a hotel room to be closer to his office and had not yet gone to Orange Court. "I let your office know immediately that I might tell Marianna I had returned."

"There is some news—"

"I believe this has been decided already," the male cousin interrupted the solicitor. He stood. "You have other affairs to attend to, dear cousin. A single woman without a father, brother, husband, or son to look after her will have enough to worry over. And your grandmother's estate to tend to. We will ensure Marianna has sufficient care and a satisfactory dowry when that time comes."

"Of course you'll be welcome to see her and correspond," the whining wife added. "We would not deprive you of that, though you should give her a little time to grieve. We'll have her send a note when she feels up to seeing you."

"She has already sent me a note. She asked me to come and be her mother." Couldn't they see how the girl longed for Dorothea to claim her? Why wasn't she here?

"She already calls me Auntie," the maiden cousin told her. The woman's pinched eyes shone greedily inside a face with cheeks dotted red.

Dorothea felt that same slow seethe that had brewed inside her all the years she stitched her father's tracts. She named it *powerlessness*. Marianna, too, was a pawn and not allowed to choose her destiny. She was aware that the cousins all stood and were waiting for her to leave as well. She did not stand, however. She was not finished.

"Why not let Marianna decide?"

The male cousin stopped at the door, his hand on the gold knob. "She has no say. She is a girl."

The solicitor shrugged his shoulders.

The cousins filed out, and after a few moments of silence, the solicitor asked if Dorothea was all right.

"I will be." Her hands shook. She didn't know if it was a lie.

She made an appointment to meet with the executor of her grandmother's estate later in the week. The following day she hired a cab to

Orange Court. At least here was something firm. She would have a place to call her own. Property mattered in Boston society. From here she could launch her campaign for Marianna and her own future, whatever it held.

The estate looked even more forlorn than when she had left. Fall always stripped the mansion bare: the porch held no wicker chairs, leaves already clustered at the roots of bare trees. The Hudson brother must have slowed in his age or perhaps no longer tended the grounds at all. She walked up the stone steps that needed sweeping, opened the mansion door and gasped. Where was all the furniture?

Dorothea walked through the house, her footsteps echoing on the pine floors, the brush of her crinolines as she turned this way and that exerted small pressure against her stockings. She heard herself gasping, taking in breath. She stopped, gained control. She would not be ill.

In the parlor her eyes went to the fireplace where a single settee and two chairs sat forlorn. The room had once been filled with chairs and end tables and three divans, ferns on plant stands waving their fronds at passing guests. Gone were the porcelains, the statues, the treasures her grandfather had brought back from Europe. She climbed the stairs to the library. Only a few books lined the shelves. *Had they sold the collection book by book?* The long table where she had taught school remained, but the ladder-back chairs had been replaced with benches. Cobwebs already gathered on the chandeliers.

She opened a bedroom. A simple bed, a nightstand, and a small armoire. A room bare of all but necessities. There were clothes inside the armoire. People lived here? In what had been her room, a single trunk sat in the center. She lifted the rounded cover and peered inside. She moved aside her camisoles, corset covers, and a pale chemise. Beneath were pens and ink, books, and older diaries that she had stored in her writing desk. And the desk was no longer in the room.

A porcelain candle stand that had been her father's lay alongside several beeswax candles. First-edition copies of each of her books made a small stack. She looked around, grateful she had not had her trunk sent to Orange Court when she had arrived. Someone lived here, someone with spare taste.

She took the path through the pear garden to the cottage. It was locked. She looked through the window to see that nothing remained, no dishes on the shelves, no pictures on the walls. She hoped she would have some personal memento of her grandmother to claim. What had happened to Benji? Without a key, she couldn't enter.

As she walked down the hill to locate a cab to take her back to her hotel, Dorothea let the high and low of her day wash over her. She had not coughed. She would find out about the stripped mansion. Greenbank had rescued her, saved her. While she faced a terrible loss on the first day of her arrival—the custody of Marianna—she would continue a relationship with the child, she was committed to that.

Potted ferns graced the executor's office, but these were well watered and lifted their fronds to the window heights. Outside, autumn scampered across the street in the form of little children chased by the breeze as they held on to their bonnets and mothers' hands. A fire burned in the fireplace, the logs crackling perhaps because they were damp from the first light snow, which had fallen overnight.

"I have a number of things to share with you, Miss Dix," the executor said. He stood taller than Dorothea, and she noted how pleasant it was to be looking up into the eyes of a man without having to crank her neck. "Would you like tea?"

Dorothea nodded and they passed the time waiting for it by discussing the weather and her book sales. He had a mole on his high cheek-bones.

"Ah, here we are then." The executor poured her tea, then returned to his perch behind his desk, where he opened a thick file.

"Your grandmother left a number of small bequests to different acquaintances throughout

New England, and she hoped you would be the one to assist me in locating the recipients." Dorothea thought that was his job but said nothing. When she did not respond, he continued. "Ah, then." He rifled through the pages, pulling up one. "She has left you her cane, hand carved and used by her very hand to steady herself. It's a fine symbol of her care for you, don't you think? Her wish to help you be a steady woman."

"I'll appreciate that."

"An English tea set she left you, which we have stored here. She said you liked tea and so wanted to be sure you had it. There are small items for your brothers who, as they continue abroad, received this information by post." He cleared his throat. "Your grandmother's bequest to you is one-sixth of the estate. Charles and Joseph will receive one-sixth each. Your brother Charles has bequeathed his share to you to manage, and Joseph's share will be managed by his uncle Thaddeus until Joseph is twenty-five. He intends to live with them at Orange Court."

"Oh? It was my understanding that half of Orange Court was to go to me and my brothers."

"Ah, and well it does. Your grandmother wanted your minister uncle and his fine wife to have use of the house for free until they died." He showed her a codicil of the will, dated while she was recovering at Greenbank. "The best way to arrange that was that I simply sold the house to your uncle after Madam Dix died. I thought it best for everyone. You are a single woman, and the upkeep of a mansion would be extraordinary. The income will be yours, of course, along with the profit from the sale of some of the furnishings. Your uncle's simple tastes meant they had little need for many of the heirlooms."

"The mansion . . . I have no claim on it? No . . . property?"

"It was in your best interest. With a small bequest left from your grandfather, the money from the sale, your own earnings, which I imagine provide you a little from your writing and teaching, you ought to have—"

"But I have no . . . home."

"Perhaps your uncle will welcome you."

Dorothea shook her head. Her uncle and aunt had been stuffy and prim when she had stayed with them. Her aunt had complained the entire time she had been with them. "I find no hope in their interest in having me be a part of their household."

"Ah, then. You will simply have to stay in hotels or inns or take rooms in Boston. Did you not rent a home on your own some years past? You can do so again."

Yes, she could do so again, but it was not his duty to tell her how to live her life. Everyone tried to tell her how to live. Except the Rathbones. They accepted her as she was.

"Is there anything more I need to know?"

He cleared his throat. "Yes, yes, there is. It's of your mother." The executor sighed, though he seemed well versed in giving clients bad news. "She has passed away in New Hampshire. I was forced to pay the burial expenses out of your share of your grandmother's estate."

"My mother is . . . dead? How?"

"Appears to be a wasting away. No known cause. I'm sorry."

Dorothea left his office like a child alone, as though walking through smoke.

The letter to Marianna was addressed to Marianna Davenport Dix Cutter. She underlined the *Dix*. Marianna answered in a day. "Please come to see me. Let us go riding if you're able. Come tomorrow. I will be waiting."

The maiden cousin opened the door, and before she could close it in Dorothea's face, Marianna ran toward her, a young woman, slender as a lily with skin as white. "Mummy!"

"She is not your mother," the whining cousin corrected her.

Dorothea held the girl, the wrap of her arms like a quilt of warm wool around her. "I will always call you daughter, whether you are legally my own or not," she whispered to the girl.

"And you will be my mother."

Dorothea nodded, held her back, and looked at

her. "You're beautiful as you always were. So grown up. A young lady at eighteen already."

"That they've tried to marry off." She laughed.

"Don't accept a suitor you don't want," Dorothea told her.

"You best come inside," the cousin said. "You'll catch your death."

"We're going riding, cousin. Aren't we . . . Mummy?"

"It's way too cold. No. I forbid it," said the cousin.

"But I don't," Marianna said.

"It'll be a chilly ride but invigorating," Dorothea said.

The cousin scowled. "She has a mind of her own."

"Definitely of the Dix line," Dorothea told her, a happy stream she would cherish in this lake of disappointment.

Seventeen

What Is Left

At the hotel the next day, Dorothea pondered her future. She and Marianna were both orphans now. But orphans who had a heavenly Father where they would always belong. She would remind Marianna of that. Dorothea had lost her mother,

her grandmother, and her home. But she had her health back, she had a now-and-then daughter, and she had been reborn in the womb of the Rathbones' love. It would be enough. She pondered the present as she gazed out the window at walkers pushing against the wind. Maybe she could visit and stay for a time with former students. The Fesser family had returned to Boston. She might winter with them. Sarah Gibbs and the Channings might welcome her. Brookline and the Heaths could be an option. They might take pity on her until spring.

What were her choices? She did not want to strain her renewed relationship with Anne. She had come to see her off, and since then there had been letters without the carping but also without the intimacy they had once had. She had no place to begin another school, and she wasn't certain that was what God intended for her as it seemed whenever she taught, her health soon declined. Both the Rathbones and the Channings expressed concern at how the schools drained her, threatened her spinning top.

She reread her grandmother's will. She could at least deliver the items left to the various people remembered by her grandmother. She would also visit a banker to help manage her finances and Charles's share of the estate. Should she buy a house? It would use up too much of the principal. She was a frugal woman and would have to remain so if she was to live without dependence on uncles or aunts or brothers or sons.

Her uncle had "generously" offered to manage her finances when she had gone back to the mansion, where a light snowfall had dusted the shrubs. Low fires burned in the parlor fireplace. The room was cool enough that Dorothea kept her gloves and hat on, not that her aunt had offered to take them or invited her to take tea. The three of them sat in the parlor. Dorothea did not recognize any of their furniture.

"Uncle, I do not approve of the arrangements made on my behalf, but I am settled that I have no recourse."

"It was done for your good, niece." His sharp nose and small eyes reminded her of a ferret. "As God would intend that we care for the widows and orphans." Her relatives had moved in soon after her grandmother's death and had been visiting in Dorchester on the day Dorothea toured the house. It was still devoid of accoutrement. Her eyes scanned the room. "We kept only essential items and sold what was unnecessary."

"Yes," Dorothea said. She noticed the hall clock that had been her grandfather's now graced the parlor. At least they had kept some of the valuable furniture. "What I would inquire about is whether the writing desk that had been in my room was sold at auction. I did not find it in the storehouse to which the executor directed me, where he said you had collected my share of the furniture."

"Let me think," her aunt said, tapping her chin. "Oh, yes, we did save that for you. Didn't we, Thaddie? It's in the guest room. We worried that it might be damaged in storage."

"I . . . I looked in the room, my old room, and didn't see it."

"You were in the house? When?"

"The day I returned. I believed it was my home as well."

"You should have come to us before simply walking in," her uncle chastised her.

"It would please me if you would hold the writing desk until I find a permanent abode. It was my father's, I believe. Perhaps my mother's."

"Oh, your mother was no writer," Thaddeus said.

She could read, Dorothea thought. *Perhaps she wrote.*

"But, of course, we will preserve it for you, for whenever you wish it sent to wherever you may go. Thaddeus is also willing to manage your finances. Aren't you, Thaddeus?"

"Of course. What is family for if not to be helpful."

She had not wanted an invitation to remain with them through the winter, but it would have been nice to have been able to decline such an offer. Still, she had their commitment for what she wanted, but then another thought occurred to her.

"I may be staying some with the Heaths, and I

should like to have the writing desk left there."

"Oh. Well. We understood there was a falling out. The Peabody sisters are so close to the Heath girls now."

"I'm aware. But we continue to correspond. And she came to see me off to Liverpool."

"Did she? I didn't know."

"I'll just take the desk with me now."

Looks were exchanged, and she knew she ought to have discussed this with Anne before simply arriving with a desk, but she no longer trusted her uncle. The desk was hers, and she didn't want them using it or deciding to sell it because it was "in her best interest."

The desk was strapped onto a carriage. Little Benji bounced around during the lifting and tying, which Dorothea helped her uncle to accomplish. At least the dog looked to be in good health. If she had a home of her own, she would have asked for the dog. Dorothea spoke her good-byes and took the carriage immediately to Brookline where Anne greeted her warmly.

"Here I am, unannounced."

"No, no, come in." Anne looked beyond to the carriage with the desk.

"I am being intrusive, I know. I can't stay, but might I leave my writing desk with you? It was my father's and one of the few items left to me by my grandmamma and uncle."

"I'd heard about Orange Court. I'm sorry,

Dorothea. I know you hoped it would one day be your home."

"I promise not to be at your doorstep when you least expect it . . . present moment excepted."

"Of course. We'll store it. It's a lovely piece. Please, stay for supper."

"I have things to do regarding my grandmother's estate. You understand."

Dorothea turned to leave, her heart a hummingbird of hope when Anne added, "You come back soon."

Dorothea spent weeks in Philadelphia. Then she moved on to Savannah because she was told it was one of the few cities in America laid out in an orderly fashion, the other being Washington DC. Her grandmother had bequeathed a vase to a woman there. The city reminded her of the painting in the Rathbones' bedroom, how the war had ravaged the town. She hoped the beautiful city would never again see such destruction. While she was there, she began to read about city planning, ways to manage the glut of tenements, and how water and sewage systems ought not be afterthoughts but paramount for public health. She wrote an article on botany that was published in a magazine. She meandered.

For two years she visited friends, staying for a few weeks at a time and then moving on before they tired of her.

As she traveled, she wrote letters to Anne. In one such letter, Anne encouraged her to give up her wandering and return to Brookline, where the two old friends could live together. Dorothea caught her breath. How she would have longed for those words years before! But now she was wary. Her time at Greenbank, being tended and loved back to health, told her that she had something else in store for her. Why else would she have survived her terrible lung disease? Resting away her days with an old friend was not the future she imagined.

She remembered her Greenbank morning routine. After an hour of silent prayer and contemplation, she wrote down a list of important work she could do: the suffering to be comforted, the wandering led home, the indolent aroused, the overexcited restrained. She sent a letter to Anne with those words included and began to see that these works of service could guide her, keep her from being "a floating wad upon the ocean of each day's events." Anne told her those last words were overly dramatic. She did not comment on Dorothea's proposed life plan. Dorothea never asked after Anne's.

Another year passed with her travels, and then Dorothea returned to Boston and accepted the invitation of Sarah Gibbs to live at the summit of Beacon Hill in her home on Mount Vernon

Street. Before long, the Channings joined them. To make room, Dorothea moved into a town-house on the estate. On Sundays at the Federal Street Church, listening to the moving words of William Channing, she began again to feel a calling to inquire more diligently as to the reason for her being. In the evenings, she would read to the reverend, awaiting something she knew not what. At Channing's request, she began teaching a Sunday school class for teenage boys at the Charlestown Navy Yard. The work made her think of her brother Charles.

"It is a great satisfaction again to teach," she wrote to Anne, "to feel that I am not wholly a burden in the social circle. I am at home and at ease here."

She sent for her writing desk.

Eighteen

The Moment

Compliments settled on Dorothea's shoulders like snowflakes in May: rare and dissipating, uncertain as to their intent. Dorothea felt her face grow hot, which only seemed to encourage John Nichols, the divinity student who shared the kind words of Dorothea's mentor as they walked home from church one Sunday.

"Reverend Channing said they warmed to you, that you had an extra affinity, a charm, that put both men and women at ease. I certainly don't have it. And besides, I really need to prepare for my debate."

Dorothea nodded her bonneted head toward the young man she had met at the Channing lecture. *So young and the world opening to him with a dozen paths.* Dorothea was nearly forty and still wandered from path to path.

"But if I agree to do this, I might be getting in the way of your mission, John."

He stopped and put both hands on his cane, which he didn't need. He stared at her. "Yes, but perhaps my asking you is helping to define your great ambition." She looked away. "Please say you'll consider it. It's just one term, and if you truly detest it, I'll take over again."

"How many are there?"

"A few dozen. They'll be in an open area, maybe a few in cells. But for Sunday school they let them come in together. It's probably one of the few times they're allowed to be with each other. They're well behaved. Not like the ones across the courtyard, those awaiting trial and the over-flow from the mental asylum."

She remembered her revulsion at the conditions of the jail in Washington when she and her boardinghouse friends had visited and later returned with books she thought might help pass the prisoners' time. She had been healthy this winter. Would teaching in a drafty jail bring back the misery? She heard a sea gull screech high above, sounding lonesome and lost. She looked for the bird and blinked into the hazy late winter sun.

"All right," she said, not certain why. "I'll do it." Who knew what might come of it?

It was a March morning, one of those days when people smiled at each other on the streets and cab drivers asked after one's health as though they genuinely wanted to know.

Back in her room, Dorothea donned her black dress and straightened the white collar, checking herself once in the boardinghouse mirror. She pulled on the ribbons of her black bonnet. As it was Sunday, no steam from the textile mills hovered over Cambridge, threatening to bring down uplifted spirits.

The women populating the East Cambridge jail gathered in a room with old benches. Dorothea could see that some attempted to keep up their hygiene, most likely by family deliveries of soaps and clean linens, as she knew these would not be provided by the prison.

A red-haired woman leaned against the stone wall, arms folded across her chest. *Show me!* she seemed to say. The other women looked curious, representing all ages.

Dorothea couldn't help but wonder what had happened in their lives that brought them to this place. Women had so few choices. She remembered her journey to her grandmother's, hoping for rescue, and the devastation she had felt when she had been turned aside. She had drawn on a resilience she didn't know she had back then as a twelve-year-old child. Her purpose had been to rescue Charles and make life better for them all. She had failed that day. Perhaps these women didn't know their purpose, hadn't been given the news that they were loved by One greater than all others, a love that could help them make a better life when they left this place. Perhaps this was what she was called to do: give these women the thread they could follow to don the cape of great hope.

Threadbare slippers scraped quietly on the stone floor as the women waited.

"Good morning." Her voice was as clear as a mountain stream. "Thank you for allowing me to come."

The red-haired woman snorted. "As if we invited ye."

"Quiet," spoke another.

"I'd like to begin with a psalm."

But before she finished, a woman with a crooked nose interrupted, asking, "Why has God forgotten such as us? We done nothing but support our husbands, do what they ask, and we end up here." Dorothea read a few more words,

205

then stopped. Her prepared lesson would be of little use. What these women wanted was comfort, assurance. Was she the one to give it?

Dorothea cleared her throat. "God has not forsaken you though it may seem this way now. It was true for those of old as well, who wondered if God had forgotten them at times. But He never does. I promise you. This is but a stop on your journey to a relationship with God who will never fail you."

"A cold stop," the red-haired woman said. She reminded Dorothea of one of her students, sullen yet haughty.

"It is that. But even in the chill, we can be warm." The room quieted as Dorothea spoke of God's love for each of them. She shared bits of her own story, from being forlorn to illness to finding friends who sustained her. She spoke of moving against a stream and the strength her faith gave her for the journey. More than one woman dabbed her eyes when Dorothea read Psalm 30, which promised mourning would turn to dancing and sackcloth changed to clothes of joy. Dorothea helped them imagine themselves dressed differ-ently, dancing instead of merely existing in this hovel. She looked each woman in the eye as she spoke. Even the redhead had loosened her arms and eased her way onto a bench by the time Dorothea finished.

"Now. You tell me your stories." She sat on a

small stool. "Maybe together we can find God and grace within them." Dorothea took time to listen, to learn where they had come from, how they had arrived here, sentenced for a year or three or more for petty theft, public drunkenness, or abandoning their children.

One woman was there for murdering her husband. "It was me or him," she said. "Me or him, and I knew my children could not live safe with him no more."

Time like snowflakes disappeared until the jailer opened the door and told Dorothea she had best be going. It was mealtime.

"Will you come again?" a slender woman with a fairly clean face asked. Her head twitched as she spoke.

"I will do my best."

The red-headed woman snorted. "Don't want to commit to such as us, does she?"

"You're Miss . . ."

"Mrs. Taylor."

"You're right in noting my hesitation. But you're wrong too. I will be back."

"Not likely." She was a woman made up of demand and disappointment.

Dorothea smiled and reached to squeeze the woman's hand. "I will not fail you." She thought she saw a flash of gratitude wisp across the woman's eyes before she pulled her hand from Dorothea's.

Dorothea walked out into the sunshine and took a deep breath. Those women, so unfortunate, and all she could do for them was bring an hour or so of goodwill. It was such a small interruption in the days of torment they faced; she hoped to leave them a bit of the psalm to remember, to set their feet to dancing if only in their imagination. But she would return. She promised herself that.

A small building across the yard caught her eye. John had said there was another jail that housed inebriates, people awaiting trial, witnesses and debtors, many who made shoes to pay off their creditors so they could be released.

"They also house those not furiously mad there," John said, "along with idiots and lunatics and insane persons—if they aren't dangerous. They bring them as overflow from the state hospital in Worcester." Dorothea knew that hospital had been built some years back, but she did not realize it had an overflow.

Perhaps it was the sense of good she might have done by meeting with the Cambridge women, perhaps it was the red-headed woman's charge that she might not come back, or maybe she heard an inner voice that had been silenced for so long. Whatever it was, Dorothea turned toward the smaller building across the cobblestones. At the entrance of the well-designed stone structure she stopped to read a marker that claimed the design was the work of Charles

Bulfinch. *He designed Sarah Gibbs' home on Beacon Hill.* Dorothea smiled at the irony. At least these debtors were housed as though they lived in ornate glory. On the outside.

She watched her hand reach up to knock. She asked to be let in.

As with other jail sites, she knew the jailer would seek coins. Tourists often visited jails and prisons. It was a way for jailers to make money supposedly put into the keep of their charges. She placed a coin in the hand of a sour-looking man who pocketed it.

"Come this way." He carried a stick. She followed him down a hall where he opened a wide heavy door.

A cold draft hit her face, and she pulled her cloak around her before she realized the stench. Filth, bits of chicken bone, and rotting vegetables littered the large room where an agonized wail beat like a metronome, rising up, then down. Bars separated her from the occupants, but she spied a man wrapped in a shirt with his arms tied in front. He was making the wretched noise. His eyes vacant and his body rocking.

Several prisoners rushed to the bars, pushing their hands through. "Bread? Do you have bread?"

Another screeched, and beside her a woman jerked away. "Can you get me out of here? Please! The insane are here!"

"Step back!" the jailer ordered.

A woman half-clothed picked at her skin and cried out, her voice sharp as a mad dog's tooth. Her hair was frizzled, unkempt. Dorothea had a momentary memory of her mother, lost inside a world of her own, plucking at her clothing.

An elderly woman looked up at Dorothea with sorrow-filled eyes. "It's very cold. Very cold. This girl will freeze to death here. And I will become as feeble-minded as she is. Can you help us, madam? I cry to you for help."

"God hears your cries," Dorothea said. Her words sounded weak even to her ears. She suppressed a cough.

The jailer rattled his stick along the bars, and the women whose fingers gripped the metal howled and stepped back. Dorothea saw another woman, stripped bare, lying on the stone floor. *Is she dead? No, her bony spine rises and lowers.* Where is the dignity for people crushed together, the feeble-minded and the debtors, required witnesses, each clutching to their sanity in the midst of this cluster of prisoners . . . people. They were all suffering people.

Dorothea took deep breaths.

The room had a coal stove, and Dorothea had seen a coal bin. She could also see her breath as she gasped. The woman picking at her skin turned a vacant eye away from Dorothea. *So familiar.* Dorothea could smell the full chamber pots. One appeared to have been spilled on the far side of the coal stove. The liquid seeped close to the woman lying naked on the stones. Dorothea swallowed the revulsion from the smells, shivered, and turned to the jailer.

"Can't you build a fire? It's freezing in here, and half of them are nearly naked."

"They tear their clothes," he answered. *Bam!* The jailer's stick cracked the metal. Dorothea jumped. So did the prisoners who scurried from the bars. "And you can see they don't care about themselves. And a fire? No telling what they would burn up. Conditions are what they deserve. It's of their own doing, why they're here."

"They are still human beings. They need to be treated as you would your own mother." *My mother.* She caught her breath as she said that.

"Truth is, the idiots and lunatics, the ones naked lying there? They know no better from cold or hot. Can't tell it. Their mind won't let them know about freezing or fire. Guess that's something a fine lady like you wouldn't know about."

Smug little man. A flash of memory pierced Dorothea. Her mother—even in her most vacant states when she slept for hours and hours—would still sigh with comfort when Dorothea pulled a blanket over her to warm her. Even when her mother was so listless she could barely open her mouth to the spoon Dorothea lifted to her lips, her mother would shrink back if the soup was too hot. It was a basic human need to seek warmth in the cold, to be refreshed in the heat. To bring comfort was a moral imperative, especially for the least of these. Dorothea felt her face grow hot, her breathing quicken.

"You are wrong, sir, about the cold not affecting them. It affects all humans, the same whether one is lost to the vagaries of the mind or fully stable before us. We all suffer."

"Not them." The jailer poked his stick through the bar and jabbed at a man who then tripped and fell to the floor. The commotion appeared to irritate the rocking person in the corner. He increased his cries, shortened the rhythm of his wails.

The jailer laughed. "There's your humans," he said. "More like dogs."

"Even dogs are given beds out of the cold, sir."

"Time's up. You've gotten your money's worth." He motioned for Dorothea to leave. She resisted, so he pushed her with his stick. The cries behind her grew louder. Something made Dorothea turn back, take one last look at this cesspool of suffering. The woman, unaware of the cold, continued to pluck at her arms, but then she looked up, her eyes pleading this time.

As Dorothea's mother had so often done.

In that moment Dorothea knew: it was beyond them to change by themselves. They could not help it, might never change at all, but each of them deserved to be treated with kindness, care,

hope. She could see that now. They needed others
—they needed her.

"I'll be back!" she shouted over her shoulder.
She had no doubt.

The jailer urged her forward. "Don't go all high
and mighty on me. You don't know what it's like.
I earn my pay."

He slammed the door behind her as the cold
air hit her face. Her hands clasped the Bible and
the basket of tracts she hadn't left behind. She
had failed with her mother, but here . . . she must
not fail. She must bring relief. She had never felt
so certain of anything. But how?

Nineteen

A Second Journey

That night Dorothea prepared a petition to the
East Middlesex court situated next to the debtors'
jail. She demanded that it provide adequate heat
and empty the chamber pots at least daily. "These
suffering souls might be your distant cousin,
your maiden aunt made low by a poor choice.
None deserve to suffer cold or want for simple
covering."

In the morning, she stood outside the court in
a drizzle that only made her more adamant.

"Finally," she said when the clerk opened the door. "I would meet with the magistrate."

"He's not here yet, miss. His schedule is taken with court issues."

"I'll wait.

"It'll take some time," the clerk said. He was shaped like a pickle and wore glasses near the end of his nose. Dorothea followed close behind him as he entered the office.

"I know. I'll wait."

"It could be weeks." He poked at the coals in the stove.

"Those people are cold now," Dorothea said. "I ought to have presented the petition yesterday when I was there, but the court, as you know, was not open. They have gone yet another night in the cold. It's paramount that I plead their case, wouldn't you agree?" The clerk leaned away from her, and Dorothea softened. "I know it's not up to you. But we have to provide at least basic dignity for all people. It diminishes us if we don't."

He nodded. "I've a sister in the Worcester asylum, and I worry over her. I can't keep her with my family, but the overcrowding . . ." His eyes focused on the petition. "I'll see the judge looks at this straightaway if you care to leave it. And I'll send word when he's decided." He rose, motioning for Dorothea to stand as well.

Maybe having the magistrate read her petition without the challenge of Dorothea before him was a good idea. He would feel less . . . intimidated. "Yes. Give it to him. But I'll still wait right here for his reply." She remained seated.

She was unaware of hunger and instead sat and prayed. Dorothea looked at her pocket watch. Two hours had passed and she had hardly noticed.

"It will be done," the clerk stood before her, his glasses pushed up closer to his eyes.

"It will?" Dorothea stood. "I mean, of course it will be done. But when?"

"They said they would see to it immediately." He smiled. "Someone has already been dispatched to build the fires."

"Well. That's excellent. Yes. Excellent. Please, thank them for me. And thank you."

The clerk patted her gloved hands. "It's a good thing you do, it is."

Tears pressed behind her eyes. *Thank you.*

"And clothing? Decent clothes to cover them?"

"Your words must have been very forceful," he told her. "I've been directed to find such clothing and to ensure that the jailer makes it available. The magistrates hope you will continue your Sunday school classes and expand them to the witness court."

"Oh, I will. That I will."

Just like that, the court granted her petition. Immediately. Fires would be built daily, along with chamber pot attention. Clothes would be provided, although the court added it was uncertain if the occupants, being feeble-minded and all, could be required to keep their clothes on. The swell of success brought a joy to Dorothea that she had not realized she had been missing.

At Greenbank, she remembered, she had assisted Elizabeth Rathbone at a charity event to help the Liverpool asylum. She had watched the woman speak to each potential donor, knowing something of each family, asking after a grandson or a niece. "Your generosity is so appreciated. I know you have many places to do your faithful work, and we are honored you would choose the asylum."

"Happy to help. Happy to. Indeed."

"We know how much the asylum means to you and William."

Words spoken as the stewards served small sandwiches and cider around the room, fluttering the hibiscus as they passed.

"Yes, it does. Your gifts mean even more to the patients who are the least of these. You do the Lord's work, you know."

"I'd say you do that," the donor bowed his head.

"We do it together." Elizabeth clasped the donor's hands.

"Indeed. If it's to be, it's up to thee."

She guided them then to where William sat, accepting their contributions.

Dorothea watched, learned, took a chance

conferring with a potential donor herself. "We are both newcomers," she said. "I understand you are from America too."

"How do you know that? Oh." The man grinned. "My accent. Virginia. Guess we do sound different than the British." After introductions, he said, "I'm a friend of Lord Thaylor." He nodded toward a man who had just written a commitment to the asylum.

"Perhaps you would like to share in his happiness at making the lives of those at the asylum better. He seems quite pleased. Generosity does the heart good."

"Ha. Well, it likely does at that." He narrowed his eyes. "Did you see me as an easy mark, Miss Dix?"

"Not at all. I see you as a fellow countryman whose charitable spirit reflects the goodness of our nation. I offer you a chance to model our country's philanthropic history and make a statement here in Liverpool. And receive the blessings of our Lord in doing so."

He grinned again and tugged at his goatee. "Well done, Miss Dix. I will do my patriotic duty and support an English hospital." He pulled a long wallet from his jacket pocket. "Pleasure to make your acquaintance. I think." He smiled and headed toward William, holding court at the table.

But this present success with the East Middlesex

court was a singular joy, greater than raising money for the asylum. Here, she knew that at least one person would be relieved of the cold because of something she had done personally, something simply giving money could not have accomplished.

She began teaching the Sunday school classes weekly, along with an additional class at the debtors' jail, where she saw for herself a low fire heating the cavernous room and the smaller cells as well. The greatly impaired prisoners had been removed, and when she asked to see where they were, she was shown to another room, where a flame rose. It brought scant warmth, but at least the freeze of the stone walls had lessened.

Still, the moans of despair and minds in peril overpowered the lingering scent of pain and degradation. It seemed to Dorothea that the people housed here needed to be in a hospital or they would soon affect the healthier cellmates. This mixing of prisoners simply was not wise. Prisoners with less reason could easily become victims of their stronger cellmates, or they might harm the other prisoners as their thoughts grew beyond spats to confused attacks.

"Required to pay my brother-in-law to sit in here and watch 'em when the fire's going," the jailer growled. Jailers were paid by the local sheriffs, and the cost of any care came from their profits, if there were any. "Hope you're happy now," he said.

"My happiness is much improved, thank you. It's especially good to see the floors have been washed. Thank you for that as well."

"Brother-in-law has to keep busy."

"And he's chosen wisely. You may find it easier to manage the prisoner demands by separating the feeble-minded from the others."

"I wouldn't push, miss, if I was you. Take what you got and leave us be."

On a Sunday some weeks later, Dorothea was approached by a prisoner awaiting sentencing and asked if she couldn't intervene on her behalf. "The woman, my cellmate, hardly sleeps," the woman told her. Her clothes hung on her. She must have lost weight during her incarceration or she wore someone else's clothes. "She hovers over me so, when I wake, she's there, staring at me. Other times she wails and rocks, her eyes jerk like a squirrel's from here to there." The woman leaned in close. "She talks to people who aren't present and sometimes barks like a dog. She can look fierce too. I worry for myself but for her too."

Dorothea had seen the woman who usually mumbled and rocked in the back corner when she came for the classes.

"Is she ever able to speak of what is happening?"

"Not that I've been aware."

"Why is she here?"

"I don't know."

Dorothea inquired of the jailer, who told her the woman had been sent from the Worcester asylum due to overcrowding.

"She appears to have picked at her arms so badly she bleeds."

"Noticed that," the jailer said. He rolled a toothpick in his mouth.

"Could we please bring in a physician?"

"That'll be another expense."

"I'll pay for it myself."

Dorothea contacted Dr. Samuel Howe, the head of the Perkins School for the Blind and a board member of the Boston Normal School. Their paths had crossed during her school-teaching years.

Howe made the journey with her the next Sunday and examined the woman. "Her behavior certainly puts her cellmate at risk. There's no telling what she might do in her mad state."

Dorothea advocated with the jailer, her compassion easing onto him, and a separate cell was found, though the jailer complained, "I don't know how long I can keep her there. I have new prisoners coming in daily and not many going out."

"We appreciate your assistance," Dorothea said. She had to be gentle with jailers or they would prevent her from visiting.

"Those conditions for the insane . . . it really needs a public exposure." Dr. Howe expressed his concerns while riding in the carriage back to Dorothea's townhouse.

"It's not something I can do, being a woman."

"You were successful in getting heat into the cells. And they allowed me to come in and separate the poor woman from her cellmate's insanity. I doubt that would have happened without your intervention. You can do more than you think, though you are quite right in knowing a woman's place." He gazed out the carriage window. "It is best for women not to be out publicly crusading for some cause."

Dorothea knew Dr. Howe was courting the beautiful Julia Ward, who was outspoken against slavery. She did not want to mention Julia's public presence. He apparently approved of crusading quietly. He was but a year older than Dorothea and had wavy hair, which he wore longish at his neck, and a beard that twisted like grass around a fencepost. He had served as a surgeon during the Greek revolution, and some called him the "Lafayette of Greece" for his later fund-raising for refugees. It was a nickname that pleased him.

"Truly, that poor woman needs to be hospitalized. Moral treatment is what she needs."

"You've read the Jarvis pamphlet?" Her excitement bubbled. "Or know of Doctors Tuke and Thomas Kirkbride who promote such treatment?"

"I do. Our friend Horace Mann invited Dr. Jarvis to write of his successes in treating the mentally ill in his home and to describe the way to bring health into schools."

Dorothea had liked the philosophy of moral treatment ever since being introduced to it while at the Rathbones'. It required treating all people, rich or poor, with dignity and compassion in a homelike setting.

"Worcester, for all its good intent, merely houses them," Howe continued. He combed his beard with his fingers. "They need more than that. They need to be in a world as normal as possible, with structure, of course, but more with love, like a family."

"From chaos into order. God's very action with the creation of the world. A garden perhaps. Work with animals, gathering eggs or grooming horses." She remembered the calm a ride on Mercy gave her. Even the Rathbones' little dog curling up against her back brought her peace during her illness. "Intellectual stimulation, listening to music boxes, employment such as the shoemakers have at East Cambridge. The prisoners have little hope of attempting to acquire a skill without proper instruction or safety." Ideas popped into her head. "A family atmosphere of compassion and caring."

"So how might we proceed in our campaign?" Howe asked. "Keeping your feminine guiles secure but using your passion of words to move forward?"

"How indeed." It was a massive challenge to affect the lives of others while maintaining the private life required of a proper Boston woman. She felt her heart quicken. Howe echoed what Channing had once told her, about every person being our brother's—or sister's—keeper. She gleaned a certainty she hadn't known before. Here at last might be her glorious ambition.

Twenty

Compassion in the Particular

Dorothea was good at classifying. Botany had given her that interest and taught her the importance of ordering and structure. And she observed well, "activities" at least, although she wasn't always good at attributing causes to behavior or emotions. But she could organize and then write of what she saw. She would be focused and direct.

Dr. Howe and she agreed on how to proceed, and then he left for Kentucky, where he worked to establish another school for the blind. His part of the goal—to get the Massachusetts legislature to provide funds for a hospital committed to moral treatment—was to write a review of the Jarvis pamphlet and have it published in the highly regarded *North American Review.* Thus there would be renewed interest in moral treatment and justice and mercy for the mentally ill.

"I will visit the jails and almshouses in eastern and central Massachusetts, becoming a witness to the condition of those who are in need of such treatment," Dorothea said. The two set about doing their separate work.

Dorothea decided early on that she would not just count people but try to see each as an individual, not accepting the words or descriptions given by the jailers or matrons, but seeing for herself how each responded to the presence of a stranger: how they communicated, even without words; what they allowed their eyes to focus on; the unmet need suggested by their behavior. She would classify those distinctions to make a final report, but she wanted always to be mindful of the particular misery of each person. "Where I can," she told William Channing, "I will relieve the suffering, one person at a time."

"You've chosen a major task, Dorothea. Pace yourself in this. Let God work through you, not where you're pulling Him along behind you."

Dorothea's shoulders dropped. She loved this man as a father. She did not wish to displease him. "Did you not say from the pulpit last Sunday that the way the insane are soothed by mere kindness is proof that love is the divine plan for all? I am merely loving them as I can."

Channing smiled. "You listen well, Dorothea. Just remember to let God's love bring kindness to you as well."

"I hope to suggest ways a hospital designed just for the feeble-minded could meet a patient's basic needs and still provide parts of moral treatment, not just housing them in cold cells. But first I want to see what is."

"Find out how often ministers visit them," Channing suggested.

"Yes. And whether they stay to offer kindness or merely drop off tracts. If I do this, I'll no longer be able to read to you in an evening. At least for a time."

"We leave for Vermont for a respite, so you need not worry over our readings."

"Oh. I'll miss you all." She hadn't been invited to join them. She would not let exclusion stumble her.

"We won't be here to make sure you eat well," he said. "So don't overdo. Remember that spinning top." He smiled then, and she didn't feel in the least chastised.

Her first visits to jails close to the city were similar to her East Cambridge experience, but as she took the stage during the summer of 1842 to hither and yon, staying at inns, rising in the early mist to write down what she had experienced the day before, she began to see true suffering in ways she had not encountered before.

"Mournfully," Dorothea wrote in her diary, "a woman extended her arms to me and asked why she was consigned to hell. Then she used our Lord's very words and shouted 'My God! My God! Why hast thou forsaken me?' "

Some of the patients were estranged from God, and here was a blackness like hell on this earth for them. The cause of such estrangement, whether sin or accident of birth or misfortune not of their making, made no difference, Dorothea decided; each was entitled to respect and human kindness and a way back to that relationship that meets all needs.

She was a witness for a woman chained to a heavy metal ring cemented into the stone wall, clothes covered with feces, fingernails on one hand chewed to the quick and on the other longer than a laundry peg. The woman scratched and gouged her own face, arms, and legs. Open sores oozed. A boy, eyes dull as old pewter, leaned against a woman who rocked constantly and was likely the child's mother. He looked up at Dorothea.

"Why is he here?" Dorothea asked the jailer.

"Nowhere for him to go."

"No relatives? No orphanage to take him?"

"Sometimes he acts as crazy as his mother. Safer for everyone with him in here."

"No, it's not," Dorothea said.

The jailer bristled. "Let's move on."

She turned back and watched the child's eyes follow them out.

At an almshouse, a man who claimed to be a former local official clung to Dorothea, begging her to find release for him. "I am not insane. I am not insane. They leave me with that." His eyes moved furtively to a body behind him so thin with hair missing in clumps. Dorothea thought the person might have died, but then she heard a swell of breath. Cockroaches skittered in a darkened corner. "I could be useful again, I could." The former official's eyes drained at the corners, and she could see that he was closer to this world than the woman. Yes, a woman beside him hummed, then screeched. How dreadful his days must be.

"Why are you here?" Dorothea asked.

"I was unable to pay for a service and was taken to court. I cannot possibly repay from in here and will soon lose my mind if I stay longer. Please, please, help me." He had sores on his hands, unhealed burns she thought. He reached out to her.

The laws of Leviticus came to her, the ones that warned that anyone who touched an unclean person would become unclean likewise. She took his hand, something her grandmother would have gasped at her for doing. The story of Mark was a stronger pull. Jesus touched a leper and healed him, a singular act of compassion.

The man gasped when she held his hand.

"Did I hurt you?"

"No, no. It . . . it's been so long. Your touch . . ." His shoulders shook as he tried to quell the sobs.

Dorothea removed her gloves and put her pale palm against his and squeezed his fingers. "It's the least I can do," she whispered.

At another jail she spoke with a man who did not seem the least bit insane to Dorothea as she asked him what work he had once done.

"Livery, madam," he said. "I tended stage horses until an injury required surgery and I healed slowly and could not pay." When she asked the jailer about him, he described behaviors she would classify as mad. The jailer said the man was jailed, not just because he had failed to pay a bill, but because he had rushed out into the cold. His family had been unable to keep him clothed or make any sense from him following his sentencing. Yet she had seen a man making perfect sense. Had that moment of appropriateness been brought on by her willingness to see what was normal in his world?

She lay awake that night considering his situation. In the morning she returned, seeking to have the man moved to a cell with fewer mentally ill persons. The resident doctor resisted at first but then complied.

"I see your point, Miss Dix," he said. "The man has deteriorated. But we simply can't move everyone around to suit you." Dorothea thought he might be miffed because she had been able to get Dr. Howe to move a prisoner earlier.

She wrote a letter to Howe seeking possible employment for the man in the stables at the school. Perhaps she could find a place for him in a normal world. Moral treatment. For the first time it was not an abstract theory of how to treat people; it was a truth she had stumbled upon, one given her as she sought to relieve a man's immediate suffering. Her touching him had seemed so small an act of kindness, and yet it brought out a response she would have herself if her hands were covered with sores, if she felt abandoned and alone and someone had reached out to her. As the Channings had. As the Rathbones had.

Dorothea sat up in bed and reached for her diary. Extending herself was the very thing keeping her from despair, from actually becoming ill again. "To stay well, I must do this work. I must paint the portrait of what the human condition is like when left abandoned. There is hope for those prisoners. If I reach them, if I can make their lives more like mine, then I will have done good work. To relieve the suffering of others will relieve my own." That thought startled her. "Moreover, if they see where my care comes from and that they can have it for themselves, then I will be meeting the Great Commission, to gather others to the heart of God where they need never feel alone."

She would ask dozens of questions about what a normal person would experience: were Sunday school classes offered? Did the local Fragment Society come to teach needlework? Would a saddle maker be allowed to continue his craft? Did patients serve meals to others more impaired? Did they go outside, breathe fresh air? Were there uplifting books available for them to read, music to soothe them?

She would draw conclusions about the nature of those insane where normal opportunities existed. It would help prove the premise that a separate treatment hospital was needed. No bars or chains, their healing coming from the borders of compassion.

As she broadened her scope to include all of Massachusetts, Dorothea became accustomed to the stagecoach's rough ride. She bounced and jostled and could not write, so she recorded in the evenings what she had encountered during the days. She tried to take notes in the jails, but she noticed the jailers offered only short responses if she appeared to write them down. She strengthened her memory for detail, not just that which the patients said, but their jailers as well, pouring out the day on paper, using up nibs and ink in far greater numbers than she had imagined.

Through the stage windows she took in the countryside, the stone fences that marked one man's border and spoke of efforts to clear ground and stack the rocks so they wouldn't tumble down. She saw women in gardens and made a mental note to consider the size of a garden one might need for moral treatment in an institution housing two hundred fifty patients. Gardens would serve as treatment but also food supply.

At the stage stop where the horses were changed before travel to the next berg, Dorothea wondered about the care provided for work animals. Surely that was something normal. She watched the men pat the necks of the big animals as they lowered the heavy harnesses from them and led the horses to the trough. The fine animals lipped the water. She saw a bond between the men and beasts and thought of Mercy. She wished she had a dog or horse, some beating heart she might come home to in the evening. But this was wishful thinking. Her life was on the road now, and even when it wasn't, she was in the home of another. What would she do with a dog when she traveled?

Instead, on a warm August evening she made a note about making sure the new institution Howe and she hoped for would have barns and sheds where patients could help the stockmen work with cows and pigs and chickens and horses. And where perhaps a small dog could be kept. Maybe more than one.

Before sending her material to Howe, Dorothea reread the Jarvis pamphlet on moral treatment.

Jarvis had written it in the third person, as though someone else described his work. "Knowing that so much depends on the influences which surround the patients, Dr. J. regulated every thing in respect to its effect on them—their food, their exercise, the places and the persons they visited or who visited them, the conversation at table or elsewhere." Most of all, he made a great case for doing away with heroic treatments, as they were known, the powerful herbs to put people to sleep, or the prescribing of painful treatments such as binding them with chains or shirts until blood stopped flowing to their arms, fingers, and feet.

She could see little difference between these heroics and torture. It seemed to her that Jarvis, too, felt that what governed all insanity were unchecked passions. She recalled a visit to a private home secured for the insane by a local sheriff. Inside, she witnessed unbridled passion unchecked as a man flailed and shouted and destroyed his meager belongings of which shards remained inside the room. But she felt his caretakers had intensified his behaviors by using brutal chains. Their violence escalated the man's violence. That had to stop. *She* had to stop it. Somehow, she would.

Dorothea had thought Dr. Howe would rework her treatise and perhaps use it to support his review of Jarvis's work for the *North American*

Review article. Instead, Howe wrote an exposé on the East Cambridge jail that was published on September 8, 1842, in the *Boston Daily Advertiser.* He reported that treatment "was disgraceful in the highest degree to a Christian community."

The resident physician of the jail objected and wrote a response to the *Advertiser*, denying Howe's charges.

Howe responded back, and others presented their perspectives with heated invective. A jailer gave Dorothea's name and said she had barely been in his facility for five minutes and could not possibly have seen what was described.

"What on earth was Howe thinking?" Dorothea asked Anne. She poked at the newspaper article. "My material was to enhance his review of Jarvis's work, not bring down the establishment on us. They'll be reluctant now to let me in to see what's going on."

"Dr. Howe is usually so diplomatic, didn't you say?" Anne knitted while Dorothea paced the room, causing the lamplight to wobble on its stand.

"I wanted this to bring a general awareness to people. Then approach legislators in particular with good evidence to back up what we want. Now the doctors and the jailers have their backs up. They see this as an assault on them rather than a cause to take different action. I never once said the jailers or the resident doctors were bad people!"

Had she misread Howe's intention? Did he have an ulterior motive, raising his own prestige for his blind school at the expense of a systematic plan for reformed treatment for the insane?

"I must write to him. And to the *Advertiser*."

She had to defend Howe's statements if only to sustain her reputation as a benevolent observer. But if she did, she was making herself public. More public than she had planned. But for the sake of the mentally ill, she felt compelled to write a letter. She said that the conditions in East Cambridge were as Dr. Howe had described them, but they were also better than in other Massachusetts prisons she had visited. She promised to reveal more of what she had seen with the hope toward changing all of it, knowing that the jailers and others did the best they could. It was the responsibility of all the people of the common-wealth to aid them in saving the insane.

The *Advertiser* rejected her submission but the *Evening Mercantile Journal* accepted it for publication. Perhaps she could put water on this firestorm after all.

She received the letter after a long day helping to quell a minor conflict between a livery owner and a man she had helped to find work there. The letter was from Sarah Gibbs, who was traveling with the Channings in Vermont. William Ellery Channing—icon of the Federal Street Church,

Sarah's brother-in-law, and Dorothea's mentor—had died of typhoid fever. Dorothea gasped, tears pricking her eyes, flooding them so hard she couldn't read the details.

Channing had been as close to her as any father could be, and now, in the midst of her first big battle, he was gone. She wished she had been in Vermont so she wouldn't have to grieve alone in the little townhouse on Mount Vernon Street, wished she could have heard his inspiring voice just one more time.

She picked the letter up and finished reading. Sarah would be selling the townhouse in which Dorothea now lived. Sarah would be staying in Vermont with Channing's widow, Elizabeth. Dorothea put her hands to her throat. She was not invited to join the Channing household. Nor, she realized, would she desire to be so. She had work here to do, though it meant grieving alone.

Dorothea's article was published the day after Channing's death, but Dorothea took little notice. Once again she was packing. Once again she had no home. But she had a plan.

Twenty-One

The Best She Could Hope For

"Relieving the suffering of others will relieve my own," Dorothea reread in her diary. She dated it November 1842. This insight led her to put some of her things—including her writing desk—into storage. She packed a trunk with the simple uniform she was known for: a black merino-wool dress with a small, white lace collar. She arranged her hair in two swooping waves on either side of her face and collected it in the back in a tasteful bun sheltered by netting. Simple and easy. With ample supplies of pens, paper, and ink, she began to travel. She visited jails up the coast to Cape Cod, then across the interior to the Berkshire Mountains and back again. The inns along the way became her home. She made sure she did not fall into the despair she had felt after her grandmother's death and the loss of Orange Court.

"As I am homeless, I will create homes for the insane," she wrote in her diary and later to Anne, when the latter urged her to pace herself and to consider living with her in Boston. "We could grow old together."

"I have things to do," she wrote. "There are those in need of me and what little discomfort I feel with a hard bed or mud-wet shoes, these are minor compared to my brothers and sisters, the insane. If I am cold, they are cold; if I am weary, they are distressed; if I am alone, they are abandoned."

She began visiting jails and almshouses, canvassing thirty-five towns in one week. She pushed herself, writing early in the morning and late at night, uncertain why she pushed so hard. She thought often of Reverend Channing, hoping he would approve.

A part of her was relieved she did not have to defend to him the very public argument going on in the newspapers about what Dr. Howe had written and about her public response. The worst part of the scathing letters going back and forth in the newspapers questioned her veracity and motives. She had hoped to remain outside the fray. Thankfully, one editorial had defended her, saying that since Miss Dix cannot vote nor stand for office, she had no motive but good to say what she did. "She has no reason to lie," the editor concluded.

She hoped this pronouncement would lower the fury and keep the subject on moral treatment and those who needed it, not on the messengers raising the issues.

She did have to deal with Dr. Howe though. A

part of her felt used that he had taken her material. Instead of preparing it thoughtfully for presentation to the legislature, he had gone on his own, purporting that moral treatment could "cure" the insane. She had not gone that far. It was out of humanity, out of Christian love, that their care should be improved. If people improved, so much the better. If they did not, they still deserved to be cared for as human beings, not wild animals.

Dr. Howe had attempted to soothe her in his latest letter and had encouraged her to acquire more evidence of the need. "The legislature will require the most recent information and the more we have statewide, the more we can engage the entire House."

It was in part why she had set out with this travel schedule that fall and into early winter. But she also needed to tell him how his actions had affected her.

Dorothea returned to Boston for Marianna's wedding. Dr. Howe was in Boston too, and she requested a visit. They met in the parlor at Dorothea's boardinghouse.

"I had thought you'd write the review and then we would work together to see about approaching legislators. Now we have jailers and doctors displeased. As I travel the countryside, I meet with resistance if people have read of the uproar in Boston. They think I come to malign them rather than help them do better work."

"I imagine that if we're successful in getting funds for the hospitals, the local jailers and the brothers-in-law they hire to assist will have their profits reduced, so we're not likely to ever have them on our side," Howe said. He looked at his fingernails, not at her.

"I prefer to appeal to their better souls. If we describe what we're doing well, they'll see the humanity in it and want the best for these people they often refer to as 'wild creatures.' "

"You are an optimist." He adjusted his glasses, smiled. "But never fear. The legislature has convened an investigative committee to look into the conditions at East Cambridge. They will affirm what you saw, what we saw. Your words have power, Dolly. While you did not know it, you *have* approached the legislature. You are approaching a singular legislator." He cleared his throat.

She frowned. *What's he talking about?*

"At least I hope to be. I am standing as a Whig for our dear Massachusetts House of Representatives. You will have an inside track at making moral treatment happen if I'm successful." He beamed.

He was running for office! That explained the timing of his exposé. She supposed that was good—should he be elected. He was benevolent. Still, there would be others who were not, and if she was to be successful in this realm of politics and policy, she needed to be a wary observer of the men who cast their votes even if she called them friends.

Marianna's wedding was a blend of vinegar and honey. Marianna made a good match with Edward Trott, the son of a wealthy industrialist. That was the honey. They planned to leave Boston and move south. That was the vinegar.

"I will miss you," Dorothea told her after the ceremony, careful as she hugged the girl not to crush the Belgian lace that lined her throat like alyssum.

"You travel so much, Mummy. Perhaps you'll come see us in Georgia."

"That could be." She still warmed at the word *Mummy*.

"When we have our first child, you must come for the baptism. You will, won't you? Edward and I want you for the godmother."

"I will be there with ribbons on my fingers."

Marianna left her to greet the other guests. Dorothea avoided the whining cousins. They had allowed Marianna to wait and marry for love. Of course that meant they maintained guardianship over her longer and thus control over a portion of Marianna's estate. She wouldn't begrudge them. They had never prevented Marianna from visiting with her, and she prayed that her husband never would either. It was the way of families: one adapted or was left out.

Dorothea didn't always have access to the latest news during her far-reaching travels, but she did learn in December that Dr. Howe had been elected to the House.

"Now," he told her, just days before the December session convened, "bring us facts and statistics to show the need. It must be a memorial, an officially written statement of facts that will go with our petition to the legislature seeking funds for a new hospital. Pull all of it together, and I will present the memorial to the legislature. We'll have our public hospital for those relieved of their reason and treat them with moral treatment. Bring the results of your painful and toilsome tour to light once and for all."

At the boardinghouse, Dr. Howe reviewed her work and made suggestions. She would spend the evening revising her report. At first, he seemed to resist her approach. "We must convince them that the policy of placing insane people in almshouses and jails is wrong and keeps people from a cure. Once they agree to that, it will be easier to move to the solution being a new hospital advocating moral treatment."

"We're not selling cures. They need to see the souls of these people. I'll not pepper the memorial with numbers but with human souls," she said.

"It's too easy for them to argue over whether there are two hundred or ten people held in chains or whether doctors come daily to check or never come at all. Those numbers are distractions. What matters are the lives of people merely surviving in inappropriate places and how their plight speaks to our souls, to your fellow legislators' souls."

"I suppose you're right." He adjusted his vest over his ample stomach. "Though some of these episodes read like your emotional children's stories."

"Stories appeal to all ages," she said. "They will remember the stories much better than if I simply list bare facts."

When she handed him the final memorial at his office, he read it quietly. Dorothea's eyes noted his framed degree on the wall; she heard noise in the hallway of busy aides shuffling here and there. He was interrupted several times by aides who handed him papers. He directed others, then returned to her pages. Lamplight flickered against the cherry wood walls. She didn't know the name of the plant behind him on the credenza, but it was lush and promised blooms.

"You do mention 'hundreds of insane persons seen in every variety and circumstance.' It's good you tell how many months of travel you've made and that your interest began more than two years previous. That's wise." He continued to read, then he looked up at her across the desk.

"You name specific places visited." She nodded, not sure if he thought that wise or not, but she thought it essential so these men in power might learn of a distant relative or at least not be able to put these sad people at arm's length. She wanted them to "touch" them as she had.

"It's a very powerful work," he told her, laying the manuscript down and removing his glasses. "You have captured the plight of the insane. It's a . . . horrifying account, actually. Horrifying."

"I only witnessed it. I don't have to live it."

"But you conclude that for many of those you've seen little improvement can be expected."

"I believe that's true. The majority are well treated, and their caretakers are doing the best they can. It's the minority I worry over, those whose lives are the saddest picture of human suffering and degradation. They are worthy of all of this." She gestured to the memorial that had consumed so much of her recent life.

He looked through several pages again. "You failed to include any note of the origins of insanity or the state's duty to care for them because of the disorder caused by our imperfect social institutions and freedoms of our modern world."

"The causes are irrelevant. Our duty is the same. Moral treatment may not cure insanity caused by sin or misfortune or even the freedoms of democracy, but the patients still have a right to be safe, comfortable, and peaceful. That cannot happen, I believe, in almshouses or jails. They need a hospital. They need a physician's care. That's what this is all about." She heard the passion in her voice and calmed herself. "I would come to the committee and tell them directly, if that would help."

Howe shook his head. "Women are not permitted. Against the feminine nature."

"My feminine nature allows me to witness the horror, to write of it, but not to speak of it to men who can do something about it?" She wasn't disagreeing with him but noted the irony.

"We must keep you as pure as we can. It's what I tell Julia, but she doesn't listen to me and insists on speaking publicly of abolition. I think it lessens her moral authority. I don't want that happening to you."

Should I be comforted by his worry over my reputation or is this yet another way for him to use my work for his own gain? What mattered, she decided, was that he would introduce the memorial to the legislature. He would be her voice and the voice of the mad in securing them a safe and humane place where some might improve. But improvement was not the goal. Being treated as a human being was.

Twenty-Two

Thousands Await

"This is astonishing," Anne told her. Dorothea's *Memorial to the Legislature of Massachusetts* had been introduced on January 19, 1843, with copies printed as a pamphlet for interested readers. A few newspapers decided to serialize portions.

The two friends sat in Anne's parlor at Brookline, newsprint spread before them. It had been months since they had shared an afternoon. During the legislative session Dorothea sat in the gallery, ready and willing to give Dr. Howe more information, should he need it. Thankfully, he had been named chairman of the memorial committee.

"Your examples of the poor suffering people," Anne continued. "I know you wrote of some of them, but to read of them here in the way you've presented them, it's quite . . . moving."

"Not for everyone, judging from the letters to the editor. There's more controversy when there should be none. Relieving suffering is part of the human condition. I so hope it moves the legislature to act."

"The story where you were asked by the insane

man if you had lost dear friends too. Do you suppose it was your dark dress that made him think you were in mourning?"

"It might well have been. And I didn't think him insane. Just lost of his reason. Temporarily."

"But did the conversation really go as you wrote?"

Even her friend questioned her veracity? "I answered him as I would anyone who would ask. 'I've not lost all my friends,' I told him. And then he said, 'Have you any dear mother or father to love you?' " Her voice caught at the memory. "Oh, Anne, his gentle question brought tears to my eyes." Dorothea brought clasped hands to her throat. "Imagine, his being lucid enough to comfort. That he laughed and paced his stall and shouted with his fists to an unseen monster right afterward did not take away from his moment of aware compassion. That he would strike to the core of my orphan state, with no mother or father to love me, to never have had them to love me, speaks to his humanity." She patted her fingers at her heart.

"One wonders if those people have a special telescope to peer into the soul of others," Anne said. "Less distracted by the demands of daily living, they perhaps can be more observant of the emotions of others."

"And might that not suggest that those whose art is recognizing human suffering might be that close"—Dorothea put her thumb and finger to within a smidgeon of each other—"that close to madness themselves?"

"Oh, posh, not you. Though I do worry over your exertions." Anne stuck her knitting needles into the ball of yarn and pulled on the servant cord to ask for tea. It was that time. Her sisters would be back from their walk soon.

"I find it interesting that your account of the baby in the arms of the vacant mother was quite different from Howe's use of it in his article last fall," Anne said. She cleared the table of books for the tea tray.

"Which did you prefer?"

"Yours," she said after a pause. She leaned toward Dorothea and lowered her voice. "I also thought he might have inflamed the baser senses by describing the half-naked man in the cell next to the young woman. The image of him pounding on the thin wall, hoping to reach 'the comely girl' to do heaven knows what damage. Well, it was quite vivid." She pursed her lips. *Mock prurient disgust?* Dorothea sat back. What could be titillating about the slippage of humanity?

"Perhaps that sort of sexual image appeals to readers of the *Advertiser.*"

"Such words, Dorothea." Anne fanned herself.

"I wanted to evoke compassion from the legislators, not fear or voyeuristic emotions. I hope that as brothers, fathers, and husbands, they

247

will see the importance of sensitivity to their less fortunate sisters, mothers, and wives. Even brothers. That man could have been a father."

"Well, the excerpts in the papers have certainly aroused comment." She set aside her fan for the tea. "How does your shawl for Marianna progress?"

Dorothea looked at her hands. "The yarn dye blackens my fingers, so I've put it off for a time in case I need to remove my gloves to make notes in the legislative gallery."

"The dye wasn't set properly if it stains," Anne said. "There is another letter to the editor today. Did you see it? From the Danforth jail officials. They're quite upset and said you wrote out of your imagination."

"I've become accustomed to such furor." Still, her stomach ached with the criticism.

"They called the memorial a series of barefaced falsehoods, false impressions, and false statements. Does it . . . bother you, that people question your integrity?"

The words hurt as much as the reviews of her book *The Garland of Flora* had. "I wish you had not told me," Dorothea said.

"I thought you would want to know the truth."

"There's little I can do about the negativity, and I'm not new to it." She sipped her tea. "Truthfully, it's an added pain to hear those words from your mouth, dear friend, even though you are just repeating them."

"Oh, I never meant to hurt you! I truly thought you would want to know."

"I know." She smiled, trying to lighten the mood she had changed by expressing her feelings. She had no one with whom she could feel safe. No one who would understand that the repetition of an untruthful statement from the lips of a friend pained her more than if she had read it herself. Psalm 57 came to mind. " 'They have prepared a net for my steps; my soul is bowed down.' Only I will not bow down. I must respond to the Danforth claims, of course. I cannot let such accusations stand now that I know of them."

"But it makes you so . . . public if you start a word war. You risk becoming like Julia Ward."

"I'm not preaching in front of crowds about abolishing slavery."

"You are becoming known, though, in a public forum."

"For the suffering," Dorothea said. "I make myself a public person for them."

She did not tell Anne that she had publicly solicited letters of support for a new asylum from hospital superintendents around the region. Nor did she tell Anne that she had replied quite firmly to an editorial that had been supportive, but the editor suggested one minor inaccuracy. They had a flurry of letters between them, thankfully not published in the paper. Facts were facts that must be defended, however minute the issues might appear to someone less informed.

She kept to herself the more positive letters she received. Anne would think her prideful, and it might feed an envy she had so casually witnessed. L. M. Sargent, a prominent speaker of temperance reminded her, "Woman was last at the cross and first at the tomb, and she is never more in her appropriate situation, than when placed precisely as you are at this moment." She reread that letter several times.

Dr. Howe supported Dorothea more privately than publicly. When he did respond to editorials or letters, he never once said that he too had visited many of the same facilities and saw the same things Dorothea described. Once he suggested that perhaps on another day things might have been much better, that the vagaries of treatment in the jails could not be pinned down quite so much as one might like.

Dorothea read his letter and felt her face burn. He was succumbing to the complainers, mitigating the horrors that were real and every day for those who suffered without treatment in cold, smelly jails. It was something of the political world she could not grasp, this weathervane mentality as she thought it, never being certain who one's allies really were or if they would stay the course or turn as the winds blew differently. If not Howe, then who could she count on to bring the memorial to its perfect solution? She could not do it herself. Her skirts could not cross the threshold of the assembly.

The memorial included a request for one hundred thousand dollars to build a moral treatment hospital. Yes, it was a quarter of the entire commonwealth budget. But she assured Howe that she could acquire donations for most of it, leaving the state to come up with perhaps only twenty-five thousand more dollars and the ongoing maintenance costs. But as a woman, she was not allowed to testify before the committee to these factors.

"I'm trying to keep the discussion of the committee from focusing on the accuracy of your descriptions and move them toward debate about a new hospital," Howe told Dorothea. He had taken supper with her. They sat in the parlor now, drinking coffee and eating carrot cake. The fuchsia plant near the window offered a spot of pink color to their surroundings.

"I do understand; I do," Dorothea said. "But in listening to the debate yesterday, it seemed that the minds of the representatives speak to expanding Worcester's hospital rather than building a separate one. You invited testimony from the superintendent, and it seems to me you made less use of my arguments—which I could not make myself. Where will moral treatment end up with a mere expansion?"

"The superintendent supported the base of your memorial. We must take what wins we can, Dorothea," Howe said. "It is the nature of politics."

"I'm not certain I much like politics," she said.

"It requires a certain masculine skill."

She accepted the rebuke. "You do know I wrote to Representative Allen?"

"Yes. Comparing his passion for eliminating slavery in the state to our commonwealth holding the insane in dungeons did not sit well with him. They are two different but very important issues."

"I appealed to his reason, or so I thought," she said. "How can he fight for the freedom of slaves and not fight for the freedom of the insane?"

"He does not see the connection. He is not a supporter. And when the vote comes up later this week, which I hope it will, I believe it will not be for a new hospital as we had hoped but for an addition to Worcester, if that."

It would be a defeat. Her work—her arrival on the public stage at risk to her private, proper feminine role, where women stayed out of the limelight, knew their place—would all be for naught.

"What could I have done differently?"

Howe shook his head. "I don't know."

In the next weeks, Dorothea immersed herself in political schemes and the vagaries of political speech. She discovered that she must provide material daily to the committee members while in session, competing with other interests for their attention. She might meet them in the morning and get a warm reception, but by nightfall someone else had slipped in and placed another bill in a higher position, and she would have to begin again. Nothing ever appeared certain.

Except the suffering of those relieved of their reason.

When the vote came, Dorothea was in the gallery. It went as Howe had predicted. She had raised the issue, kept it on the minds of many, but in the end, only one hundred fifty more beds added to the existing two hundred fifty at the Worcester State Lunatic Hospital would become available. Only one hundred fifty of those hundreds caged and forgotten in the almshouses and jails from Cape Cod to the mountains would have access to a better existence. And none served by the moral treatment approach.

She had reduced the suffering of a few. Thousands more waited.

Twenty-Three

To Ask for More

With Reverend Channing gone and the campaign for the hospital on to new phases that did not need her, Dorothea pondered her future. She wrote to Marianna and to Anne, being honest but cheerful. She kept in touch with the Channing children and Sarah Gibbs, their aunt, writing that perhaps her memorial was not such a failure. After all, she had gotten more beds set aside for the mentally ill, and in the process she had established relationships with several asylum directors in the region, a few of whom had already formed an association. "This could be a powerful group to get behind my objectives to separate the insane from jails and almshouses and move them into moral treatment facilities," she wrote to Sarah. "Though I'm unsure of their acceptance of a woman's contribution to the cause."

She would approach her next steps as a military campaign and look beyond the immediate battle to the larger war to combat human suffering.

"I'm going to travel," she told Dr. Howe when they met at the end of the session. "Expand beyond Massachusetts and focus on those who cannot be treated, the hopeless cases who nevertheless deserve lives of dignity, free of pain and degradation."

"A noble effort. Keep me informed, would you? We might be able to pick up where we left off if we have new legislation to consider."

"What would we ask for? They chose expansion over a new facility."

"Think big," he said.

She would think hugely but never forget the individual lives she might make better through her specific interventions. How long she could juggle both she did not know.

She spent the next six months visiting small towns in Vermont, New Hampshire, eastern Canada, and Rhode Island, bringing her inquisitive eye to the almshouses and jails. Her pattern was to find a reputable inn and interview the innkeeper about the local leaders and their interests, who the pastors were, and what charitable groups helped keep the town on an even keel. She used that information to identify civic-minded men she could solicit for support and to meet their wives. Women were the streams that fed the ocean of action. She needed these men and women to sustain her work and keep it brewing after she left, or she would be setting fires with-out andirons. She would meet with them and gauge who could be helpful, as Howe had certainly been, but she'd be wary with them too. As political beings, men could also change their minds or temperature of support, and she might not anticipate when they were so moved.

Weekly, she checked her ledger books, careful of her spending. This crusade was at her own expense.

As she unpacked her bags in Providence, Rhode Island, she considered how distant she was from her brothers, but she stopped those thoughts—an activity she found she could control if she kept busy and focused on the needs of others. It kept her from despairing or self-pitying. Her brothers both had families. Joseph had their aunt and uncle. Charles had his shipmates. Even Marianna was happily married. Dorothea's family was now the insane.

She found in some small towns that her reputation preceded her. The controversy over the memorial and her legislative success with the expansion reached many towns and villages.

"Dix," an innkeeper said aloud, looking at her sweeping script that embellished the fine-lined pages of the yellow guest book. "Aye. Heard of you. Work with the imbeciles." She would nod agreement and wait to see what they might say next. "Got a niece. In the Providence jail. Didn't mean to do anything, but now she's there. Needs help I can't give her nor her mother either."

"I'll visit and see what I can do."

The innkeeper himself carried her trunk to her room.

While renowned educator Horace Mann and his new wife traveled in Europe, and Samuel and Julia Howe joined them on their honeymoon, visiting the castles and glories of Italy and France, Dorothea rode the dusty roads of villages nestled in the mountains of New Hampshire or spent her evenings in a quiet guesthouse on the Canadian border, writing of what she had seen. When she finished a tour, she provided copious notes to each state's interested parties with the hope that the asylum movement to provide moral treatment and to address the needs of the incurable would move forward village by village, state by state.

She visited private asylums as well and recognized a stiffness in some of the superintendents. "Most everyone is curable with medical treatment," one told her.

"Bloodletting and castor oil are no treatment, sir."

"Neither is putting raving imbeciles in an asylum of their own. It would prove a madhouse. No, those are best left to caretakers in rooms where they can be contained. Small jails where they can be watched and kept from harming themselves or others."

She would watch those superintendents. She was not surprised when her legislative contacts told her they had been visited already by these men who did not share her views on the value of moral treatment.

Dorothea's back would ache by day's end, after hours spent on dirt floors or standing beside barred cages, sometimes offering small suggestions to the jailers. She sought permission for a musician to come and play slow tunes to calm the inmates. She suggested a relative be allowed to visit and read to an inmate. "Soft voices can often relieve their agitation," she assured skeptical jailers. Then she would read to the inmates, and the shouts and cries of the confused stopped when they heard her melodious voice.

"It must sometimes feel like you're imprisoned too," she ventured once to a jailer in Berlin, New Hampshire.

"I get paid." He was a burly man with a part of his ear missing.

"Yes, but is there pay enough to every day witness the downtrodden, those whose mental faculties are in peril? I say you suffer too. You who care for them and cannot make their lives or yours better."

Sometimes they would scoff at her, but more often the grizzled jailers would scratch their beards, cock their heads, and soften their stares. "How do you know that?" they would ask.

"We suffer, too, who want to make things better but seemingly can't," she said. "I know you work hard. I can see it." She might reach out and touch a gloved hand to their knuckles. Tears welled in the faces of men who let this woman feel that side of them they dare not admit existed, for to do so would be to admit that they were powerless.

"I intend to help the legislature see how difficult your work is and how much we need to place some of your . . . residents in a hospital. That's where they should be, not here, not harassing other inmates or adding to the damage of your long days."

They would nod and show her the most despicable cases that would cause her to gasp with the stench but also propel her onward. So many suffered. She had so little time.

Twenty-Four

Polishing the Soul

"So he's a miser," Dorothea said.

"Indeed. But you might, with your gentle charms, relieve his purse of a few coins," Providence minister Edward Hall commented. Several other prominent Rhode Islanders nodded and murmured their assent as they spoke of Cyrus Butler, renowned miser, or so they said.

Dorothea entertained these guests at the Oakland Inn where she had stayed off and on during March 1844. Mrs. Hall paused behind the settee, listening and saying little, but Dorothea knew her to be both wise and kindhearted like her husband.

"His contribution could put us forward on a facility for the indigent insane, get them away from the almshouse and into decent quarters for care." This observation came from yet another civic leader.

"Why has he not been approached before?"

"Oh, he has; he has," Reverend Hall said. "But none of us has had the least bit success in relieving him of even a penny. For any worthy cause."

"I've always liked a challenge," Dorothea told the men. She rubbed her gloved hands as though at a fire and the men smiled. Her challenge wasn't in getting the money, though, but in finding out what pained the man to make him so unaffected by the needs of his community.

"If he would give you twenty-five thousand dollars, that would go a long way toward a new hospital," the cleric said.

"He's elderly and without issue?" Dorothea asked. Heads nodded. His legacy would weigh on him as it does with all men. What is earthly success when the last moments are spoken between a man and his Creator? "He suffers."

One of the men laughed. "I'd like to suffer with his bank accounts."

Dorothea turned to the man, her blue-gray eyes piercing. "We all suffer. And when we give reason to be generous, we relieve a modicum of that terrible distress. Did our Lord not say it was easier for a camel to pass through the eye of a needle than for a rich man to enter the kingdom of heaven? But we who open that tent gate, that eye of the needle, make a way for the souls of men to move toward a closer association with God. It is our duty to do what we can for such men."

"Well, Edward. It seems it's your duty to relieve a wealthy man of his coins." The men chortled.

Dorothea's face grew warm with the mocking. She must temper her opinions.

"Let's consider this. I've prepared an article for the *Journal*," Dorothea said. "If published, it is my hope it will soften the hearts of potential donors such as Cyrus Butler. I would approach him after he has had the opportunity to read it." She hoped there would be few distractions with letters to the editor since she wrote about an area so far from the capital. Accessing private money might be more productive than convincing legislators to expend public funds. She did not want controversy; she wanted compassion. "It's about an unfortunate man, Abram Simmons, whom I met in Little Compton—"

"You went that far in your research?" Mrs. Hall interrupted. "Little Compton is so remote. Near the Sakonnet River?"

"Across the bay from Massachusetts," Dorothea confirmed. "To the far corners, yes. A countryman rowed me over the river to the almshouse."

"Was it safe to travel so far south?" Mrs. Hall persisted, a blend of curiosity and admiration in her voice. "The citizens are a . . . quirky lot, are they not?"

Women are capable of so much more than we're allowed. "Quite safe." She handed a copy of the proposed newspaper article to Reverend Hall, but Mrs. Hall came from behind the settee and intercepted it.

"Let me read this to us all," she said. The men affirmed, allowing her to read. " 'It is said that grains of wheat, taken from within the envelope of Egyptian mummies some thousands of years old, have been found to germinate and grow in a number of instances. Even toads and other reptiles have been found alive in situations where it is evident that they must have been encased for many hundreds, if not thousands, of years.' You capture us, Miss Dix, with this interesting opening image of tenacious seeds and frogs. It says nothing about the insane."

Dorothea smiled and urged her to read on.

" 'It may, however, be doubted whether any instance has ever occurred in the history of the race where the vital principle has adhered so tenaciously to the human body under such a load and complication of sufferings and torture as in the case of Abram Simmons, an insane man, who has been confined for several years in a dungeon in the town of Little Compton.' " Mrs. Hall looked up. "You will use his name?"

"I must. God named all whom He loves. Abram Simmons will be seen for who he is: an individual who clings to life despite the wretched conditions inside his coffin-size cage with frost on the stone walls and his teeth chattering constantly from cold."

Mrs. Hall finished and into the silence, a bird in a cage in the boardinghouse chirped.

"Our God awaits us to act on His behalf."

"What would you have us to do to help?" Reverend Hall asked.

"The article is scheduled for publication on Saturday, the tenth. Would you set up a private interview for me with your Mr. Butler after that? And come join me, of course, to make the proper introductions. But let him have time to read of Mr. Simmons and let God work within the man's heart."

As the visitors were leaving, Dorothea stood on the stairway leading to her room. She had to educate even the supporters. She overheard Mrs. Hall say, "She is a shining example of womanhood, self-appointed critic that she is. She's strong and quite beautiful. I suspect Butler will be well taken with her."

"Right on all accounts, my dear," Hall told her.

Self-appointed critic? Is that what she was? Dorothea pondered that as she finished her climb to her second-floor room. That was not a bad observation. Critics changed things, and that was what she was about. On this journey to change the lives of the insane, she must never be in doubt.

Cyrus Butler welcomed them to his Providence estate a few days later. Considering his assumed wealth, the home was modestly furnished without the usual silver service prominently displayed on a sideboard. Dorothea saw an open Bible there instead. An industrialist, he had accumulated his wealth "by himself," he was known to say, and he did not want to interfere with the paupers who would one day want the pleasure of saying they had made their own way too.

"To what do I owe this visit of the gentlewoman from Massachusetts?"

Dorothea decided to be direct. Men of means liked that, though they might not expect it from a woman. "We have come to ask for a bit of your money."

Butler laughed. He wore a waistcoat with a high starched white collar. A diamond pin sat at his throat. "As do most who walk through my office doors. Hall here has been trying to get me to donate to his churchy functions for years. Haven't you, Reverend?"

Hall nodded meekly. "She insisted on seeking a

consultation with you. You know how women can be."

"And what charity do you represent, Miss Dix?"

"None. I come on behalf of the insane. A voice for the mad who cannot speak for themselves. The ones who are in a paupers' jail when they belong where they can be properly cared for."

"Ah, that Simmons man in Little Compton. I read of him."

"Yes, for him and thousands like him. And I come for you."

"Me? Ha-ha!"

Although he laughed, Dorothea could tell it was from discomfort not disdain.

"Let us take coffee, Miss Dix." He pulled the servant cord for the maid to come.

They spoke of small things then, of the roads along her travels and the weather. She let him set the pace, smoke his cigar, until he said, "So you've come for the weak and you've come for me, eh?"

"I've come to offer you a way to polish your soul of the tarnish of years and choices."

"And you have knowledge that my soul needs polishing, do you?" That same *ha-ha* followed.

She used her most gentle voice. "Here's what I know of you, Mr. Butler. You treat your employees kindly. You do not hire children. You have not wasted your profits on bobbles but have put them back into your business to improve conditions. There are troughs outside your offices for horses to drink from in the heat. You hired someone to keep the troughs cleaned and filled. You do not like to see suffering. I can tell that."

He eyed her. "Sounds like my soul is in pretty good shape then."

"But you buy and build larger, working to have yet more profit, and you hoard your cash. Cash that could serve the least of these." Reverend Hall had been sitting quietly and now fidgeted in his chair. "I know you know who else you serve when the indigent insane are comforted." She nodded toward the open Bible. "Unless that book is just for decor."

She thought she might have gone too far when he cast a quick glance toward the illustrated Bible on the sideboard. A back mirror reflected the colorful artwork on the page, a depiction of Jesus giving the Sermon on the Mount.

" 'One thing thou lackest: go thy way, sell whatsoever thou hast, and give to the poor, and thou shalt have treasure in heaven: and come, take up the cross, and follow me.' " He quoted a verse in Mark. "Are you suggesting this is what I should do, my good woman?"

"I, sir, do not suggest it. I only offer you a way to relieve your suffering." Then with the quiet voice she knew could still a room, she added, "I know you suffer."

He said nothing as the clock ticked a few

seconds in silence. "Do you now? You know I suffer." No laughter this time.

"I do." Dorothea noticed Hall's eyes grow wide with her boldness. "I see it in the darkness below your eyes. I see it in the tremor of your hands. I feel it in the drapes blocking out the sun that might shine upon your face. I hear it in the quiet ticking of your Thompson clock. There are no other sounds of living happening here. For all your wealth, you are a lonely man, Cyrus Butler. I recognize this as I was lonely too, until I found my true ambition: to be the voice of those who cannot speak for themselves. I invite you to help give them a voice. Let your money talk, and may it speak for the Abram Simmonses of this world." She softened even more. "May it speak to your good heart, Mr. Butler." She reached out to touch his hand and he allowed the comfort. "We are all on the same journey to discover why we're here, to find meaning. I offer a path to that end."

She considered rising and walking to the windows and thrusting open the drapes to let the sunshine in, but something told her to wait. This was not her work now. She recognized this. It was her work now to get out of the way.

"How much would you need?" he said finally. "And for what specific purpose?"

"Eighty thousand would build a hospital." She heard Hall choke on the cookie he had just taken a bite of. "And it could bear your name,"

Dorothea said. "It would serve the indigent insane, those needing care for whatever reason, regardless of whether their insanity arrived at birth or from some disease or some disaster or of their own sin. The hospital would serve without judgment. If you gave fifty thousand dollars now, it would be an enormous start."

Butler gazed past Dorothea, then looked straight at her. "I need time to consider," he said. "Will you come back? In two days?"

"I will." Dorothea stood. "I'm grateful for your careful consideration."

"Well, best you pray for my soul," he said. "Use your polishing rag."

"It will be my pleasure."

Dorothea did hold Cyrus Butler in her morning prayers and in her evening prayers too. Abram Simmons had touched her deeply with his tenacity, and she hoped she had brought his needs before the industrialist in such a way that the misery of both men might be relieved. If Cyrus Butler could relieve the suffering of many, he would relieve his own. She was becoming more and more certain of that.

"I will give you forty thousand dollars, but only then if it can be matched by others who, as you say, are like me in needing a bit of polishing."

"I believe that can be arranged. Wouldn't you say so, Reverend Hall?"

Hall could not speak, but he nodded his head. Dorothea could barely keep herself from reaching out and embracing the man.

"Fine then. We have an arrangement. I will have the bank transfer forty thousand dollars to an account set up to be drawn upon only when the figure reaches eighty thousand dollars. Agreed?"

"Excellent," Dorothea said. "We'll call it the Butler Hospital for the Insane account."

"If you insist."

"I do." She reached out to take his hand in hers. "Abram Simmons thanks you. And so will hundreds like him. You are a good man, Cyrus Butler."

"Well . . . I thank Mr. Simmons for his part in"— he cleared his throat—"getting my soul to its proper sheen." His eyes glistened. "Is there . . . Are there things I can do before the money is matched?"

"Invite your friends to do likewise," Reverend Hall said.

"That and, yes, if you are willing, there is always need for books, for people to be read to in the jails. And your business eyes will be valued for the design and operation of the hospital as we prepare. That is, if you are willing to serve on such a committee."

He nodded. "Please let my secretary know so he can schedule such a visit. I do have books."

Dorothea thanked him. She wanted to swirl

around the room, but she kept her composure. It had not been her doing, after all. She had only been the messenger. She and Reverend Hall left, but not before she noticed that Cyrus Butler turned to pull open the curtains and let sunlight flood the darkened room.

Twenty-Five
Thwarted Ambition

In the fall of 1843, with the leaves just beginning to turn, Dorothea made her way to New York. Another campaign called to her. Despite the fact that she was now forty-one years old, she felt invigorated. She had raised funds for the Butler Hospital, met with countless dignitaries and jailers about conditions, and swept her skirts into dank cells, bringing quiet and peace to those devoid of their reason. She crisscrossed the state, visiting sites of concern, traveling day and night, covering sixty counties in ten weeks with nary a cough or momentary weakness to remind her of when she had once avoided the Bible study meetings with Reverend Channing because of the cold night air. She lamented her avoidance of the senseless parties her cousin had dragged her to when she was younger. She might have made more contacts so she could see future industrialists whom she might all these years later win to her cause. But Dorothea did not linger at the dock of regret, for that boat had long ago sailed. Now, she was in deeper waters. She must find new ways to push her ship forward.

A family member of an insane person in New York called her to do for New York what she had done for Massachusetts and New England. The book royalties that had once gone for her mother's care now came to her again, and she used them to fund her travel and her work, setting aside small portions for the occasional music box she left at an almshouse or a complete set of Reverend Channing's books, which she gave to a jail or an asylum.

In New York the challenge was not in building a new asylum. The state had authorized one at Utica some years before, but it had never been com-pleted. It served only two hundred fifty of the insane while the census of 1840 recorded twenty-three hundred patients needing care. The Utica hospital also took people who had become insane within the past two years, leaving those who had been suffering the longest writhing in almshouses and jails. Dorothea's tour of the many counties confirmed the great need. Institutions choosing to treat the most recently impaired worked to show that they cured people, thus demonstrating that the investment had showed progress. But that left others to linger longer in the abyss of mental desperation. Dorothea mentioned this observation in her New York memorial, expressing concern over the practice.

She submitted her report and wrote as convincingly as she could that it was the incurable insane whom she spoke for most fervently. She added a note of challenge in her report to the legislature: "Insanity is the result of imperfect or vicious social institutions and observances. Revolutions, party strife, unwise and capricious legislation, brought on by the United States government in part, causes mental illness. The lack of order and structure presses people into insanity."

She had written that last late into the night, finishing as she checked her lapel watch. Structure and order, those were the hallmarks of sanity, of good health. Discipline of the mind was what was needed, by first disciplining the body. She kept her own disciplined order by rising early, wearing the same simple black dress, eating sparingly of sugars, contemplating Scripture, mending, sewing new undergarments as needed, and drinking ample amounts of water (or beer, if fresh water wasn't available).

Two things she accepted as interruptions of her daily order: travel exertions such as muddy roads or frightening waterway crossings, and the time it might take her to wind up a music box and set it before a half-dressed woman hunched in a cold cell corner. Such interactions were necessities for the polishing of her own soul. The slightest change in the size of the woman's iris or the slowing of her breathing as the music plinked inside those barren walls or the calming of shrieks might keep Dorothea from her appointed schedule for an hour or more, but she would be rested by the belief that, if only for a moment, one person suffered less. Dorothea would move on only when the woman calmed. Later, Dorothea set aside the knowledge that she saw within the crazed woman's eyes her mother. At other times, she saw herself. Order and structure, a passion and a goal, those would keep her sane.

Dorothea's New York memorial to the legislature was again excerpted in the newspapers. As a result of her experiences, she changed her approach, staying with the facts and using fewer personal stories. The latter, she realized, might appeal too much to sympathy. Dealing with legislators, she found, required a delicate balance between appeals to emotion and appeals by facts. She presented as fact the causes of mental illness, suggesting that government and society were major causes. But even this less emotional appeal drew criticism.

"Only physicians have the understanding and ability to know the cause or to treat the insane," wrote a superintendent at Utica. "Perhaps, dear lady, you should return to your feminine role as teacher or writer of children's stories rather than acting as reformer of things beyond your knowledge."

Dorothea grabbed her quill and with a hard press began a retort she finished but did not seal. She would send the letter not to the editor but to the superintendent personally. If she responded in kind publicly to his rebuke, he might escalate the criticism and make matters worse. She wrote instead that she agreed physicians ought always to be in charge of the treatment of the insane. Her only intention was to give them the most recent information so they might proceed on behalf of those who suffered, especially those long-term patients who were neglected and forgotten in the far-distant almshouses or village jails. She said nothing about the superintendent's suggestion she return to a proper place for a woman.

The superintendent did not respond to her letter, but she learned later that he had expressed his opinions to legislators, diminishing her work. He saw her as a threat. Imagine. Her, a woman, a threat.

The New York legislature voted no funds for a new hospital nor even to finishing the existing one. "The legislature even failed to pass a vote of thanks a good Whig had offered for my effort and expense," Dorothea wrote to Sarah Gibbs.

Despite the cool day, she found a stable and

rode. Astride she could think. Her New York work had resulted in nothing, no changes for the suffering. She took in the woods, bent beneath a hanging branch, sat firm when the horse shied at a rabbit. "But I'm gaining perspective and skill," she told the gelding she rode. "So I suppose all is not lost."

The coal stove worked against the February wind in Albany, attempting to warm Dorothea's room. She prepared a small bag and readied her traveling writing desk—an indulgence she felt necessary. She wasn't certain where she would go next, perhaps to visit Marianna or stay a few days with Anne Heath at Brookline. One of her former students lived in the Oregon Territory, the wife of a missionary there. Shelley Mason had invited her to visit. But she wasn't ready for the long ship ride around the horn that would be necessary to arrive in the Oregon Territory. What would she do on the Willamette River where her former student labored? There were so few people in the wilder-ness that mental illness must be absent.

A knock at the door interrupted her packing and planning. She opened the door and lifted an envelope from a woman's fingers. The seal bore an official emblem, but not of the state. Rather the merchant marines.

"It is with deep regret that we inform you that Charles Wesley Dix has died off the coast of

Africa. He was buried at sea. We extend our deep remorse for your loss." It was dated some months previous.

Dorothea sank onto the chair. She hadn't seen Charles in years. His letters had trouble finding her, as did hers finding him. He was her closest relative, the one to whom she had given her heart as an older sister, the one she had mothered as best she could, defending him against an abusive father and an absent mother. Now he was gone. She had been without his physical presence for years, but with his death she felt anew the sharp knife of separation and the heavy cut of abandonment.

She became aware of the room cooling. She had let the fire go out. If she knew such anguish without a loving family to mourn with, what must it be like for the forgotten insane who were separated from those they loved? She must never find out.

Twenty-Six

To Be Miss-Dixed

"Pennsylvania is interested in having me," Dorothea told Sarah Gibbs. Her old friend had come to Philadelphia to visit friends and invited Dorothea to join her. Dorothea had not reached out to anyone since the news of Charles's death. She had grieved alone.

She had written to Joseph, who still lived at Orange Court with the Harrises, but only to inform him. She did not suggest an invitation where they might hold a memorial for their brother. Neither did Joseph suggest one. Joseph did report that he was doing well with his export business and that he hoped she would continue to permit him loans with no interest as "you'll now have Charles's share free and clear." Joseph did not ask for money then, but he alerted her to that possibility soon, as he hoped to marry in the following year and planned to purchase a home. "Everyone needs a home of their own," he had written. He did not suggest there would be a guest room for her.

The same Philadelphia boardinghouse where Dorothea had stayed before welcomed her back. Dorothea and Sarah strolled the street not far from the house; the sun shining through the scalloped lace edges of Sarah's parasol formed busy patterns on her face. They spoke of Oakland and their trips to Newport and the sea, and then Dorothea told her of Pennsylvania's request.

"Pennsylvania legislators actually want to build an asylum there, and supporters believe I can lend credibility to the need if I commit to a survey for them. They passed a bill in 1840, but the governor vetoed it."

"Will you go?"

"How can I not? I get restless without a task in front of me."

"Mr. Channing called you a spinning top, if I remember," Sarah said. "A spinning top that would fall over if it stopped."

"I think if I stopped I should go mad."

Sarah placed a gloved hand on Dorothea's arm. "You wouldn't."

They walked the cobblestones and stopped at a café with wrought-iron tables painted red, and took tea.

"I will do one thing differently in Pennsylvania, though," Dorothea told her. "This time, the superintendents and physicians will be on my side before I begin. I'll not have them undermining the work because they think I am out to ruin them."

"Learning from experience. This is wisdom," Sarah said.

Pennsylvania in the spring and summer was a balm to Dorothea's grieving soul. She was welcomed in the state and given free rein to visit most everywhere she liked for as long as she liked. She saw individual efforts to make the lives of the insane more humane with coal in the stoves and food served on trays with plates, where one could tell what was being served rather than a hodgepodge of meat and who knew what else mashed into one patty and shoved beneath the cell door. She also visited a few prisons and interviewed wardens about proper ventilation, keeping food supplies safe, and having adequate physician assistance. She made copious notes.

At one point she learned that more than thirty-five Pennsylvania counties did not send their mentally ill indigent to almshouses but rather put them up for auction. Impaired men and women and older children would find themselves slopping hogs on a distant farm or following a mule behind a plow, and then end their day with the mule in the barn and barely a bread crust for supper. Those that were not confined were often too frightened to run away with nowhere to go. She could not visit private homes to see how such "auction items" fared, but she knew. She saw the faces of those suffering mongoloid souls as she passed the farms on her way to the next almshouse. Sometimes those sent to the prisons were better off.

"At least," she urged more than one warden, "separate those who are mad. Don't let them be the bones that the larger, stronger dogs salivate over, chew on, and bury."

To publicize her efforts, she gave speeches at women's events and carefully described her presentations as education lectures and not harangues that some might think beneath a proper lady's role. She thought of Julia Ward

Howe still speaking out for abolition, although less now that she was married. She did not want to be associated with society's radical elements. Her words were even, studied, and she made sure she smiled often to the crowd that they would find her efforts worthy of a natural feminine role. She wrote articles about treatment at the request of the physicians of some private mental hospitals. She was often asked to settle discussions about how a hospital might be organized or what strategies were best suited to the moral treatment model.

"Does it not appeal to you that you have become an arbiter in the halls of men?" Anne asked during one of Dorothea's short visits to Boston.

"No, it does not. It takes me away from seeing with my own eyes the needs of people."

"But by settling disputes, you make way for many to be helped."

She could not describe to Anne how a raging soul seemed to calm her in ways that talking with legislators or wardens did not. Still, she did listen in the halls of the assembly. She needed to know what other bills might divert a Whig or a Democrat from attending to her legislation.

Winter came upon her as she traversed Pennsylvania, surveying sites in all fifty-eight counties. Before she finished, a resident of Salem, New Jersey, wrote and asked that she might undertake a survey for that state. Assemblymen were ready to assist her once her memorial was completed.

She moved back and forth between two states, then sometimes ventured into western Ohio and parts of Indiana. For two weeks she visited in Virginia and then Maryland, always making notes, comparing, spending less time with individuals in need and more time with jailers and superintendents. She slept fitfully, more than once seized by bedbugs in the small inns in which she stayed.

At a crossing with a bridge out, she pondered whether to enter a tiny boat with a smelly bear of a man who would row her across, or hire a wagon. She chose the latter. The wagon had no springs, and every rock in the road of the sixty-nine-mile journey jabbed at her backside, tore aches into her shoulders like arrows. But she listened carefully to the driver, learned of his family and hardships, and admired his care of his horses, despite the weather and distance. Rain pelted them at times, and then they endured spitting snow. She wrapped her cape more tightly around her and held an umbrella over their heads. These were good people who were making do with what they had. When she told the driver of her survey work, he thanked her. "Good of you to care about those you ain't ever met."

"I believe we're required," she told him.

"It's a new law, is it?"

"An old law, of loving others as we would love ourselves."

Once while attempting to visit a village jail, she surprised the warden, who kept the door open but an inch. "I would see your most troublesome prisoners," she said.

"They'll eat you alive! Can't you hear the fighting?" She could hear the screams and shouts, the smack of fist to face.

"Show me."

The warden threw the door open, stomped to another, and swept his hand as though she were a queen stepping onto a velvet carpet. "Be my guest."

She scanned the room of burly men, all of whom smelled rank. They had interrupted an assault on a smaller prisoner who walked on his knees to the bars and clung to them. His narrow eyes seeped tears, his tongue lolled, too big for his mouth. He was a mongoloid. "Thank you! Thank you!"

"Who's in charge here?" she spoke to the prisoners, not the jailer.

"I am." A wide-faced man with long hair and a longer beard, which could have been a nest for a pack rat, sauntered to the cage door where she stood. No one else claimed leadership. He dug at his ear, pulled out a fingertip of wax, and stared at it.

"What influence you wield. No one disputes your leadership, Mr. . . . ."

"Who's askin'?"

"My name is Dorothea Dix. I'm here to improve conditions for you."

He flipped the earwax at her. It dropped and hit her shoe.

"Here now." The warden reached for the man through the bars, but he stepped back.

"It's all right. What I wonder, Mr. . . . What is your name?"

"Jackson," he sneered.

"Mr. Jackson. What I wonder is how a man of your strength and leadership came to end up here."

"Theft."

"That temptation does happen to even the most capable of men. But I would urge you to use your abilities that are obvious, that of leading men, to good purpose while you're here. Do you read?" He nodded that he did, though he looked stunned at her gentle words. "Perhaps you could teach those who don't."

The warden scoffed. "Miss Dix. This is a waste of your precious time."

"If one man is prepared to return to society with better tools, we will have served a purpose beyond ourselves. Don't you agree?"

The warden shook his head, but Dorothea handed the ringleader a book. "You're responsible for what you gain from your time here," she said. "Let it be that you share the goodness you have and not give in to the momentary temptation to do evil. Especially to those not able to defend themselves." She nodded toward the mongoloid shivering beside him.

"I'll bring you other books," she said, handing him the novel *Paul Clifford* that she carried with her that day. "Read it to your . . . followers."

Jackson took the book through the bars, opened it, and read: " 'It was a dark and stormy night . . .' "

"You are in such a stormy night. But you will see light one day. I believe it."

"Yes, miss." He turned to his cellmates and continued to read, stumbling at first, then gaining confidence with practice.

The mongoloid crawled closer, and she stooped to meet his narrow gaze. "I will pray you will be safer now." She held his pudgy hand through the bars. She hated to stand and leave. There was so little she could do.

"You tame the wild beasts," the warden told Dorothea in the foyer. He held no sarcasm.

"I seek their inner angels," she said. "Sometimes I find them."

That evening, after a day of awakening at 5:00 a.m. for tea and a biscuit, a light noonday meal of vegetables and a piece of chicken, and soup for supper, Dorothea collapsed in her room with barely enough energy to brush her hair before retiring. A tightness in her chest and a small cough alarmed her as exhaustion crept along her shoulders and settled like a snake curling around her.

Still fatigued in the morning, thinking her lung disease was returning to overtake her, she wrote to her friend George Emerson, "My strength of will threatens to be insufficient for my stern purposes of self-extinction." She lay the pen down to reread what she had written. *Dare I expose such despair?* Was she trying to extinguish her life through interminable exertion? "Please forgive my self-pitying," she resumed writing. "I have no one else to whom I can relay my inadequacies."

"You are as a daughter to us," Emerson wrote back. "Our home fire will always welcome and warm you. But be wary of your health."

Dorothea read concern in his words, but most of all she savored the word *daughter.* She would have to reassure him that the illness was of a mind fatigue drawn from talking to assemblymen, possible benefactors, lawyers, and trustees, and he was not to worry. There was so much to do, and she had to work *with* others and *through* others. She would fight off this cold.

Twenty men crowded the drawing room at her Philadelphia boardinghouse in December 1844. The Pennsylvania assemblymen sported watch fobs on gold chains dangling over portly vest coats. Dorothea listened to the talk of territories petitioning to become states, of slavery issues, of the apportionment of land in the West.

Then she began. She flattered them for their efforts of taking a census of indigent paupers. "Many states have not," she told them. She complimented them on their obvious interest in creating committees to look after these important policy issues of prisoner care and those relieved of their reason. She cajoled them into identifying all they had done well, and then, when they finished exchanging smiles, she praised them again for how they were relieving suffering. Then she added in her softest yet clearest voice, "Sadly, you still have work to do. I've nearly finished my latest memorial." She added, "I am confident that with this information you will alert your colleagues to the dire circumstances within your districts and what can be done about it. You cannot slip back into looking at information only and praising yourselves for accumulating it. Such information must propel you to action."

"What would you have us do, Miss Dix?"

"I'd begin—"

"It's all hypocrisy," a western Pennsylvania legislator interjected. He had listened to Dorothea with a smirk, and now his words burst like a firecracker over a Fourth of July celebration. "Humbug and poppycock. There aren't that many imbeciles, and even if there were, we've done our duty by housing them. What more can you ask the good citizens of this state to do?"

The room grew silent, and Dorothea suspected that he spoke what a number of others had not had the courage to say.

"I'm familiar with your district," Dorothea said. "Let me tell you of some of the abuses I personally witnessed. The auctions are the hypocrisy, sending paupers with limited mental faculties to become the slaves—I use that word advisedly having seen slaves in the South better treated than these wretched souls. Will you wish to stand before your Maker at the end and explain how you failed to act to rescue the least of these, turned the impaired into slaves?"

"I'm familiar with Scripture. I don't need you to preach at me."

"Of course you are. It's just that we are all so privileged here in this room, so more is required of us." She went on to give another five examples of deplorable conditions within his district. "Sadly, the same could be said of any district. These examples of suffering are meant to appeal to our humanity, not to shame. We wear finely tailored clothes, and some might even suffer from gout caused by too much rich food. But those who are relieved of their reason, the indigent insane especially, are often half-clothed and starving through no fault of their own."

"She has you there," a colleague said. "Your gout, I mean."

The legislator laughed.

She spoke for more than an hour. She told of how a simple book could bring comfort, how giving meaningful work returned dignity to even the basest human being. "God expects more of those to whom He's given much. Let me begin to share with you the conditions of the insane in your prison system." Her throat was sore and her chest tight.

The assemblyman pressed his hands to his ears. "I don't want to hear any more! I am convinced, convinced!" More than one colleague raised his eyebrows. "You can decide for yourselves," he told them. "I will vote for your hospital, Miss Dix. But I want you to come to the legislature. 'Miss-Dix' our Pennsylvania senators." The other assemblymen laughed. "I mean for you to inform them as you have me, though you might choose examples from other districts."

"That I will do," Dorothea told him. "And I must say that as a teacher and grammarian, I find it quite inventive of you to form a verb from my name."

"Verbs are actions, are they not?" he said. "And being Miss-Dixed has brought about an action. I will vote for your legislation. But tomorrow, you must be on the train to Harrisburg. I'll have the Speaker of the Pennsylvania House and the president of the state senate there, and you, dear lady, shall 'Miss-Dix' them on the train and then move on to the halls and the conference rooms."

The next morning, Dorothea rode that train, and with her most diplomatic efforts, she "Miss-Dixed" the Speaker and the senate president until each agreed. "Pennsylvania shall have its indigent hospital for the insane."

New Jersey acted first. The legislature accepted her report in December, substituting it for the usual committee report.

"I am honored," she told the assemblyman with whom she had worked. This would surely shorten the debate. On the day the legislation was introduced, the Salem County poorhouse burned to the ground. Eighty paupers housed there survived, but now they had nowhere to go. Their need was more desperate than ever.

The usual legislative wrangling occurred, but this time Dorothea stayed. She did not travel to Pennsylvania to move that bill forward. She felt something good about New Jersey—namely, the people's commitment to those who had no voice. She met with many assemblymen, served tea to their wives, appealed to their humanity, even their egos, that this might be the first public hospital for the indigent insane devoted solely to moral treatment. It would be something to be proud of, she told them.

During a weekend lull in the session, she hired a carriage to drive her to the countryside, to clear her mind of the facts and figures and fatigue. She passed fields with melting spring snow that looked like white doilies on a cherry table. She had breakfast at a country inn where she chatted with guests from faraway places. When asked her name, she noticed one or two nod and say they had heard of her work and were grateful she had taken up the cause. She would have gone on to the beaches, but she couldn't risk not being at the statehouse on Monday morning. No one ever knew about the New Jersey weather or roads. There might be more questions, and she did not want the bill to fail for lack of answers.

On March 20, 1845, the measure for New Jersey to build and fund a public asylum came up for a vote. Dorothea was in the gallery. All her work, would it be for naught yet again? Her shaking knees trembled the book she used to count the votes as each name was called and she heard an aye or a nay.

"It's passed!" She jumped up. The book hit the floor. Heads turned, and she sat back down. "It's passed," she said again. She couldn't erase the smile from her face. The clerk read the vote then. She was right. A New Jersey state lunatic asylum had been authorized. At last!

In the hall outside the chambers she accepted the congratulations of legislators, chatted about the Trenton site, and basked in the praise for her part in this success. She hoped she wasn't being prideful. That evening at the boardinghouse she wrote in her diary: "This is the first new hospital to be built with public funds for the indigent insane who will receive moral treatment. I am so grateful that God has given me a small part in bringing comfort to my family for that is who my true family is: the mentally ill, and I will do whatever I can to reduce their suffering. God grant me good health that I may continue in His service."

There would be much to do. She had been appointed to the implementation committee for the Trenton hospital. She would help determine the site and structure, maybe even have a say about the pictures on the wall. Most members had not ever seen even a private asylum, as far as she could discover, and knew little of Jarvis's or Kirkbride's work designing structures to enhance moral treatment. But their hearts were in the right place, and together they would help the county programs expand immediately to meet the needs brought on by the almshouse fire while they moved forward with building. Private hospital physicians were on their side this time.

Back at her boardinghouse, she danced around the room to the music of a tinkling music box she had purchased in celebration. She planned to give it to the local county jail in the morning, but this night it would accompany her celebrating heart.

Pennsylvania also passed its hospital bill, the "Miss-Dixed" assemblymen and senators deciding it was necessary for their citizenry. Perhaps the auctions would be discontinued. That would be her hope.

"Father" Emerson wrote to say her accomplishments were extraordinary, given the rumor that Pennsylvania already had a debt of forty million dollars.

Dorothea wrote back with the lament: "I should have suggested a larger facility. I'll need a place there myself if I must work daily with legislators."

She hoped it wasn't a premonition.

Twenty-Seven
To Absorb the Goodness

With no other states seeking her advice, Dorothea became restless. She began a book titled *Remarks on Prisons and Prison Discipline in the United States*, which included her theory that lack of discipline was the primary reason for prisoner incarceration and for the poor behavior of prisoners behind bars. She supported the separation movement, which advocated keeping prisoners isolated from each other so they would meditate on their actions without distraction while they worked alone. Not all agreed with her assessment once the book was published, but she did not remain in Pennsylvania long enough to participate in the war of words among the book's many reviewers. Instead, she headed to Kentucky, where the Eastern Kentucky Lunatic Asylum solicited her help in lobbying for a new hospital.

"Surely you won't go there alone. The state is a backwater," Anne Heath said. The two friends sat at a quilt frame in Anne's room. "Did you enjoy meeting your brother's wife? I'm so sorry you weren't able to attend the nuptials. Perhaps the invitation could not find you with all your travels?"

"I sent a gift along," Dorothea said. She poked her finger with a needle and sucked on it. "And I did meet her. Quite lovely. Joseph is happy I think. He keeps a tight lid on his thoughts. He did ask for a loan, which I granted, though he doesn't seem to realize he's used up his portion and is now into Charles's and mine." She sighed. "But I'll not let money interfere with even a loose family tie. So I'm on to Kentucky. As for taking wagons and coaches to the hinterlands, Kentucky can be no more challenging than the distant regions of Rhode Island. I survived those. I shall sail through the jails and almshouses and provide needed information to the legislature to see if they will act."

What she did not know until she arrived in Lexington was that Kentucky followed out-of-door relief. Many of those in need were housed in private family settings rather than the public jails and poorhouses. Determining the state of the insane in private homes was not an avenue she had walked before.

When a dry-goods owner told her he knew of a mentally ill person living nearby with an aunt or uncle, she knocked on the door but was not invited inside.

When a boardinghouse cook whispered, "There be a mad woman in the shed behind the saloon. I see her when I pass sometimes, staring out the window," Dorothea made her way to the saloon and asked outright. Perhaps it was her height, her self-assurance, or the quietness that followed when she entered some establishment suited for men only. This time the barkeep twisted a rag and nodded. "My sister. We feed her well, and she ain't chained."

"But does she have a way forward to become better?"

"As much as I can give her."

Dorothea saw the compassion in the brother's eyes. He was doing his best, but his best was not sufficient to treat the woman's condition. "And if a hospital in Lexington would serve her, would you let her go? Bring her there for care?"

"I would."

In the mirror behind the bar Dorothea looked at the faces of the men she had silenced with her entrance. "Will he?" she asked them.

"I think he'd take her," one said and other heads nodded in agreement.

"May I meet your sister?"

The barkeep came out from behind the shiny oak bar and took Dorothea to a shed fit for a horse or a mule. A chain held the door shut, but inside, the woman was free to move in the small space. A little dog looked healthy and panted atop the single bed, which was covered with a quilt. A coal stove vented to the outside. A window let in pale light. A thunder bucket sat ready to be emptied, but it appeared this happened daily. Small wooden figures lined a shelf, and knives and other tools covered a table. A fragile woman was dressed in cotton. She was slender as a noodle and rocked from foot to foot at the back of the dimly lit room. *How odd he trusts her with knives and yet keeps her confined.*

"Her name's Madeleine, after our mother, what died when she was borned," the barkeep said.

"You carved these, Madeleine?" The woman nodded.

"She has a gift," her brother said. "Just can't keep herself from running naked in the streets sometimes. Have to go find her, or she would freeze to death. I confine her 'cause I have to."

"These are lovely." Dorothea picked up a carving of a child whose face held the expression of Madeleine's sorrow.

"She will have a better life in the hospital we propose." She thought to ask Madeleine if she wished to move to such a place, but she felt it unfair to give hope when she could not assure it. "Until then," Dorothea said, "make certain she has clean clothes weekly and perhaps some books. Can she read?"

"I can read," Madeleine answered.

"Can you?" Dorothea turned to her. "I'll send some books before I leave."

Madeleine rushed at her, grabbing at the table as she passed it. For a moment, Dorothea thought she sought the knife or would push past her brother and out the door. But instead, Madeleine stepped so close to Dorothea that she could see a piece of green stuck in her teeth when she grinned, her eyes wild. Madeleine handed her the carving of the sorrowful child. "In return for the books. And your visit."

"I am moved by your generosity."

"I am generous. Yes. I am."

Back at her boardinghouse, Dorothea packed some books and sent them to the brother. In a quiet moment, she fingered the delicate carving. The woman was an artist. She might know of an outlet for the woman's carvings, and Madeleine could perhaps support herself if her unpredictable condition could be treated successfully. Maybe carving brought her discipline and order, and so she could endure until the mind tricked her and had her ripping off her clothes and running through the cold. How difficult it must be for her brother to see her as sane as any of his bar patrons and know that at any moment she could be another person, her suffering catapulting her into danger and his life into chaos.

"We are all deprived by these people stored in sheds and basements," she wrote to Anne. "The woman's carvings are exquisite and without a hospital there will be no hope anyone else will ever see them nor that she might one day live the noble life she so deserves."

Dorothea traveled all of Kentucky's forty-four counties and submitted her memorial in January 1846. She did not ask for a hospital to humanely house the incurable insane, but rather she asked for one to *treat* the insane. The incurables might need to be overseen by private benefactors, such as herself, because she failed to see how she could ever convince the legislators to fund a hospital for the most severe cases, including people who were ensconced in attics and sheds. They were out of sight of the legislators and unlikely to ever cast a vote. A hospital would bring hope to the Madeleines who had families who cared for them and who would bring them forward.

"The legislature voted five thousand dollars and set up a committee to find a site," Dorothea wrote George Emerson. "They must do more for the carving woman, but I do not know when. Each state has its own problems, and the suffering of the insane is on the bottom of their lists. I am becoming cynical in my older age that anything will ever change in the ways that are so massively needed throughout this country."

Many states in the South called on Dorothea as her reputation grew. Alabama, Arkansas, Georgia, Louisiana, Mississippi, and South Carolina, as well as Missouri and Illinois, lured her to bring her notebooks and traveling desk to their counties. She also carried with her Madeleine's tiny carving in her bag. Dorothea commissioned music boxes in every state, returning to pick them up and deliver them to patients who drew her to them, their wide eyes or disheveled stares stopping her as she otherwise whisked through the various institutions and took notes. Suffering pressed on her as if she were one of the pansies she laid between the pages of her books, and the memories lingered.

She wrote a brief memorial for Illinois, seeking a hospital and a new penitentiary. The asylum was funded, but the penitentiary was not. She saw vast needs and pushed for memorials in every state she visited. She Miss-Dixed assemblymen over fine dining in her boardinghouse or on the plantations with slaves fanning her impassioned face with palms. In Nashville she successfully submitted a memorial written in four days. Supporters had four thousand copies printed and distributed. The memorial moved quickly through the legislature, and it was adopted in 1847. Tennessee joined Louisiana in the reform work, one more state moving to relieve the suffering of many.

"I cannot believe you talked me into coming here for Christmas," Anne told her when Dorothea met the stage in Nashville. "Transportation is wretched. I am all the more amazed that you travel as much as you do and still remain healthy and sane."

"My sanity is not in question here."

"Mine is to have made this trek." The women laughed. Then Dorothea introduced her to Jane and John Bell, the former Speaker of the House and now a newly elected senator. The Bells had invited the women to stay with them.

"Any friend of our dear Dorothea is a friend of ours," Jane Bell charmed. "Our Sewanee plantation awaits you where the Cumberland River winds by like a lazy snake. Here, let Jeremiah get your bags, dear." She motioned for a slave to place Anne's luggage in the wagon. Anne's eyes grew wide.

As they rode by fields with slaves bent to pick cotton, Anne's mouth tightened. She scowled despite Jane's questions about her travels and life in Boston. When Dorothea knocked on Anne's door later, Anne pulled her in and showed her that the room overlooked an orchard.

"I had no idea you were staying with people who own slaves," she hissed. "How could you, Dorothea?"

"It's their way of life. They're good to them. You'll see how healthy they are."

"It's deplorable. I . . . I didn't realize. I thought you were in a boardinghouse or I never would have come."

The words stung. "They are gracious, gracious people. They were instrumental in passage of the bill for the hospital. Their slaves are fine. Truly."

"Dorothea, you're blind. They're as captive as your insane you worry over so."

"The insane have no one to speak for them. The slaves have the Bells and people like them to make sure their needs are met."

"But they don't meet their needs." Anne shook her head. "Do you think happy, well-tended people risk their lives to come north? They're . . . not free to come and go. All the arguments about whether new states come into the Union as free or slave, have you been deaf to that? It's deplorable. No human being deserves to be left in someone's will to a niece like an old bed. Remember how you hate the auctions in Pennsylvania of the mentally ill?"

"This is different."

"No, it is not. It appalls me that you cannot see it."

"Even Reverend Channing thought their plight

exaggerated by those in the North who knew nothing of their ways in the South." He had said as much in St. Croix, hadn't he?

"He changed in later years." Anne sat at a dressing table, her hands clasped in her lap. "How good that he is not alive to see you here among these . . . people."

Her precious Reverend Channing had become an abolitionist? He would be upset with her? *No.* She hadn't seen one mistreated slave in all the time she had been here or anywhere in the South.

"It's not that I wish the institution of slavery on anyone," Dorothea said. "It's just that those relieved of their reason need me more."

Anne sighed. "I know where your heart is, but I will not be comfortable here."

"Give your body rest after the long journey. The Bells are wonderful people. Their cook creates ambrosia for the gods."

Anne sat as tight as a guitar string. "And is their cook a slave?"

"I imagine . . . I never asked." *Why is this so upsetting to Anne?* "I'll be going back to Boston when the Bells leave for Washington. I could travel with you. Give you hints of my survival skills on muddy roads and small inns." Dorothea smiled, hoping to ease the strain.

"No. I'll arrange to leave in the morning."

"Please, don't let this come between us."

"I'll try not to, Dorothea. But it is beneath your Christian heart not to see the degradation of all involved with this despicable thing. As much as it degrades us all to allow the mentally ill to be mistreated, so are we diminished by tolerating slavery. Both place people in bondage, and we are called upon by our Lord to care for each afflicted person as the 'least of these.' You must come back with me."

Dorothea blinked nervously. "I only have the call to serve those deprived of their reason."

"I understand. But don't close your eyes to the subtle support that staying on a slave-run plantation truly is. We are all called to be awake and to seek justice, wherever we find it. There is no justice for the Negro. You must not forget that. It is an issue that will come to a head one day, and you do not want to be on the side of evil."

PART

Three

Twenty-Eight
Battle Preparations

A hole formed in Dorothea's thin leather soles. She would have to find a cobbler to repair them and then order another pair. The many muddy trails, wet-bottomed boats, cold snows that she stepped into while traveling thousands of miles over the past seven years of surveying had not been kind to her feet. She stoked the small coal stove in her room at a Nashville boardinghouse. The two black merino dresses she rotated were looking thin in places from the many brushings. If she stayed a week or more here, she would have them steamed, but lately she rarely stayed that long anywhere. She checked the black dress for tiny holes she could repair and decided that she would stop at the nearest dry-goods store to purchase wool. She would delay her trip for a few days and sew a new dress. Her crinolines needed refreshing as well, perhaps she needed two new ones so she could avoid the hoops that made movement so expansive. It wouldn't do for her to look threadbare or too frugal. She must look feminine and formidable when she met with the men who made the nation's laws to put forth her most ambitious plan.

This was where she stood: ready to pursue her life's purpose in a powerful way. She was forty-five years old, and her new hope involved living in the belly of the beast: Washington DC. She planned to arrive in the spring of 1848 and to stay at Mrs. Birth's boardinghouse, where the Bells had landed after John was elected to the Senate. They had already written to her of the lovely accommodations. Hope rose as abundant as the lilacs that would be blooming then. She had learned how to move through the maze of politics and would emerge victorious for the Abrams and Madeleines of this great land so flawed by its blindness to those relieved of their reason.

Dorothea supposed she was blind too. Anne was right about slavery. But Dorothea could not enter into that foray. The mentally ill had her passion. She had let Anne leave without her, remaining with the Bells to strategize about her grand idea until they left for Washington DC.

After another week in Nashville, with new clothing and two pairs of shoes without holes in her trunk, she left by train, heading first to New Jersey for the opening of the first asylum she had helped construct. Trenton was beautiful in May, and the grounds leading up to the mansion-like building wore emerald green like royalty. The Delaware River sparkled off to the side. Landscaping suggested tender care, and the rooms inside were bright and airy. Dorothea was ecstatic with the Trenton hospital and humbled by Superintendent Horace Buttolph's personal tour, along with Thomas Story Kirkbride, the architect who had become synonymous with moral treatment.

"Here we are," Buttolph said on the third floor as he opened a door to a sitting room. Dorothea could see a bedroom beyond.

"I don't remember this in the plans." She turned to Kirkbride.

"We thought it a good addition."

She let her fingers linger on the wainscot shelf. A small kaleidoscope could rest there one day. Through the window she saw a horse and rider lope across a field. It reminded her of Marianna's drawing. "Yes. An apartment for the superintendent to stay when needed. It is a good idea. There are always emergencies."

The superintendent shook his head. "I have quarters on site. This apartment is for you, Miss Dix. Should you ever be in need of a place to rest your head. These rooms will always be here for you. You may furnish them as you like, of course. They are yours for the rest of your life."

Dorothea's throat thickened. Tears threatened to dribble down her checks. She reached to wipe them with her gloved fingers.

"Are you all right, Miss Dix?" Kirkbride touched her elbow.

"I am. Yes, I am. It's . . . to see this place, after

all you've done to speak of moral treatment and to create this lovely atmosphere . . . the wings staggered so light comes in. Art on the walls." She spread her arms to take it all in. "And to have created a small apartment that will surely be available for residents or students spending time here."

"It will be known as the Dix Apartment," Buttolph insisted. *A place of her own.*

"I . . . thank you."

They toured the other rooms, and then she offered, "I have a writing desk. It was my grandfather's and is quite an heirloom. It would fit nicely here. If you like, I'll have it shipped."

Dorothea left for Washington and reviewed her notes along the way, wistfully resting her hand on the traveling desk as she recalled the lovely apartment she might one day call home. While she had resisted having hospitals or wings named for her, or even a bust, as Jane Bell had wanted, the idea of "home" appealed. She inhaled deeply and returned to her notes.

She had done her homework. She no longer wished to charm or beg state legislators who were always strapped for funds. Those wishing to reduce the suffering of the mentally ill had to compete with other state needs while assemblymen parsed out meager funds to those making the greatest noise, or worse, offered bits to those who would help them win election, like mother birds feeding their babies to silence their constant chirps.

Now, her target was Washington and a report by the US General Land Office stating that the federal government had title to almost one billion acres in the states and territories. A billion acres! The end of the war with Mexico had brought a half million new acres into the public domain. Plans were underway to open up the Oregon and Minnesota Territories for more settlement, but nearly a billion acres were not yet spoken for and promised incredible development for the still young nation. For Dorothea, the land promised a way to finally fund hospitals across the continent, where asylum supporters would no longer have to seek unreliable state funding every year. She had drafted a plan to provide long-term funding for a national system of public mental hospitals. This was her greatest goal.

She had written the national memorial a bit differently than those she had prepared for the various states. She would ask Congress to set aside five million acres of public land to be divided among the states, which could then sell the land for the sole purpose of funding public mental health hospitals for the indigent where moral treatment would prevail. None of the proceeds could go for housing the insane in almshouses or jails or even private hospitals, and none would fund care in private homes. This democracy, with all its lack of discipline and order, had helped create madness among its people, and it must be required to assist in relieving the suffering of the Madeleines and Abrams of this land.

There was precedent. Congress had already set aside land for schools and for universities in the year she was born—1802—and two states had later received donations for deaf-mute schools. She could build a case for need, show precedent, and then describe the solution: land grants and sales. She just had to work *with* others to make it happen.

She already knew several legislators she called colleagues if not friends. Many she had worked with in her state campaigns were now representatives and senators. John Bell, two representatives from Massachusetts, and Horace Mann, her old mentor, had been elected to the House, the latter succeeding the late John Quincy Adams. She had met Jefferson Davis while traveling in Mississippi —he would not be supportive—and she knew Henry Clay as the founder of the Whig Party, having met him at a horse stable in Lexington, where he practiced law before his many incarnations in government service. There were others. Her task would be to win over the reluctant, such as Davis, and give sound reasons to the supporters not to lose faith in the battle. For it would be a battle, she knew that.

"I think both parties will find value in my proposal," she told John Bell at the boarding-house. Jane knitted on the settee, and John picked at his teeth with a toothpick. His stern eyes belied his compassion for the downtrodden as well as his passion for the federal government's role as a tool to benefit individuals across the nation. He had been in the House of Representatives and had sided with those who wanted public land sales to fund things such as canals and roads. Most of the Democrats, however, wanted the federal government to stay out of the states' affairs, especially with regard to issues of property, which included land and slaves.

"I think not," John said. "We Whigs will favor it, but the Democrats resist any federal moneys being spent inside the states. They want the land sold and the money given to them to do with as they see fit. The western states are already glum, because they have not been able to sell some of their land at the federal minimum of one dollar and twenty-five cents an acre. We may have to propose lowering that price."

"And they will fund what? Not mental hospitals," Dorothea said. She placed her delicate fingers on the white lace collar of her dress. "As for the land prices, anything less than a dollar twenty-five will not bring in enough revenue to sustain the hospitals. Maybe we should ask for more land."

"The Massachusetts delegates might agree with you. They would like the proceeds of western lands to be given to them, by apportion, precisely because the New England states have little public land to sell."

"But the North is not so committed to moral treatment," Jane Bell said. "You have been more successful in the Dixie states."

"New Jersey and Pennsylvania were the first to move forward," Dorothea pointed out.

"That's hardly New England," Jane said. "And what you propose is a new national charity approach. It's a wonderful idea but it's never been proposed before." Dorothea knew this. It was what made her stomach churn in the night when sleep evaded her.

"You'll have to reach out to New England with the land distribution support rather than appeal to their benevolent nature," Senator Bell said. "The proposal really does benefit them more than the western states. And there will be many knocking on the door of free land. Homesteaders. States for new colleges and universities, all to advance the nation, none for the indigent insane or for the poor at all. The Free-Soil Party wants confirmation that slavery will not darken the new territories. And the railroads." He poked at the air with his cigar, smoke curling around his face. "They will be your biggest competition. New Englanders may eventually see a benefit to them in their long struggle to win distribution rights from federal sales." He pulled on the vest stretching over his stomach. "You must win over the Democrats. We Whigs alone cannot carry your bill."

"I have a plan to reach the biggest Democrat: the president," Dorothea told him.

"Have you now?" Jane looked up from her knitting.

"Oh, I know you have little time for President Polk," Dorothea said. "Though he is a Tennessean."

"The worst thing Tennesseans have perpetrated on the country. The man has little time for Whigs," the senator scoffed.

"Yes. But his *wife* has an interest in my work. At least I heard that, so I have boldly asked for an appointment. She has invited me to tea."

Bell grunted. "I have no such luxury of opportunity."

"Oh, Dorothea! What a coup!" To her husband, Jane said, "We women are forced to work through wives and others, as we are excluded from the halls of Congress."

Bell turned to her. "And have *you* been approached by some Democrat seeking my attention?"

"I have not. And if I did, I would tell you. But I do have ears. I do hear things."

"Indeed." He smiled, then turned to Dorothea. "And for whatever you can tell me of Mrs.

Polk's husband's state of mind, I would be most grateful." He stood and made a courtly bow to Dorothea. Under his breath he added, "On more than one occasion, I believe, the president has been relieved of his reason."

"Oh, John!" his wife protested as she and Dorothea exchanged smiles.

Sarah Childress Polk wore maroon, which set off her olive skin and hair as black as piano keys.

"Welcome, Miss Dix. I have heard such wonderful things about you and your work in our South. I'm so pleased you asked for an audience."

"And you are so gracious to have invited me to a tea instead." Dorothea noted they were the same height and, from what she knew, nearly the same age. A nephew had been taken in as a ward because the president and first lady had no children of their own, another thing they shared.

"It's lovely to spend an afternoon with a well-informed and intelligent woman," the first lady said. She motioned Dorothea to sit, and a dark-skinned man brought in a tray of cool drinks and small sandwiches. "Sweet tea is my favorite but I must serve it without liquor to set an example here in the North, my husband tells me."

"I'm sure I'll enjoy it." She nodded to the server. *Was the waiter a slave? in the Executive Mansion?*

They spoke of the president's ward, Dorothea's

travels, the first lady's fine education in North Carolina.

"So few women were allowed schooling," Dorothea noted. "It's getting better."

"Yes, I was most fortunate. Some men are threatened by an educated woman, but the president is not." She appeared stern, yet her voice was warm with a southern lilt and welcoming.

"We are most fortunate to have him in the seat of power."

"He agreed to serve only one term, you know. I suspect it helped him defeat Clay in the end, but he will have to be productive to annex Texas as he wishes and deal with the British over the Oregon argument. He has some ideas for fiscal changes as well."

"I didn't realize . . . I am hopeful he might take my little project under his wing."

"You have a national interest for the mentally ill? I was not aware. I thought it was in the states you worked."

"I propose that some federal government land might be sold and the proceeds would go toward publicly funding hospitals for the mentally ill."

"Oh my, that is a grand scheme. Everyone seems to want land, don't they?" She smiled then, and Dorothea saw she had large teeth, which might account for her stern look when she did not smile.

"Perhaps it is a scheme, but for a worthy cause. You are a Presbyterian, I believe." The first lady nodded. "So you know of justice and mercy. It's really all I seek. I feel we are all responsible for those impaired of their reason, but regardless, they deserve a decent life. Our Lord asks this of us."

"Indeed He does ask us much. But how justice is derived is one of those issues that could put another crack in the Liberty Bell." *Does she speak of slavery?* "After all, we are not all responsible for the mentally ill. They bring it on themselves."

"Do you think so? I would disagree, respectfully. Yes, some overindulge in ale. But many more are born with disparities. And others we make for them, our freewheeling democracy leaves people uncertain and increases anxieties. Dictatorships do not speak of the mentally ill. Things are certain in their world. In ours"—she raised her hands as though saying "this or that"— "I have met many a legislator in need of treatment from our freewheeling ways."

The first lady laughed but turned it into a cough when she realized Dorothea was serious. "It would make an interesting dinner conversation with physicians and jailers and superintendents of such institutions," she said. "And a few of those legislators."

"It would."

"If the occasion arises, I will speak with my husband. He is always interested in an intelligent woman's point of view. Now, tell me, how do you find your accommodations at Mrs. Bride's? I hear the boardinghouses can be quite charming in the city, almost like one's home. And where is your home, Miss Dix? I have heard of your travels but never much about where your people came from. I'm sure it's an interesting family story."

Twenty-Nine
Praying a Grant of Land

For the first time in years, Dorothea was weakened by flu. In June 1848 she desperately wanted her *Memorial Praying a Grant of Land* to be presented to the Congress. She wrote from her bed, coughing and achy, while Mrs. Bride's little pug rested at the foot of her bed. She shortened the document to thirty-two pages. She wanted it in a New York Democrat's hands. His name was John A. Dix, but he was no relation. She thought her strategy ingenious: pick someone from the party most likely to object as the bill's sponsor. She had courted the Democrat early in May for that reason.

"Are we related, Miss Dix?" the senator asked when she sought a meeting with him in his walnut-paneled congressional office. Lamps with multicolored shades cast a rainbow of light in the interior office lacking windows. He had gentle brown eyes, and they studied her face in the surrounding light.

Dorothea lowered her eyes. "It would please me to be your relative, but I am not." She almost flirted, flashing her eyes at him and offering a generous smile.

"More's the pity. What can I do for such a reforming woman?"

She described her proposed memorial and how she thought the government might fund public mental hospitals across the nation, sprinkling her speech with vivid images of the lost and forgotten, the epileptics and the insane. They spoke for the fifteen minutes he had allotted her. He was silent when his aide began to usher Dorothea out. Then he asked, "Might I join you at your quarters for further discussion?"

"I'm staying at Mrs. Bride's. Please invite your lovely wife."

At the boardinghouse, they spoke well into the evening. She knew he had seen suffering in the war of 1812. Dorothea had taken tea with his wife, Catherine, and knew they were Episcopalians, which led Dorothea to believe that he was both a born leader and a man grounded in faith. He would be a perfect sponsor for her bill.

"There is someone in my life," Dix said, his voice softened by the piercing memory. "An aunt. She lived with us for a time, until my mother could not provide for her. There were visits to

318

private hospitals, the constant vigilance of making sure she was well tended. It drained my mother terribly. I was the oldest child. It was difficult enough with resources. I cannot imagine what it must be like for the indigent, the untreatable insane."

"You have suffered," Dorothea said. "That's exactly why I want you to introduce my memorial."

"I've had my annoyances with President Polk," he said. "As you know, we walked out of the Democratic convention when they failed to endorse the Mexican Territory as slave free. Someone else might be a better sponsor."

"I believe your wisdom and your heart will bring attention. I am meeting with Whigs, but I know fewer Democrats, and you are the majority party now."

"We will have work to do," he told her. They explored whom she ought to meet with, who might be malleable or who could be "Miss-Dixed." She had told the couple of the comment from the Pennsylvania assemblyman and her success with the Speaker and the senate president. "I charmed them into changing their minds."

"Miss-Dixed." He smiled. "Some might think we are related."

"We could let them believe we are brother and sister."

"I, the older brother, and you, the adorable younger sister."

She smiled and let her eyes twinkle. "I shall address my letters to you in that familiar way, if you consent."

"Likewise." He stood, pulled at the sleeves of his waistcoat that were a bit short for his long arms. "We'll spice the political soup with it then," he said. "What better endorsement than a Dix support the famous Miss Dix. Let them think it is a family affair." He bowed to her.

In June her room smelled of illness as she finished the memorial through a blizzard of handkerchiefs and honey-laced elixirs brought to her by Jane Bell.

" 'I have visited epileptics, imbeciles, the insane in all but three states and have traveled sixty thousand miles,' " she read to Jane from the memorial and suggested that more than ninety percent of those relieved of their reason lacked critical care. She thought deeply about whether to comment on the causes of mental illness in the document, even though most people agreed the very nature of democracy and America's style of political freedom played a part in causing mental strain.

"Now this next sentence I believe sincerely, but I wonder if I ought to include it. 'A high incidence of insanity among politicians is caused by the many varied and intense "excitements" in the political sphere. Even a presidential election will adversely affect the mental state of the people.' "

Jane laughed.

"It is fact," Dorothea defended as she hacked through another attack.

"Oh, Dorothea, I know." Jane straightened Dorothea's pillow, adjusted her writing desk, and freshened her water. "You have no sense of humor, my friend. We shall hope most legislators do."

"I speak of those legislators already in mental hospitals, mostly private ones. People I've met."

"I know. But they may be looking across the aisle at one of their colleagues and wondering about his mental health." Jane laughed.

"But it is not meant to be funny. It is all true. The government does have an obligation, and the excitements of political life can cause mental derangement. It is one reason why women ought not be public. We have to guard against such excitements."

Jane stared at her. "You are a public figure, Dolly. And you are not mentally impaired."

"I am not public. I am careful about protecting my femininity. I am—"

"Oh, you are no raving Julia Ward Howe, and I have not heard you rail against rum, but surely you see you have influence and power as a woman participating in public discourse. Your presence when they introduce the bill will cause applause and notice. You must know that."

Dorothea coughed. She made a few more changes, then in a breathless voice she finished reading from *Memorial Praying for a Land Grant.* " 'It is the duty of the government to exercise its civil obligation on behalf of the mentally ill as well as to demonstrate federal compassion. I ask for the people that which is already the property of the people.' " She dropped the papers on her lap. "True greatness of a nation is not found in war, Jane. It is found in Godlike attributes which sanctify public life." She lay back on her pillows. "What do you think?"

"Add that last part, about war and Godlike attributes. Then I think it's ready for your *brother,* Senator Dix, to make the introduction. Now just get well so you can be there to hear it."

Senator John Dix read movingly from the memorial, though he did not read aloud all thirty-two pages. Dorothea was nowhere in the chamber. She still suffered from a flu-like illness. But by the end of that day, knowing the deed had been done, her fever broke and her cough silenced.

Jane Bell told her later that Senator Dix had given notice to her by name and there had been applause. "So sad you were not there to hear it."

"I must remain out of the fray lest I become the object of discussion as a woman reformer rather than keeping the focus on those who need the reform."

Her health much improved, Dorothea could now track her *Praying for a Grant of Land*. She had suggested that the memorial go to a select committee set up by Senator Dix rather than the committee on public lands, with the hope her memorial could be voted upon before the close of the session in August.

Dorothea followed the progress through the *Congressional Globe*, a published record of the ongoing debates in Congress. She noticed on the same day Dix presented her bill that a railroad sought land to lay tracks from Lake Michigan to the West. So the first volley had been fired: her land needs for the mentally ill would compete with transportation, and the argument of economic and national advancement over the needs of the least of these.

Notes back and forth about the committee acceptance or debate from John Dix enhanced the *Globe*'s notations.

"We are at the point of contention," Dix told her a few weeks before the August recess.

The Bells took after-dinner coffee at the boardinghouse, and with John and Catherine Dix and Dorothea, they sat on the wide porch overlooking a lotus pond in bloom with pink and white water lilies. Festive fans met the sultry July air, keeping the mosquitoes at bay.

"The western and southern states object because my proposal will help the northern states more than theirs," Dorothea said.

"You have it, clear as Mrs. Bride's broth," Dix said.

"It's ridiculous, dear brother. The Senate is supposed to be the chamber of consensus, coming to agreement on behalf of the people. Can you not influence your New York colleagues?"

"The railroaders are in the Senate offices daily," John Bell said.

"Then so shall I. And I will spend a little more time with the select committee. Might that help?"

Senator Bell shrugged. "Hard to know. They are generally supportive. Jefferson Davis and Thomas Hart Benton have come along. The two of us, you know, are supportive."

"It is just so frustrating!"

"The very middle name of politics," Jane Bell said.

Over the next week, with time running out, wrangling persisted over the territories issues. Dorothea's bill sat like the spectator she was, while men argued about the role of the federal government within the territories. John C. Calhoun used his reason and eloquence as twin daggers attacking the very features that Dorothea needed for her bill to succeed. She would have to wait. That's what legislation was about.

Meanwhile, she rose early, wrote letters while she ate a light biscuit, and garnered support from private and public asylum hospital physicians and superintendents. She urged them to write to their congressmen and senators. She sat outside committee rooms in order to confer with aides during breaks, bringing facts and figures and stories to support their discussion—when it was of her bill. She lamented to Anne her frustrations, sent pressed flowers in her letters to Marianna, and increased her correspondence with Joseph, deciding that even if he did not write often, she would.

Optimism buoyed her one day, despair threatened on another. She felt powerful when asked for advice by legislators and committee members, but powerless when they failed to incorporate her ideas. *Why ask?* The session wore on with only the passionate debates about the territories and slavery filling the galleries. In between were tedious hours of sitting, waiting, hoping to catch a senator or congressman she might win to her side. The summer heat stifled her like a tight corset. A fan was her constant companion.

"My dear sister," John Dix wrote in early August. "I have failed you. We are about to adjourn, and I have been unable to secure your land."

Dorothea read his words, his sense of failure

seeping through them like blood through linen, dark and foreboding and suggesting permanence. *It cannot be.*

"You did your best," Dorothea wrote in reply. She must encourage him. There would be another session. "I have learned there are always obstacles, and it is a mark of one's character how such challenges are met, how we allow them to shape us. You can reintroduce it again in the winter session."

She did not hear back from him by letter, but two evenings later Senator Dix and Catherine appeared at Mrs. Bride's. "I came to tell you myself."

"What more bad news can there be?" Dorothea spoke cheerily. "We will find the good news inside the bad." She said he could reintroduce the bill in the winter term. It would be fine.

The sadness in his eyes caused her heart to pound. He inhaled deeply. "I am resigning from the Senate." Dorothea gasped. "I've broken with the Democrats. In November I'll be the Barnburner–Free-Soil candidate for governor of New York State."

"Oh." She sank onto the settee.

"There is some hope," Catherine said as she petted Mrs. Bride's pug. "Polk won't run again, and the party is split between Democrats and Free-Soilers."

"The Whigs may win, so you could then have

your friend Horace Mann introduce the bill in the next term," Dix added.

"Yes. Senator Mann. From Massachusetts. That'll agitate the western states." Dorothea had so wanted a Democrat—the opposition party—to sponsor and guide the bill through Congress.

Dix sat across from her, leaned forward, clasping his hands between his knees. "I cannot not do this," he said. "It's as though my voice in the wilderness cries to me to take this risk. New York cries out for a leader. I know you know what that is like, dear sister."

She did.

"Well, it is what it is. I wish you well in your new ambition." She looked up at him and forced a smile. "But you will still be in the political world and run the risk of insanity yourself."

Without the likelihood of passage of her *Praying for a Grant of Land*, Dorothea felt herself removed from politicking. She knew she would have to gird herself for the next battle, that she had not yet lost the war. Planning ahead, she arranged to have her rooms kept for the winter session, and she declined an invitation to spend the fall in Boston with Anne. Before he left, she spoke with Senator Mann, as Dix had suggested.

"We'll get something introduced," he told her. "But you must know that slavery is the issue of this time. Until it is eliminated in the new lands and forever, we face the wrath of God for our lack of justice seeking."

"God's wrath is not limited to slavery," Dorothea said on the veranda of Mrs. Bride's. "He has His eyes on all sparrows, especially those relieved of their reason."

"I am certain you are right," he said.

"All that has happened," Dorothea wrote to Anne in September, "is that Oregon has been named a free territory thanks to the Free-Soil Party. Congress rejected the railroad request; did not even consider my prayer for the grant of land. Then everyone went home."

At least they had homes to go to.

Thirty

A Change of Fortune

Dorothea donned her traveling clothes and headed to North Carolina, one of three states she had yet to survey. She also inspected almshouses along the way.

The South gave her solace. She loved the scents of magnolia and jasmine, the thick spanish moss hanging from the branches of so many trees. The beauty and orderliness of the sweeping planta-tions appealed to her sense of propriety, but now she felt guilty with Anne's words about slavery still ringing in her ears.

She spent the winter at Raleigh and drafted a memorial for the legislature. Her Whig friends told her the bill would be defeated because the state was poor and lacked resources. Undaunted and encouraged by prominent North Carolinians and people of faith with personal concerns about the insane, she implemented the same strategy she used in Washington: she selected a member of the opposition party, "Miss-Dixed" him with her passion and her charm, and convinced her Whig friends and their colleagues to support him when he introduced the bill in the state senate.

The bill passed, and she allowed herself a celebratory moment with a glass of tea at the Raleigh boardinghouse in which she was staying. There, she toasted herself. *How can I get these bills through the states and fail so dismally at the national level?*

Brother John Dix lost his bid for governorship of New York, and James K. Polk would still be the nation's president until March. On a positive side, Zachary Taylor, a Whig, had won the election that fall, and his vice president, Millard Fillmore, was a New Yorker. Brother Dix knew him and offered to make an introduction for Dorothea. Meanwhile, her *Memorial Praying a Land Grant* was still in place from the previous congressional session, having languished with the committee during the lame duck session. Yet bigger issues demanded the national attention: settling the issue of slavery in the territories, especially as people flocked to California at the news of a gold rush.

As for Dorothea, she was less concerned about the issue of slavery in California and more concerned with what was said about the future of the country in which people abandoned their homes and families and livelihoods to seek nuggets across the continent. This was just another example of how undisciplined the world was and how these future prospectors were gold crazy— or soon would be to leave everything they knew for the minuscule possibility of some measure of wealth. Couldn't the country's leaders see what lay ahead? The country would need asylums more than ever, because the nation seemed to be coming apart at the seams. She would discuss that with the vice president when she met him.

"I hope you don't mind, dear lady, but my wife, Abigail, and our daughter, Abby, have heard of your work and said they would be honored to meet you. Our son is away at boarding school."

"I'm the honored one." Dorothea had been ushered into the living room of the vice president–elect's residence at the Willard Hotel.

"Likewise." Abigail had flaming red hair and

sparkling green eyes, and Dorothea could see devotion in the looks exchanged between the politician and his wife. She had heard they had met while he attended a small academy. There Abigail was a teacher whom he swept away and married many years later.

"You're a teacher," Dorothea said.

"Indeed. I even worked after Millard was elected to office in New York. Quite the scandal, you know, to be a working wife." She smiled and her sausage curls danced in delight. "Teaching is my first love. Well, perhaps second. Books are what I adore most. Books and music and my family. May we sit?" She directed Dorothea to a settee. The Fillmores stayed here when Congress was in session. "My ankle is a bother," Abigail continued. "It gives me fits when I have to stand in receiving lines, so I hope you will forgive me for needing to rest." Millard lifted her leg onto a brocaded stool and revealed a soft slipper instead of a shoe.

"I'm of an age," Dorothea said, "where sitting is quite lovely." She turned to Abby, a pretty young woman of about seventeen. "Will you be following in your mother's footsteps?"

"As a teacher? No. But I love music as she does. And books."

"We shall have her play the guitar or harp for you one day," the vice president–elect said.

"I would very much like that."

Dorothea took pleasure in this quiet interaction

with the Fillmore family. A fire burned in the brazier as a cold wind whipped the trees outside the hotel. The family appeared to genuinely care for each other, to give as well as receive. There was a sense of home here. To simply sit and be still was a luxury she had seldom allowed herself. What cost might there be if her top stopped spinning? Yet she must take advantage of this moment. How could she not?

"Was there something you wished to discuss with me of a congressional nature?"

"I don't wish to compromise your wife and daughter's feminine sensibilities by speaking of public matters—"

"Nonsense. Tell us what you are up to now, Miss Dix." Abigail rubbed her hands as though before a campfire.

"Mother loves a good story," Abby chimed in.

"There's a bill titled *Praying for a Grant of Land*. It is being introduced on behalf of those who have been relieved of their reason, the epileptics, the mad, forgotten people. I have come to the conclusion that asking each financially strapped state to provide funds to establish public mental health hospitals—to remove from the terrible almshouses and appalling jails people who need instead moral treatment, not incarceration or worse—is futile and not in the best interest of all the people." She paused. "My bill requests federal land be sold and the proceeds going into each state's coffers for the purpose of funding such humane hospitals."

"A national charity." Abigail quickly discerned the intent.

Dorothea nodded. "Senator Dix introduced it, and the select committee approved it, but it has gone nowhere."

"You know there are many pressing issues before the Congress. Will California enter the Union as a slave state? Will the other territories be free or not? Will fugitive slaves from the South be required by law to be returned as property to their owners?" Fillmore ticked off the items from an imaginary list. "Will the federal government assist in that return though it be against the morals of those who receive the escaping slaves? Should other states carved out of the Mexican accessions decide for themselves about slavery or ought there to be a wider federal policy? These are highly controversial matters, Miss Dix." The vice president–elect raised his eyebrows. "You do understand?"

"I know. But for those desperate souls who have no one to speak for them, I must be their voice. *We* must be their voice, Mr. Fillmore."

The politician sighed. "I suspect I will be presiding over a senate as cantankerous as a bull with a nose full of porcupine quills."

"Will there be any room on your agenda for my bill?"

He was thoughtful. "It falls under the rubric of land use, Miss Dix. Land and property are the issues of note, those and the role of the states and the federal government. But please know that I am sympathetic to your cause."

"I thought you might be."

He nodded. "I believe it is the role of federal government to put its resources to good use for the whole nation, 'to form a more perfect union,' and not dribble things state by state, like a patchwork quilt."

"And the president-elect?"

Fillmore hesitated. "He is a southern slaveholder. I doubt that the issue of the insane has come to his attention, but we will see what we can do with your bill, Miss Dix. We can work on it together, perhaps go around the president if need be."

Dorothea knew her smile was broader than it ought to be, but she was heartened by the vice president–elect's words. She had a champion at the highest level of government. God had given her another man of faith with whom to work.

"Meanwhile, it would please Millard and me to have you to tea each week, should your schedule permit," Abigail offered. "We can keep up on the progress of your bill, and perhaps you will enjoy a little concert now and then."

"I will indeed."

She would happily sit through a young girl's

harp playing, knowing that music soothed the raging souls of the insane. She was hopeful again about her memorial. "Maybe the Senate should consider music to begin their day," Dorothea mused. "It might reduce their cantankerousness."

"Oh, if only that would do it," Fillmore said. "I should encourage an executive order immediately."

Thirty-One
Hooked

The weekly teas, which the vice president sometimes attended, nurtured a growing fondness for young Abby Fillmore, reminding Dorothea of her teaching years. She found friendship with the spirited Abigail when they discussed books, and Dorothea silenced those moments of aching envy when she watched a husband treat his wife with gentleness and admiration. If this was what marriage could be, then it was indeed an institution worth considering. They were like the Rathbones and the Channings in that way, spouses who mutually cared for each other.

Away from those idyllic moments, however, Dorothea grew impatient with still more wrangling over land during the lame duck session. March could not come fast enough for the inaugural and Millard's—as she now thought of the vice president—impending influence on behalf of her bill.

A February drizzle threatened to keep her indoors, so she forced herself to survey prisons in the Washington area instead. She also visited acquaintances to solicit funds for books for several jails and for the almshouses she had visited before. She heard several music boxes play during her inspections, confirming that they had been distributed since her prior visits. The cacophony of tunes playing simultaneously suggested to her that she might intersperse the music boxes with kaleidoscopes. Dorothea believed these would bring ease to people, along with magic boxes that popped up to delight. She found a shop displaying inexpensive prints of flowers and landscapes. She had them framed and gave them to the jailers and the asylum superintendents to offer the promise of spring in a world stuck in winter.

Dorothea met with legislators, wrote letters, even corresponding with her brother Joseph, telling him of her current social status in the capital and her weekly meetings with the vice president's family. She compared her life in Washington with tedious stagecoach travel, though her journey through the halls of power was not nearly as likely to bring her to her desired destination. She stayed in the city for the inaugural and spent the last days of the congressional session listening to arguments that did not advance her cause. At the end of the session, she packed her bags, hooked her glass shoe buttons tightly around her narrow ankles, and moved on to the next campaign. By her calculations, fifty of the sixty senators supported her bill. She would push it again in the next session, after things had settled down for the new administration.

Dorothea headed south again, spending nearly seven months traveling. In November 1849 she arrived in Alabama. She did her usual work, cajoling and telling stories of the needy in her gentle yet mesmerizing way. "I was almost successful here in Mobile," she wrote to Abigail Fillmore. "But then the statehouse burned, and when the assembly reconvened, of course, they had to fund reconstruction rather than my state mental hospital."

She next headed to Mississippi, hoping for better results. These came about in March 1850 when the state set aside fifty thousand dollars for construction of the asylum the legislature had agreed to construct two years prior. "They want to name the institution after me," she wrote to the vice president. "But I have told them in no uncertain terms I will not allow it, and my forcefulness has prevailed."

"I have need of you!" Horace Mann told her. He championed her bill during the present term. "What were you doing in Alabama? You have to be here, be present. You never know when something will come up that can mean the life or death of your bill."

"All the talk has been of slavery," Dorothea defended. "Even rumblings about secession roll across the magnolia and jasmine, though I think it much exaggerated. No one speaks of those who have lost their reason. The vice president's kept me informed, as have you."

"Quite." Mann brushed the air dismissively. "You're here now. I have arranged for you to have an office in the Library of Congress. You may use my franking privileges and those of Senator Bell to write the necessary letters to once again gain support and move the bill forward. Write to Kirkbride. Get him to get the hospital superintendents behind this."

"That's . . . quite accommodating of you, Horace. An office? I will make good use of it and your postal benefits. I'm . . . I apologize. I simply could not sit in the gallery each day and hold my patience. I feared I would leap up and shout out at the futility of so many political speeches. I had to get away and make something happen."

"I understand." His voice softened and he patted her gloved hand. "I've thought of screaming once or twice myself. But we are now trying to find a way to soothe the western and southern states that object to the land distribution arrangement in the bill. They resist the New England states receiving money from federal lands in *their* states. They want to keep it all. We have to forge a compromise."

A compromise? "No! I've determined this is the only way to fund this! If we lower the federal minimum for land sales, there won't be enough money for the institutions. You know the western states will want to give the money from the lowered acreage and keep the remaining for their projects that might not include the insane."

"It would be a start, Dolly."

"Watered-down soup lacks nutrition even if you intend to later add meat. We must begin with a full-bodied meal."

He sighed. "See who you can persuade then."

"I shall sit right outside the Library of Congress, and I'll . . . I'll hook them."

The thought had just come to her. She would use the small end of her shoe buttonhook to lightly grab at the congressmen's sleeves as they rushed to their next meeting. She would pour on her charm, let her eyes twinkle. "I'll invite them in for a moment of their precious time, sugar." She took on the drawl of southern women quite easily.

She noticed it worked to get a gentleman's attention, and if it didn't, the buttonhook would.

Mann laughed. "Well, we might place the bill into the land committee, where those details could be worked out."

Dorothea shook her head. "No, it remains in the select committee or it will be muted."

"Stephen Douglas managed to get three million acres set aside for the Illinois Central Railroad. Think about that!"

"Did he?" Dorothea sat forward. "That bodes well, doesn't it?"

"He succeeded by confirming that the railroad would extend to Mobile. There are always terms, Dolly. Always compromise."

"And they did that? Pure politics." She sat back, crossed her arms. "I will not stoop to such measures."

Mann softened his voice. He was being reasonable. "If it was in the land committee, Dolly, you might see opportunities like what Davis managed. It's how things get done here."

"This is a good bill. You know it is. The Senate has just given three million acres for a railroad. I ask for little more for the insane. Is there not a higher authority than politics these men should follow?"

"Unfortunately," Mann told her with a long sigh, "the wires to that higher authority are strung by men."

Hooking anyone during the debate that came to be known as the Compromise of 1850 seemed futile, but Dorothea continued to sit outside the halls of Congress, chatting with anyone whenever the doors opened from the heated meetings. The men, however, either avoided seeing her, as they rushed by or paused and spoke of things deemed appropriate for public conversation with a woman. How was she feeling? Was her brother well? Did she like her office furnishings? All of this was a diversion from the work at hand, and Dorothea knew it. Each time, she brought the subject back to explore who might have personal concerns about someone relieved of their reason.

Yet the tediousness of the debate about lands and slavery upset her, and she undertook writing a bill to have two million acres set aside for schools for the blind, deaf, and mute.

Horace Mann chastised her. "You are weakening the position of your own bill by going off on these other tangents, however important they may be."

"I have to achieve something."

"We need your bill to go to the land committee." His high forehead, sharp jaw line, and erect posture reminded Dorothea of a statue. "There is precedent now with the railroad acreage set aside."

"We have discussed this. I will not give in to another congressman's or senator's pet project to get mine through. I won't have it. My bill stands on its merits. It is worthy, and I will not diminish it with politics."

Mann brushed his white hair behind his ears with both hands. "You can be stubborn beyond good reason, Dolly. It does not always serve you. At least consider adapting it to make it more acceptable. Talk with Daniel Webster."

"It will pass this time." She adjusted the doily pinned to her hair and worn for modesty in public. "I have confidence in *your* committee, the virtue of this bill, and God's good graces."

In the humid summer, she chose a Democrat in the House to sponsor the bill, sticking with her original strategy of getting the party less likely to support her cause to be the one to introduce it before the session. The only changes she made were to ask for ten million acres instead of five.

"Webster suggested it," she told Mann when he expressed exasperation with the change.

And she chose a war hero from Illinois—William H. Bissell—to introduce her bill in the House. "Did you not know that he criticized a Mississippi regiment during the war?" Mann asked her. "This resulted in the regiment's commander, Jefferson Davis—yes, *that* Jefferson Davis—to challenge him to a duel. Davis will never go along with a bill associated with Bissell."

"God will be our mediator," she insisted. She

kept her choice of Democrat to sponsor the bill. In the Senate, she chose a Marylander to push the bill. Then she waited and resisted the heat by wiping ice cubes on her wrists and throat. She wrote to Anne, "My heart pounds during my daily trek to the halls of Congress. Perhaps I shall collapse and not have to see the fate of these machinations in our capitol." She quickly added, "But my baby—this bill—calls me forward, and of course, I will not abandon it."

The Fillmores invited Dorothea to attend a Fourth of July celebration with them. They sat beneath a canopy that did little to protect them from the sweltering heat. Ice from Boston had been shipped down, and chips were added to tall glasses of water, which they all drank liberally. President Taylor and his family sat beneath a neighboring canopy, eating cherries and drinking iced water too.

"I feel like a sieve," Dorothea told Abigail as the two employed fans and wiped at their perspiration. Dorothea tugged at the collar of the brown linen dress she wore, still dark but hoping not to trap the hot sun as her black merino wools would. She perspired and looked forward to a cool bath whenever she returned to her quarters.

Joseph Henry, the head of the new Smithsonian Institution, and his wife, Harriet, were among the Fillmores' guests. They were also Dorothea's hosts in the city. She had given up her boarding-house life for the pleasantries of the Henry family and for their kindness in allowing her to invite prominent legislators to meet with her in their parlor. She also loved their wonderful conversations about the Smithsonian mission of "disseminating knowledge among men."

"Will President Taylor ever resolve the slavery issue so we might move forward?" Dorothea leaned toward Vice President Fillmore and whispered. Firecrackers snapped in the distance.

"He is torn. The president is more independent than either Whig or Democrat," Millard told her. "He sees both sides, which is a horrible affliction for a man of political persuasion. It can make him look weak."

They enjoyed the parade and festivities and sauntered back to their quarters at day's end. Dorothea was tiring of Washington. Nothing happened here except heat and stirring, but there was no baking or final bread to take from the oven. Only the friendships of the Fillmores and Bells brought her any comfort. She sighed as she slipped into a cool bath and washed her arms and legs with lavender-laced soaps.

Four days later, while enjoying her weekly tea with the Fillmores, Dorothea heard the news that was rocking the capital. Before Abigail joined her, Abby said, "The president is ill and has asked for his wife to prepare herself."

"Prepare for what?"

"His death."

Dorothea gasped. "Is he so ill?" She had heard that the president had come down with a case of ague after the celebration on the Fourth and that meetings with several congressmen had been canceled.

"He complains of his stomach. Perhaps the water . . . Cholera? No one knows."

"How is your father?"

"Well. He's well. And Mama and me. You aren't ill, are you? We all drank the same water."

Dorothea shook her head. "I'm fine. But our ice came from a different bucket. It might have been . . . but no one else has taken ill? The first lady is all right?"

Abby nodded. She blinked back tears. "He's such a good man. So fair. Should he die, it will put much weight upon Father."

Three days later Zachary Taylor did die and Millard Fillmore assumed the presidency.

As much as Dorothea grieved the loss of this popular president, so popular that more than a hundred thousand mourners lined the streets to honor him at the passing of his hearse, Dorothea was also hopeful. She renewed her assurance by reading Scripture that morning, Romans 8:28: "We know that all things work together for good to them that love God, to them who are the called according to his purpose."

Millard Fillmore was not conflicted about preventing the spread of slavery to the new territories, and he believed as Dorothea did that the federal government must play a role within the states regarding the treatment of the mentally ill. She grieved the president's passing but also thanked God that He had placed her friend Fillmore on the ticket. She would have her bill passed at last.

Thirty-Two
Compromise

The new president moved quickly on the Compromise of 1850, breaking Henry Clay's proposals into smaller pieces. Each passed, mollifying the South and quieting talk of secession. Dorothea's friend the president appealed to veterans, providing land grants to them. Oregon Territory settlers were offered free land, and the federal government ceded federal swampland to the states in which they lay. People were thinking about land, and Dorothea was certain her bill would pass and be signed into law by her powerful friend.

"All in God's timing," she wrote to Marianna.

"I expected Senator Davis to object," Dorothea told Fillmore after a day of debate when her bill was introduced. They shared tea in September 1850 in the family quarters. "He does not believe the federal government has any role in the states. He purports the federal government is only a trustee of the states' rights."

"At least his old argument of constitutionality held less sway this time," the president told her, "given that other land grants have been accepted. But the western states still object to the distribution. You have got to find a way to help them see your light."

"I simply cannot compromise. It annoys me that people think I can." She fanned herself against the late summer heat. "How's Abigail? Has she begun the library in the mansion yet? That was such a grand idea to ask Congress to fund it."

The president set his cup down. "Her ankle aches, but she finds herself lost in the best of ways by selecting titles for the shelves. Your books are already there."

"Oh, well, that isn't necessary." Dorothea felt her face grow warm.

"Dolly, this stance of yours, not to negotiate"— the president leaned toward her—"not to find ways to appease the states who object to issues in your bill. You must reconsider. It is not a sign of weakness to understand the ways in which bills become laws and adjust accordingly."

"I appreciate your wisdom, dear friend. But the virtue of the bill itself will be sufficient. Anything less is a concession against those in greatest need and, truly, I see compromise in this as an affront to God."

"Oh, Dorothea." The president shook his head, a sympathetic gesture.

"I will continue to bring my full will to bear. I believe you shall have the bill this session to sign."

Fillmore leaned back and pulled at his watch fob. "I admire your certainty." He rose to leave, nodding to his daughter. To Dorothea, he added, "But I pray for your reversal."

Dorothea left Washington days after the delay of her bill yet one more time by a member of the select committee who said he needed time to study it.

"Outrageous," Dorothea wrote to Sarah Gibbs in Vermont. "He has already had two years or more to study it. Now they have scheduled it for debate in the *next* session. I no longer expect anything to happen as proposed."

The president invited her to a tea of consolation. Abigail and Abby helped serve. Legislative attendees attempted to soothe her disappointment. They commented on Dorothea's stature as a prominent public figure, having tea with the president, how she brought important cultural and social issues to the front of political life "as a woman." They tended to emphasize the last. How rare it was for a woman to walk the halls of power.

She took small pleasure in the accolades after failing yet again to fulfill her greatest purpose for the Abrams and Madeleines of the country. She had wielded her power for benevolence, for the good of others, and that was woman's greatest role. Women gained influence in their charity, Dorothea knew. Such kindness should sway the legislature.

"You have decided not to allow Mrs. Hale to write of you in *Godey's*?" Abby asked after the politicians had left.

"I would think allowing this woman to highlight your accomplishments in her magazine could only assist with your campaign for the mentally ill," Abigail said. "It would bring in more of the public interest."

"Never." Dorothea rose and stared out a window at the green expanse of lawn. Sheep grazed to keep the grass clipped short.

"But she believes in the education of women, in helping young girls become fully prepared for their roles as women," Abigail said. "As teachers, this can only help our own cause for the future Abbys of the world."

"A lovely thought, yes. But delicacy and modesty must prevail." Dorothea turned from the window. "I object to making celebratory stories of women or using our feminine sides to promote causes. The cause itself ought to lead the parade for change." She smiled at Abby. "Mrs. Hale may write of me when I'm dead."

Sarah Josepha Hale, however, ignored Dorothea's objection and published a biography of the reformer, using the occasion to advance her own cause of federal land to be set aside for normal schools for women teachers rather than for the mentally ill.

"You should have let her write of you, Dolly," Abigail told her at their next gathering. "Perhaps she would not have pushed her own cause quite so hard."

Dorothea punched the magazine article with her fingers. "I did what I thought was right."

"You always do."

Dorothea spent a week at the Trenton hospital in the apartment provided for her. She walked the grounds, checking on the growth of the pear trees. She ate meals with the patients and marveled at their table manners. Moral treatment worked! She could see it in their smiles and on their faces. This humane approach was needed in every state in the nation.

Her bill, however, languished in Congress again during the winter session, until January 1851, when a sponsoring senator disputed Senator Davis's constitutional concerns by pointing out that the sale of public lands would increase economic development and add value that was every bit the role of the federal government as a trustee of the country, thus improving the condition of state lands.

Dorothea nearly cheered from the gallery. What a gallant and inventive argument! His argument carried the day, and her bill passed the Senate, carrying New England and winning thirty-five to sixteen votes. She praised the senator effusively when she hooked him outside her office door. "Brilliant, just brilliant."

"It is only the truth, dear lady," he said. "Only the truth."

Dorothea waited anxiously for the House bill to move quickly as well. An argument to deal with the states' rights advocates was at hand and had been used successfully by the Democrats. She was so hopeful that they, too, would see it as "only the truth."

Instead, amendments and delays and referrals stalled the bill. *How can this be? We are so close.*

She waited in her office for some positive note. She wrote letters furiously, requiring frequent refilling of her sandbox. She thought of the Madeleines and the Abrams, how this grand plan would help them and all who came after them. Here was her life's work laid at the hands of men with factions pulling them left and right. Had she kept the needs of the suffering always before them? Had she done enough to champion the argument that would push them to her side?

"Dolly?"

Horace Mann entered her office.

"Yes?" she answered, rising from her chair.

"I'm so sorry."

"What? What!"

"Benton, on the select committee."

"He was in favor."

"He thought he needed more time. The opposition grew." Mann cleared his throat. "There were so many amendments, motions, delays, requests for the Speaker to reschedule. Then one of the representatives—from our beloved Massachusetts —rose and said he had voted for your bill that day as often as he could, and now he felt they should take up other, more important measures before adjourning."

"It's dead." She sank back into her chair.

"Until the next session. Are you all right? We did our best."

"I am aware of your great efforts." She was a clock winding down. She would have to find a way to wind herself back up. She rubbed her temples with her fingers, then sighed. "My efforts were simply not enough. I was not enough." Failure was as familiar as the face in her mirror.

The southern states still had causes: Alabama supporters asked for her help once again in passing legislation for a hospital there. She packed her trunk, boarded a stage, and bounced her way to South Carolina, Georgia, and Florida.

"You're from where? Massachusetts?"

The innkeeper frowned at her. She had always been greeted graciously in the South. Now this man in Florida acted as if she were there to assault him rather than purchase food from him.

"Yes. But I have spent a fair amount of time in the South. I love it here."

"Spying on us?"

"Why, no. I—"

"We don't need no northerners telling us what to do or how to think."

"No, of course not. I am here to assist the mentally ill—"

"We take care of our own."

She wrote to President Fillmore and others of these sentiments. "Abolitionists visiting here have upset the people, and there is secessionist talk that borders on the extreme. People appear to think all northerners are abolitionists."

She did not receive the usual invitations from her friends to visit their plantations and stay with them. Instead, she found rooms at boardinghouses while she did her work for those who had lost their reason. Once or twice while mending a tear in her skirt or stuffing her shoe soles with newspaper, she wondered if perhaps she had lost hers.

Following the midterm elections, she returned to Washington to learn that the Whigs had been greatly diminished. The president's support also waned with the change in the government's complexion.

In her office at the Library of Congress, she conferred with her colleagues about what these changes might mean for her bill. They shook their heads. Predicting the weather was easier than forecasting how legislation would fare through Congress.

While she awaited word on the status of her bill, she wrote another memorial, this one for Maryland to help them replace a psychiatric hospital. Not able to twiddle her thumbs while waiting for congressmen to act, she learned of a move to provide funds for a psychiatric hospital for Washington and for veterans. She thought about getting involved . . . it was a worthy cause. But if she did, would it appear she was less committed to her own bill? Horace Mann's chastisement of her earlier diversions for deaf schools was still fresh in her mind.

"There's an amendment attached to your bill," Mann told her during a session break. "But I think it will pass anyway. It resolves the question of the distribution so the western states are satisfied."

"You know how I feel about making any concessions that might weaken the overall resources for the national asylum centers," Dorothea said.

"For once, I trust you will let practical politics prevail."

She ran a cleaning rag around the ink bottle on her desk. She wiped errant sand into the palm of her hand and returned it to the sandbox. "I won't protest the amendment, but I will have an ache in my heart always if it passes."

The bill passed the House with the amendment intact. Since it had passed the Senate previously, and the changes would only appease not distress the Democrats there, Dorothea waited hopefully for word that in August 1852 she would at last see her dream accomplished.

Instead, the Senate refused to vote on the bill because of the railroad amendments attached to it.

"But the railroad amendment was supposed to further the bill along." Dorothea stood before the president in his office. Aides hovered in the background.

"Things happen. But you will be back," Fillmore told her. "Next session for certain."

"Like lemmings to the sea, you mean? Yes, I imagine I will come back. And you, will you be back?"

The president harrumphed. "I am hopeful. I would like to be elected for my own full term. I know my signing of the Fugitive Slave Act has distanced my northern Whig friends, and my position on the Caribbean invasion has disgruntled my southern Whig friends." He shrugged. "Perhaps you will outlast me, Dolly."

"I need you."

"And I will try to be of service." He nodded to her and an aide touched her elbow to usher her out. The president was a busy man, and only friendship had allowed these few minutes for him to offer his time to a passionate woman who had again failed in her attempt to promote a piece of legislation.

Amazingly, the federal hospital in Washington that she had declined to assist was approved, and while Dorothea had not championed it during the session, she saw the authorization of the hospital as a first step in recognizing the federal government's role in treating the mentally ill. She decided to remain in the city and see what she could do to support "my district hospital." She had a cause for the summer and the fall, until once again she would champion her bill and hopefully Millard Fillmore, as the newly elected president in his own right, would sign it.

In 1852 the Whigs did not nominate Fillmore for a run at the presidency. And the Democrat nominee, Franklin Pierce, won the presidential election.

"Perhaps we can still get the measure through both houses in the lame duck session that I might sign it before leaving office," Fillmore told Dorothea. He did not appear all that disappointed that he had not won his own term in office. She commented to him about that, and he nodded.

"I have done what I could do to serve my country. I will go home to New York now, with my dear Abigail and Abby, and when this session is over, I shall become a country squire again."

"You shall always be involved in public life." Dorothea smiled as he poured her a cup of tea.

"Perhaps. But it would please me to see your bill through, Dolly. It would be a solid and memorable period on the sentence of my presidency."

She smiled, and for a moment she thought his look was one of endearment, perhaps more deeply than merely as a friend. She felt her face grow warm. He cleared his throat and backed away. Admiration as a colleague, she decided. That was what had passed between them.

To the end of having him be the president who would sign her bill into law, she lobbied daily, buttonhooking legislators. She was doing it for the country's insane but also for her friend the president. In both houses, the bill languished, however. Other bills were attached to it, or it was moved to be attached to some other issue related to land. It was squeezed into discussions that seemed unrelated, though championed by some senators as a pet project. Nothing, absolutely nothing, moved closer to resolution. Still, in the wee hours of the last day of the session of March 3–4, 1853, a final effort was made to pass the bill so Millard Fillmore could sign it.

Dorothea knew the president had spoken to

many congressmen on her behalf. She had agreed to changes related to the western states, and Dorothea was still there in her office in the Library of Congress as the voices of debate droned on, hopeful that this tiny bit of compromise would be the ticket to the railroad of hope she had been riding these past few years.

She waited for the final vote. The clock ticked. She stared out a window, urging spring forward.

The last act of the Thirty-Second Congress, however, was a vote to kill Dorothea's bill.

Thirty-Three
Lessons of Loss

She kept a smile on her face at the inauguration of Franklin Pierce, watching as the Fillmores took their seats on March 4, 1853, a very cold day in Washington. Inside, Dorothea burned. She had to be optimistic, had to assume these small wins and defeats were part of some larger plan. She could not make enemies of the new administration. So she nodded her feathered hat toward the new president and his wife, smiled, then slipped in next to the Fillmores in the seat they had reserved for her.

Snow spit over them, driven by a relentless east

wind. The canopy erected to shelter the dignitaries did little against the icy cold, however.

Dorothea had dressed warmly, with a winter muffler close around her neck. Even though March often announced the coming of spring in the city, today it spoke of a winter unwilling to leave.

"I may as well attach this handkerchief to my nose," she told Abigail.

"Like a grain bag for a horse."

"Exactly."

Abigail shivered and coughed, her auburn sausage curls bobbing as she huddled on the dais as required of the former first lady. The speeches dragged on, and then the parade began. Even the horses looked chilled. Was that frost forming on their noses?

"I hope you'll forgive me, but I'm going where it's warm," Dorothea said through chattering teeth. There were hours of festivities left to come, many of them outdoors.

"I would if I could," Abigail said and sneezed.

Dorothea wrapped her knitted muffler around Abigail's neck, patted her arm, and said she would see all of them later in the week. At her boardinghouse, she took tea before a warm fire and added a splash of brandy for inner warmth. She considered her strategy. Her friend Horace Mann and a few other supporters had left Congress with the last election.

Senator Bell had cooled toward her too, though

she did not know why. Maybe because she had given in on the amendment that had doomed the bill. Or perhaps he was beginning to see all northerners as abolitionists. Now that they lived in different boardinghouses, she had not seen much of Jane Bell either, and she missed that but did not have the time to change it. Her bill held her hostage.

As she placed another coal on the fire, she realized she was tired. Tired of the effort, the wrangling, the uncertainty. She had other choices. Maybe the legislative defeat in the last session was a message for her to stop this compassionate crusade. Maybe God had something else in store for her. Her eye caught Madeleine's carving. She lifted it and sighed. She had other choices to make, but the Madeleines of the world did not.

She was just sad that her friends the Fillmores would soon be leaving Washington. She would miss them. They were like family, each one.

Dorothea spent the next few days going over the congressional committee assignments, deciding which legislators to invite to tea when she began her next charm campaign. She still had an office in the library, but her franking privileges had left with Horace Mann. President Pierce already had made his cabinet appointments, which gave her cause for some optimism. John A. Dix, her faux brother, had been chosen along with an old friend, Senator James C. Dobbin, who was named secretary of the navy. He might not have much influence on her land bill, but he was a voice inside the cabinet at least.

Suddenly, however, former senator Dix was asked to take a subordinate position to appease a faction, so he wouldn't be in the cabinet after all. Worse, her states' rights nemesis, Jefferson Davis, was appointed secretary of war. Sitting next to the new president, Davis would have a strong and ready voice against her land bill.

Still, Dobbin and the Bells cared about the mentally ill, she was certain. She would find more legislators and charm them into polishing their souls through caring for the unfortunate. She opened a letter from Nova Scotia and read a plea for her to explore a site for a new mental hospital. Imagine, another country she might assist. Maybe after this congressional session ended. It was good to have somewhere to go and be restored.

"Letter for you, Miss Dix," the landlady announced as she knocked at her door. It was three days after the inauguration, and Dorothea opened the door, anticipating an invitation from Abigail. But the letter wasn't from the vice president or Abigail. Instead, Abby's hand informed her, "Mother has taken ill. You must come to the Willard Hotel where we're staying until Mama improves."

The wretched inaugural day weather! The requirement that former first ladies remain in the outdoors while subject to freezing weather. Propriety overruled common sense sometimes. Decorum also had prevented her from testifying to Congress, when her words could have brought insight to the otherwise uninformed. She grabbed her heavy wool cape and hailed a cab.

Her quick trip out of the boardinghouse began a vigil. Dorothea visited daily, tending to her friend whose color was as pale as old teeth. The effort of her breathing brought tears to Dorothea's eyes. She would shoo Abby out to give the girl some relief, and she told Millard to do likewise. Abby would sometimes leave, but Millard sat across from her and held Abigail's hand, his eyes deep sockets in his caring face.

As Abigail's breathing rattled and slowed, lines of suffering grew on Millard's face. Dorothea prayed for his comfort, prayed Abigail would recover.

"Maybe you should get some rest yourself," Millard told Dorothea after several days of tending. "Congress is in session. You do not want to lose out on the debates."

Dorothea shook her head. "You know as well as I do they will not be taking up our bill anytime soon. And besides, caring for a friend is a higher calling. You have been like family to me. I could never desert you now."

Millard nodded. "It's good of you."

Abigail had not spoken since Dorothea's

arrival, and her glassy eyes no longer followed her around the room. Together, Millard and Dorothea listened to her labored breathing. Dorothea read psalms now to comfort Millard and Abby more than Abigail. Doctors whispered about pneumonia and a high fever while Dorothea wiped her friend's hot forehead with a cool cloth.

In the evening of March 29 she returned to the boardinghouse to freshen up. When she returned to Willard Hotel, Abby sobbed as she opened the door and clung to Dorothea like a frightened baby to its mother. Her friend Abigail had died. Dorothea simply held Abigail's child.

On March 30, both houses of Congress adjourned and public buildings closed in Abigail's honor. Abby allowed Dorothea to wrap her arms around her as they sat in a pew. *Oh, such a terrible grief to lose so loving a mother.* Dorothea allowed Millard and Abby's sorrow to mingle with her own, blessed the days she had known Abigail as a friend, and tried not to ques-tion the why of things. That evening, alone, she read Shakespeare: "Give sorrow words: the grief that does not speak Whispers to the o'er-fraught heart and bids it break." She would urge her friends to speak their grief, and she would write down her own, mingling Abigail's passing with her mother's.

Dorothea traveled with the Fillmores to Buffalo, where Abigail was buried and where the decimated Fillmores would remain.

"Your presence has been a gift," Millard told her as she prepared to leave. "Maybe you should go to Nova Scotia now, become restored by doing something constructive rather than return to the vagaries of national politics. Maybe the halls of Congress are not a place for women, after all."

"It's been my honor to be allowed to share in your family's joys . . . and grief. If there is ever anything I can do, please, call on me."

Millard nodded. He had lost weight in the days since Abigail's death; his collar was no longer tight against his throat. He held her hands in his. "Be well, Dolly. Think of us when you can." He looked away and Dorothea watched as he struggled not to weep, uncertain how to comfort him. He cleared his throat. "I will later help as I can with the bill."

"I know you will."

"Go now. Do the good you always do."

If only she could.

Dorothea did leave for Nova Scotia. She needed to see the faces of the mentally ill and to confer with those on the front lines of this war, which was how she thought of it. She needed to speak with superintendents and physicians and let the hands of the insane touch her soul.

Unexpectedly, on Sable Island, off the Nova Scotia coast, she found horses and felt the sting of sand and sea as she raced one against the lifting of the morning fog. Feral horses dotted ponds as she rode by. She had never ridden in surf, and something about the ocean and the equine beasts with manes waving in the wind restored her. She recognized that the stable boy who helped her was a mongoloid from the nearby asylum. They practiced a kind of moral treatment on Sable Island, and Dorothea saw once again that what she hoped for in her country was worthy of her efforts.

"The new president will hope both houses defeat your bill so he won't have to veto it," Millard Fillmore said. Abby served tea and sat quietly, dark circles beneath her eyes signaled her ongoing grief over her mother's death. John Dix visited as well. Dorothea had stopped to visit on her way back to Washington. "I fear for the fate of your bill."

"You think he would veto if we got that far?" Dorothea frowned.

"Davis will push the constitutionality issue," Dix told her. "Pierce is . . . a weak president, elected without full party support, so he has to appease everyone. That's why he withdrew my cabinet nomination."

"At least you'll have his ear. He must respect your judgment, dear brother."

Dix nodded but offered no other encourage-ment.

"As a distinguished woman of benevolence, you'll be received at the mansion, so you might diplomatically gauge his level of support." Millard scraped sugar into his tea and blew on it to let it cool.

"They've remodeled the mansion," Abby said. They all turned to her, the tone of her voice so flat.

"Yes, that's right. It will be different for you when you visit. But the doormen are the same. They'll remember you," Dix said.

"Would you like to visit with me?" Dorothea turned to Abby. "We could stay together for a few weeks."

Abby shook her head. "Father has need of me here."

"Of course."

"He's become involved in a new party formed by the Whigs who have been devastated," Abby added. "I'm sure he'll keep busy. I fill in for Mama—" Her voice cracked.

"As you did at the President's House." Dorothea sat beside her and held the young woman's pale hand, the lace of her sleeve limp against her wrist. She was not starching her lace. *Maybe I should remain here, help Abby through her sorrow.* "You are his greatest friend, Abby, and deepest comfort."

"That she is." Millard smiled at his daughter, pain still raw inside his eyes. "We will be all right,

Dolly, knowing you keep us in your prayers. And you have work to do, my friend."

Dorothea spent a week at Trenton, writing and gazing out the window at the Delaware River. She thought of the losses in her life as a train chugged past fields and lakes. Ducks made V shapes as they paddled to the far side of the water. Nothing remained the same. Everything changed, and yet she could not get this one change through Congress. *Am I doing something wrong? Are you still in this, God?* Had she misread what she had been called to do? Had she failed to heed another way to relieve the suffering of so many? But to stop now would be an amputation of her spirit. She had to go on.

The doorman at the Executive Mansion remembered Dorothea on the day she had arranged to meet with the president.

"I hope your day goes well, Mr. Samuel."

He welcomed her with a wide smile in his dark face and ushered her toward the aides who would take her to the president's office.

"What can I do for you, Miss Dix?" Franklin Pierce stood behind his desk—a desk Millard Fillmore had left behind.

"I would be so grateful if you might encourage your congressional supporters to assist in the passage of my land bill for the mentally ill."

"I sincerely regret that it did not pass in the

last session." The president stared at her and did not offer a chair. "I shall be glad if it passes now."

"I . . . that is such good news, Mr. President." She could not contain the joy in her voice. "I'm sure—"

"But I really have not gone much into the matter."

He looked at his watch and moved from behind his desk as a sign of his dismissing her. "I have a busy schedule, as you might imagine."

She found herself escorted out. He had given her less than two minutes, had not even invited her to sit while he remained standing. She did not see how he would ever go "into the matter" when he declined information about the bill from a first-hand, passionate source. She thought back to her New York visit. Her friends had sounded despondent as they spoke of the hope of her bill with this new Congress; now she realized they were being optimistic. Still, the president had said he wished it had passed the previous term. Political speech was its own language, and one had to translate intent. She took his words as a sign of support and would relay that support to her congressional supporters. She may well get this bill signed after all.

Thirty-Four
Men in High Places

Arguing over land was the staple of congressional fodder, but now slavery and states deciding on their own whether to come into the Union as free or not slanted the discussion. Dorothea rubbed her temples as she listened to the debate over whether *any* federal lands should be sold or instead given outright to any settlers to encourage emigration to the west, which western and southern congress-men thought prudent.

One of Dorothea's former students, Shelley Mason, had headed overland to Oregon in 1852 via wagon train. Dorothea wrote to her, asking what rumors circulated out there about land and the federal government's role in doling it out. The information mattered little; it would take weeks for any response to find Dorothea.

She found yet another sponsor to introduce the bill in the Senate while she wondered whether competing homestead bills and repeal of the Missouri Compromise, limiting slavery in the North, would ultimately press the air out of her legislation like a giant ape squashing a bird hoping to take flight. It was a constipating session: nothing moved. All the arguments took place in back rooms, where Dorothea was not allowed.

Then with spring came new energy. Newly introduced bills began to move in both houses. Millard had warned her that nothing would be done until the issue of slavery was determined, but both houses advanced her bill more quickly than they ever had. She saw this as God's timing, that at last her life's work would bear fruit.

"I'm amazed," she told Representative Bissell of Illinois, who had introduced the bill in the House.

"We may well discover how the president feels about the homestead bill based on how he responds to the passage of yours," said a representative from New York.

"He's not made himself clear about the homestead bill?" The congressman shook his head. "Then it isn't only me that he chooses to keep in the dark."

"I fear not, dear lady. What I do fear is that he may well veto your bill at the end and use it as a platform from which to speak about other issues."

"But with both houses passing it, surely he would see it as the will of the people wanting this." Could it be that after all this work a president would not accept the outcome?

"That is not how it works, Miss Dix," Bissell told her. "A few senators may vote for passage because they believe the president will veto it. He may have told them as much. He won't see passage by both houses as a mandate for action but rather as a political move on the part of the parties."

"Why would they vote for something they don't believe in? That lacks . . . integrity."

The representative gave her a pitiful look. "Miss Dix, I would think you had learned more in all your time here."

From the gallery she listened with a cautious ear to arguments on land issues and thought it good that the Dix bill was often mentioned in the conversations. At least until she heard the silver-throated James Murray Mason from Virginia suggest that the Dix bill would open doors for the federal government to dominate all state institutions with impunity.

"Oh, for heaven's sake," Dorothea said. Another gallery visitor shushed her. "Well, that's simply not true!" she hissed back.

Mason had introduced the Fugitive Slave Act, and Dorothea realized exactly what he was arguing: if they passed her bill, they were also agreeing to allow the federal government to regulate slavery within and between the states. Slave states would never agree to that. Surely someone would counter his argument. She looked around the floor. No senator rose to object. Dorothea's stomach felt heavy as stone.

On March 8, the Senate approved the bill and sent it to the House.

Dorothea hooked numerous representatives and assured them that the Senate bill did not open the doors for the federal government to decide state issues. A few legislators listened, but all seemed grateful when a colleague came along and took them away from her.

Her chest ached when she heard a North Carolinian representative lament that the government had no power to legislate even for benevolence on behalf of "lunatics, paupers, Negroes, or anybody else." She did not speak out loud in the gallery, but she wanted to shout!

In her diary, she wrote: "What do those men think they're doing in Congress if not to make laws to benefit the people! Aren't laws the gateway for the people to pursue their own paths to life, liberty, and happiness? All people? This very system of ups and downs is enough to make a person insane." She broke a nib, she wrote so hard.

On April 19, with barely a quorum and those present hoping to adjourn, Dorothea's bill came up for a vote. Whigs held firm. The bill passed. She wanted to be excited but feared it was just another sucking step in the muck of politics. She looked at how the vote had gone as a measure of how Pierce would respond. The southern states, as expected, had opposed the bill on constitutional grounds. The Whigs supported it on humanitarian grounds, and the northern Democrats were divided. But it had passed, and even the newspapers commented that it was the only land bill that had been triumphant during a session of dissension. All that was left was for the president to sign it. Surely he would see the light, as would the thousands of men and women locked in a world of darkness, suffering alone.

"There is a rumor," Anne Heath wrote by telegram. "Has Pierce returned the bill to Congress with his veto?"

"He's done nothing. It sits. Request for consultation with Pierce denied. Pray common sense and the plight of the least of these will prevail."

If Pierce held the bill and did nothing for ten days, it would become law. If he didn't want to sign, he could save face by doing nothing. But Dorothea prayed that he would sign it. It would mean so much more in implementation if the president were behind it. How she missed Millard!

Dorothea woke with a sore throat and wondered if her dry cough would escalate into lung troubles again. She overheard Senator Bell tell his wife— they were back to sharing boardinghouse space —that Pierce "will likely veto it and it will kill our Miss Dix." *No, it won't.* If he vetoed the bill, there would be enough votes to override it in both houses. She kept a careful tally. And yet, her sore throat worsened. She pulled the cotton sheet up to her chin. She'd like to stay in bed all day . . . but she wouldn't.

"Pierce will be haplessly crushed by his veto being overridden, should he veto my bill," she told the Bells over supper. They exchanged glances with each other. "Truly. He is unaware of the mountain of support and won't know until he's under it."

John Bell sounded like a man speaking to a widow when he said, "All that has gone before in the votes, Dolly, does not foretell what would happen with a veto. Overrides are . . . political sausage: no one knows what they're made of and few want to eat them."

"I appreciate your sentiments, John. But I have faith."

"Only a handful of vetoed bills have been overridden in the history of this nation," Bell warned.

"I am aware of that. But God is on our side here. Surely He won't allow all our efforts to help suffering people go for naught."

"At least you have your past successes in the states, Dolly." Jane dabbed at her lips with her napkin. "You could continue in that vein. Forget the federal ideas."

"No. If he vetoes it, I will get both houses to override his veto so the suffering insane poor

374

can have a stable future." It was part of God's plan. She had to believe in that.

On May 3 the president vetoed the bill. Worse, he included a statement of concerns.

Dorothea pored over the arguments Pierce provided for the veto, noting that he carefully did not either support or deny the homestead bill, which would distress *that* bill's supporters to no end. Instead he resorted to Jefferson Davis's states' rights argument. *Jefferson Davis. I might have known.* Pierce wrote that certain federal land grants could be investments, grants that enhanced the surrounding state lands, for example, as with the railroads. These were constitutional. But national charity bills, such as land for a school for deaf-mutes, was an unworthy act on the part of Congress, and the past president ought not to have allowed it. Miss Dix's bill was of that ilk and therefore had to be vetoed.

"National charity is an abomination, he says." Dorothea paced in her office as Horace Mann attempted to calm her. Her friend was no longer in Congress, but he came to Washington to console her and help her think through the override attempt. "Having the indigent insane in a safe place doesn't enhance the value of a community? It does. It makes it more likely people will come to a state that cares for those relieved of their reason. Does he think only poor people have insanity in their families, wretchedly ill people who need care regardless of where they live? I . . . he said he wished it had passed the previous session!"

"His words carried a different meaning than you thought, Dolly. If it had passed last session, he wouldn't have to deal with it now."

"How could he have written so bold a veto that now puts the Democrats firmly behind sustaining it and the southern states already thinking states' rights trump every federal action. I won't get enough votes!"

"Dolly, sit for a moment." She did and pressed her hand to her chest. He spoke as though to a child. "You have moved within the halls of politics in powerful ways. Your efforts at the state level amaze everyone."

"Yet my greatest ambition, to get a national land bill passed on behalf of the mentally ill, is lost without the override." She stared at him. "Will they even bring the bill up for consideration of an override?"

"They likely will, but it will be a vote of loyalty to the president. He vetoed it. It would smack him mightily if they overrode his wishes."

"Smack him mightily! What of those who wait in the dungeons and almshouses? They have been smacked for decades."

Horace shrugged. "Prepare yourself, Dolly. It is the way of things."

"How can you be so callous?"

Horace sighed. "Dolly, I care deeply about the mentally ill. I do. You know that."

She nodded, clasping her hands in her lap. "I know. I have no right to impugn your motives."

"But in this democratic world good men differ. We may think it's less important to respond to homesteaders heading west than the needs of the insane, but that does not make it so. It's not just the outcome that matters, but how we carried on, whether we were faithful to our own calling."

"But we failed." She nearly wailed.

"We did not achieve this goal. *You* may call it a failure, but I prefer to think of it as . . . schooling. For the next campaign. We will never know whose life has been touched by the campaign itself, by your articles or the letters or the greater association of the physicians and superintendents. You must not discount those experiences nor your work in the states. The very act of discussion contributes to democracy and the betterment of its citizens. Let's not forget that."

"I might not forget, but what of those who suffer?"

"We find new ways, Dolly. New venues. Pray. Listen. Wait."

She looked up, a wry smile on her face. "I still have a two-thirds majority when they vote for scheduling or minor issues. They might yet override."

"Dorothea, prepare yourself."

•••

For the next sixty days Dorothea rarely left the halls of Congress. She arrived each morning that summer at 6:00 a.m. and remained until midnight, eating only soup and biscuits when she returned to her boardinghouse. She buttonhooked legislators, wrote letters, even served tea in her office to legislative aides. She did what she knew to do, remembering Elizabeth Rathbone's words: "If it is to be, it begins with thee."

On July 6, a day so hot and still it brought on talk of an offshore storm, people hoping one might deluge the city to wash away the summer stench and refresh it at last, the Senate voted.

The president's veto was sustained.

Dorothea's bones felt cold despite the dense swelter of the city. Back in her boardinghouse, she read once again Pierce's comments, trying to see where she had misread. Her heart fluttered when she reread a letter to the editor saying that her bill had become the vehicle for those disclaiming any federal role in charity or even the states. It made it likely that the ban on slavery in the territories and the new states would now be repealed "because of Dix's bill."

She sat down next to her partially packed trunk. Her northern abolitionist friends would be heartsick. She trembled at the thought that Anne might again rebuff her or that Julia Ward

Howe and the other abolitionists would hold her and her bill as a nail in the coffin of their cause. It had not been her intent. All she had ever wanted was to relieve the suffering of the mentally ill, not extend the suffering of slaves. Unlike Horace Mann, she could not yet see her efforts as a schooling that might later show results. "I am so sorry," she said to no one. "So very sorry I have failed."

The spinning top had stopped. No new bill would pass, however cleverly she might have worked with the southern states. A lifetime of effort had been overturned with one loud vote of nay.

Dorothea lay on the bed, her arms crossed over her chest. She wanted to scream "No, No, No!" and in her heart she did. So many years, so many hopes now dashed. If she was not meant to do this thing, then how had she come to succeed at the state level? How had she, a mere woman, been allowed into the halls of Congress? to have tea with the presidents and their wives? Yet God had said no to the very heart of her life's work. And she didn't know why. Anger, like the day she'd demanded heat in the freezing cells of East Cambridge, swelled inside of her, but it wasn't the magistrates or even the congressmen to whom she sent her wrath. It was God.

She pulled herself up from the boardinghouse bed and made her way to St. Alban's Episcopal, a newly established church. She sat. She prayed.

And hours later, she surrendered. She had done what she could. She was not in control. How had she missed that simple truth?

She set about leaving Washington, not sure where she would go. She didn't want to remain in a city laid out so orderly yet where nothing seemed orderly inside the houses of government. She could stay and help implement the new hospital in Washington. Instead, she gave her inkstand and sandbox to the young superintendent she had recommended for the position. She would go to Trenton and walk the grounds, share conversations with the patients, write on her precious desk. She would find a way to serve and, in so doing, be relieved of this emptiness. She just didn't know how.

Thirty-Five

The Bridge

Dorothea's departure for Trenton was interrupted by a letter from Millard. "My dear Abby has died," he wrote. "We worked together on a university to honor Abigail, and now she's gone too. My heart is broken."

She left immediately for Buffalo and threw her arms around Millard as he sat in the parlor, shoulders closed inward, arms clasped to protect his heart and soul.

"They're gone." He raised his head to hers, his eyes red, the lines beneath them deep as furrowed rows. "I've only my son left."

"I know. I know."

He leaned against her, silent, racking sobs shaking his shoulders, his eyes narrowed with tears. "I could do nothing. So helpless! Cholera. The dreaded cholera."

She held him like she once held Charles when he had cut his knee and sobbed in pain. She held him as she had Marianna when her mother had died. Dorothea stroked his white hair. "We have no say in these things. We are simply left to grieve and let our friends and loved ones help us through the sorrow. Remember the psalms. They will bring comfort."

He wiped at his eyes, nodded, and pulled a handkerchief from his vest pocket. Then he stood, his back to her while he blew his nose.

"May I assist with the arrangements?"

"All . . ." He cleared his throat. "The burial is tomorrow." He turned back to her. "I appreciate your coming. Thank you. I didn't expect . . . You have your own grief to live with. I am so sorry Pierce vetoed our bill."

"That you would claim it as your own soothes me. We mourn what might have been."

"As with Abby. So young. Such promise." His

eyes filled with tears again. He turned to business, the rawness of his sorrow needing respite in work. "What will you do now? There are states awaiting help with asylum design, moral treatment questions. Prison reform?"

"I don't know." She pulled off her gloves and looked for a chair, though he had not invited her to sit. "The road I've been on has come to a cliff. I've yet to see the bridge God will build for me to cross it."

Millard stepped toward her, clasped her hands in his, and looked into her eyes. "You are a dear friend who trusts there will be a bridge to more in life. It will remind me to trust likewise."

His hands warmed hers, and for a moment she wondered if perhaps this would be her path now: to stand beside a good man as he worked in education to continue his wife's legacy, help mourn his daughter's death. She could be a good helpmate. He would accept a strong woman. Abigail had been so. "I . . . could stay for a time. Assist you." Her hands were damp inside his.

She saw in his eyes not love but fondness, kindness. "And you would do it well, my friend, I'm certain. But I must not interfere with what you have been called to do. Your great ambition is not over. I sense this." He squeezed her hands and then released them. "You will find the next world to conquer, and those who adore you will bask in the glory of your star."

•••

She returned to Massachusetts for brief visits with Anne and spoke with George Emerson and his wife about their plans for a European trip. Horace Mann was busy with educational endeavors. She returned to the Trenton asylum, the place she now called home, and from there she wrote letters to Millard, begging him to understand that writing helped her grieve the loss of so lovely a young woman as Abby. She wrote daily. He did not respond. Grieving Abby's death helped her lament her failure in Congress.

But now what? She checked the garden plots of the asylum, wandered the halls, spoke with the residents, helping one to use a stereopticon, assisting another to weave a basket for hair combs. Daily she walked to the farms and spoke with the patients working there. She didn't ride but spoke softly to the workhorses, who dropped their big heads over the half doors of their stalls. Back inside the hospital she heard few shrieks and these were silenced quickly with a nurse's kind gesture. She conferred daily with the superintendent, who knocked on her apartment door to ask questions about storing food or changes that might enhance sunlight into the interior or ways to address issues involved with moral treatment. She felt useful but not uniquely so. Anyone could do what she was doing here.

In the morning she watched the Delaware River

roll seamlessly to the sea, and at night she slept in her narrow bed and felt befuddled about her future. She was a top no longer spinning. What had helped her in the past move through the discouraging times? She remembered an old proverb Elizabeth Rathbone once shared: silence is the fence around wisdom. She would seek prayer in silence and perhaps wisdom would arrive.

She boarded the ship *Arctic* in September 1854, expecting an arrival within ten days as the steam line had advertised. Based on Dorothea's notoriety, the steamship owner granted her a complimentary ticket and private stateroom. "How lovely," she told the captain, at whose table she ate daily. And then, because she could not receive without reciprocating, she said, "And in return for your generosity, I have decided to take out a life insurance policy on myself, with the Trenton asylum the beneficiary."

"You are a generous lady," the captain noted, raising a toast to her. Her face grew warm. She had not intended for her announcement to bring praise; it was only a way of giving back.

In her diary, she wrote about what she might have done wrong in her campaign to help the mentally ill. Had she been too willful with the bill's passage? Should she have compromised earlier? Had she chosen the wrong men to be the sponsors of her bill? Perhaps, but she had done her best. What else could a woman do?

The rush of the hull against the water soothed her. She leaned at the railing, watching the water split by the ship. The vastness of the ocean in her view placed her where she was: a woman alone on the sea of life, and she had done her best but had failed. Was she still worthy? That was the question. The verse from Jeremiah that she loved suggested that God had an expected end for her and it was to find a place of peace. "For I know the thoughts I think toward you, saith the LORD, thoughts of peace, and not of evil, to give you an expected end." She must trust God's intentions, not her own.

Elizabeth Rathbone herself greeted Dorothea when the ship arrived. "Goodness, you look wonderful! You haven't aged a day." Her voice and her head shook a little, and Dorothea recognized it as the palsy that comes with age.

Dorothea bent to kiss the woman on either cheek and waved good-bye to a few of the passengers with whom she had spent time on board ship. To Elizabeth she said, "It has been almost twenty years."

"And, oh, how you've done so much in that time. We are all so proud of you."

"But . . . I failed."

Elizabeth patted her hand. "You have letters

awaiting you from a Dix family. And the American minister to London during the administration of your friend Mr. Fillmore has sent a letter of introduction to the Earl of Shaftesbury on your behalf."

"The Earl of Shaftesbury? Isn't he the head of the national Commission in Lunacy?"

"Every county in England and Wales has a mental hospital because of him. You'll have things to talk about." She laced her elbow through Dorothea's. "Oh, I know you came to rest. And you shall, you shall. But it is also time you took in the celebration."

"Celebration? For what?"

"For the work you've done your entire life."

Elizabeth stepped up into the carriage but waited while the workers loaded Dorothea's trunks from the dock. Sea gulls dipped above them. "We can't celebrate failure," Dorothea said.

"You brought incredible changes for the mentally ill, Dolly. Your national land bill didn't go through, but you cannot discount what you did accomplish. Nearly every one of your colonies, I mean states, now has a hospital because of you. Patients formerly locked up in cellars have a home and treatment. I cannot begin to imagine the suffering you've relieved."

"It's just that I was sure God wanted me to do the congressional work. Certain of it. And yet I failed. I was not enough to make it happen."

Elizabeth laughed. "You are the elder brother to the prodigal."

Dorothea turned to look at Elizabeth's round face framed by her winsome yellow bonnet.

"Don't look so surprised. The older brother did everything asked of him, was faithful to his father and obedient. He knew it wasn't works but grace that saved him. Yet he never opened his arms, never celebrated the way the younger son did on his return." She leaned toward Dorothea. "Not because he did not deserve that father's open arms or because the father didn't want to reach out to him; he did! The elder brother just never thought he'd done enough to deserve that loving embrace. That's you, Dolly."

"But—"

"You did everything you could." She patted Dorothea's hand. "God asks nothing more—nor less."

"Am I finished with my life's work then?"

"Of course not. You'll always be working for those who suffer. It's who you are. But you can also secure the blessings for what you've already done. Come now. We have a gathering prepared for you, and then, tomorrow, you'll meet the earl. Who knows where that acquaintance will take you?"

Thirty-Six

Acceptance and Reward

The long, winding driveway to the Greenbank estate brought tears to Dorothea's eyes. "You know I suggested the drive design toward the Trenton hospital with this lovely road in mind. Trees to pass by. Planted areas. A clear pond with swans. Then this." She spread her arms before them as the carriage stopped and she stepped outside, the cobbled stones smooth against her thin leather soles. "This incredible building that speaks of comfort, safety, and home."

"So it shall be for as long as you like. I'm so pleased you accepted our invitation. Come along. William awaits with guests."

"Guests?" Dorothea held back.

"Only a small reception."

Although Dorothea was weary from the long journey, neighbors and guests she had met long ago all greeted her like a long-lost relative returning home. None were critical of her colossal failure with Congress, and their unconditional acceptance was a salve relieving a terrible bruise. She told stories then of the voyage and even began to speak of the nuances of American government, making light of her buttonhooking and how, in the end, it had not helped.

"What will you do now?" one of the guests asked.

"She doesn't have to achieve anything," Elizabeth Rathbone answered, "except discover how to receive."

"She's not finished." William Rathbone winked at Dorothea, his white eyebrows wiggling like tufts of cotton above clear blue eyes. "When she was with us before, so ill, remember? Even then she continued to work. I had to remove her writing materials from her."

They reminisced then. For Dorothea, this was a safe place, the perfect choice for her at this moment in her life. When people grieved or suffered, they needed a place of respite. She would rest and then see what bridges appeared on the horizon.

Scotland spread its arms in the spring with the blessing if not the authority of the Earl of Shaftesbury. He asked her to use her considerable experience and gifted writing to survey conditions in Scotland and report to him.

She found the air of Aberdeen and Glasgow bracing as she visited the royal asylums, writing to Anne that while she thought the American facilities equal if not superior, she did appreciate that the country had rid itself of coercive treatments and responded to people with dignity and compassion.

"If you would, please, I should like to see a private home facility in this area." They were in the center of Edinburgh, not far from Andrew Square on a glorious sunshiny day. Dorothea could smell the sea from where they left the eatery, having just had a meal wrapped inside a pastry that Dorothea declared "bonny."

The men she traveled with exchanged glances at her request. "That's much more difficult to entertain, milady."

"I understand. But I would be remiss if I overlooked your large system of home care. It is a worry, you must know, that such care is not supervised by physicians. A necessity in my view."

"Yes, and why you want national asylums," one of her companions said.

"As do you. Am I correct?"

He nodded. "But not all share our opinion."

"You wouldn't be a Scotsman if you agreed on everything."

The men exchanged what Dorothea took for English spoken with rapidity and brogue. She could not decipher what they said. The spokesperson was a man with a mustache that flowed like white streams on either side of his wide mouth, forming a pool in a goatee at his chin. "We'll need to go to the other side of the city."

"Nonsense. Just take me to the home closest to here. I won't stay long, and I won't be intrusive. I've done this before, gentlemen. In Kentucky and Mississippi and all across the United States."

The two men spoke again, with the spokesman sighing. "Very well. There is one off Thistle."

"Then let's have at it."

Dorothea thought she could stay in this tidy city with the smell of the sea always in the air. The Scots' commitment to learning and religion soared above the streets in castle-like spires of the universities and churches. The women she'd met spoke their minds and the men didn't seem to object but rather grinned in admiration. Yes, she could find a place here if she could convince the naysayers that she wasn't intruding but rather helping them. She pulled her cape closer around herself against the cool February air and ignored the scent of garlic emanating from her companions' wool vests. They stopped before an industrial-looking building.

"The night watchman lives on site," she was told, "and cares for a young insane person."

Dorothea knocked at the heavy door. After a second knock she was greeted by a small man with rheumy eyes whose hair was mussed as though they had awakened him from a sleep, though it was near one in the afternoon.

"The superintendent of the Royal Lunatic Asylum has asked that our American visitor take a look at the conditions of your patient," her spokesman said.

"At this hour of the day?"

"Yes, now." He used his cane to push his way through the partially opened door.

Inside, the air smelled of old onions and dread.

"If you'd come ba' later I'd have tea for ye," the watchman said. A small table, two chairs, and a bed furnished the room. A picture of the sea in storm hung on the wall.

"Not necessary. Just wish to note the conditions for your patient."

"It's not easy," the watchman began. "Strange little beast that he is." He was wringing his hands now. "You have to understand, I get very little for his keep."

"Just take us to his room."

The watchman's eyes darted toward a door. Dorothea moved to it and opened it as the watchman cried, "You should let me go in first!"

Her eyes adjusted to the darkened space that might have held potatoes and sacks of grains. Inside a small figure hovered in the corner. He wore a dirty canvas jacket of straps and buckles. The boy couldn't be much older than five or six, and his eyes were filled with anger that flashed to fright. A mattress on the floor and a pot for waste sat a distance from him.

Dorothea's heart began to throb in her temples

as the suffering of this child bridged the emptiness in her heart.

"Remove the jacket." Her voice was calm but firm.

"I don't think that's a good—"

"Please. Remove the buckles." To the boy, she said, "We've come to see how you fare here. We'll not hurt you. You've been hurt enough."

"He don't understand anything. He'll be wild if I release him."

"He's wild because you don't release him. What is his name, please?"

"Charles Denton."

He was close to the same age as Charles when Dorothea had told him to wait and she would bring rescue to him when she ran away to Orange Court. She had not rescued her brother then. She would not let this Charles go without relief.

"Bring me a chair." One of her companions did. She sat. "I'll wait here. These men will remove your restraints. Then we'll talk."

With great reluctance the watchman and one of her companions unbuckled the straps and chains. When they did, the boy leaped across the room like a chimpanzee and wrapped his skinny legs around Dorothea's waist while he grabbed at her bonnet and her hair. She was thrown back against the chair when the men rushed forward, pulling at the slender child dressed in a dirty nightshirt.

"Get back!" Dorothea told them as she grabbed

the boy's hands in her own and held them between hers, hands to chest. He tried to bang his head against hers, but she bobbed, then pushed her head into his forehead, the pressure halting him. Still holding his hands in fists between them, she spoke in a voice as soothing as a pigeon settling for the night in the belfry of an Edinburgh church.

"Shoo, shoo, shoo, Charles. Shoo, shoo. I will not harm you. I come to bring relief, yes? I am going to move my head away from yours so I can see you, Charles." He tightened his legs around her waist. "You may sit on my lap just as you are. If you understand, blink your eyes."

He lifted his head, and for a moment she thought he would bang his forehead into hers. Instead, he blinked once.

She nearly cried for the look of anguish that filled this small child's face. No one deserved such suffering, least of all a child. His mouth hung open, with his tongue limp across his lower lip.

"We will find clean clothes for you, Charles. Would you like that? Just blink if you wish to say yes . . . Good. And make it safer for you. Would you like that too?" He blinked again. "Until then, your . . . caregiver will offer you more food—"

"I can't—"

"I will pay for it myself. And bring him a music box to listen to. And a toy. Perhaps a carved horse. Would you like that?"

Charles blinked.

"I am going to touch your tongue now, to remind you to pull it back in. It is the polite way to be with others. Is that all right?"

He blinked.

"He'll bite!"

She released his hands and brought her finger to his tongue. The moisture and sponge of it and his acceptance of her touch brought tears to her eyes.

He swallowed, pulled his tongue back and closed his lips.

"I want to brush the hair from your eyes, Charles, so I may see you better. May I?"

He blinked.

She removed her gloves and touched his face with her warm fingers, tugging the hair behind his ears. He leaned like a small dog into her hand so the back of her palm would caress his cheek.

"We will make things better, Charles. I make that promise. I must go now. But I will come back."

He blinked and again his tongue lolled forward, but he released his grip around her. She helped him stand, wobbly as a new colt.

"Keep him locked in if you must, but give him things to do to keep his mind open. He understands though he may not speak. You must treat him like the boy he is. It is the moral way to be."

Dorothea touched her own tongue then, and the boy responded by pulling his back into his mouth and swallowing. "Yes. You learn well. Be brave. I will be back."

Dorothea gave the watchman additional coins and assured him that she would return. "I see how much he needs, and you simply don't receive enough to tend him well, try as you might."

"Aye, try as I might."

"What will you do, Miss Dix?" her companion asked when they left.

"I shall head a campaign to put all such people under the care of a Home Secretary–appointed commission on lunacy that can oversee asylums, public and private, and home care that is supervised by a physician. As England and Wales has. That child has promise."

"But you're an American. We must make this happen through our sources."

"True. And why haven't you?" *If it is to be, it begins with thee.* "We will do this together, gentlemen, but I will see it accomplished before I leave the Continent." She could feel her old energy returning with an important purpose laid out, led by the needs of a child.

She prepared a petition to the English government that day, insisting that only a system with physicians in charge, with asylums for those relieved of their reason, both private and public, with proper national oversight, would prevent the lifelong suffering of children like Charles or the others she had seen in private care. It was as though they were imprisoned for their mental condition, then left to languish until they died.

Two breathless supporters stopped at her rooms in Edinburgh less than a week later, while she finished her report for the earl.

"Miss Dix, a member of Parliament has heard of your survey, and he's going to present a petition tomorrow to the assembly that will denounce your work and what we want to accomplish."

"Tomorrow? In London? Well, I must go there."

"There's no time, milady. The stage's already left for London town."

"Is there no other way?"

"The mail train is all. They don't usually carry passengers, especially not ladies."

"See if you can get me on it. I'll leave at once. Rather, as soon as I telegraph Shaftesbury and ask for a meeting with his Scottish counterpart. Hurry! Send the telegram while I pack a bag."

She traveled through the night, her first-ever visit to London and her first-ever meeting with the Duke of Argyll, where she would press her petition and hope to thwart the powers that be from leaving Charles and others to languish without a voice.

She sat beside mailbags, the feather on her hat weaving and bobbing to the rhythm of the train clacking on the tracks. She dozed and once woke surprised at where she was, nestled among canvas in a darkened car. What would her grandmother say about her granddaughter without a dowry now riding between sacks of missives? She hadn't needed a dowry. She had married her ambition to relieve suffering, and like any marriage, she imagined, there were bumps and bounces in the road. But if she could bring humanity to the Charleses of Scotland—or even beyond—she would believe she had done enough.

She arrived in the early morning in London without an opportunity to refresh herself. More disheveled than she preferred, she curtsied to the earl while gushing her admiration for his work. Then they crossed a cobbled courtyard to meet the Duke of Argyll. The stately man listened and nodded. The earl interjected his support. When she finished, unlike President Pierce, the duke assured her that he understood and agreed with her concerns for Charles and others like him in Scotland.

"We will make this happen," he said, "and be forever grateful that you have raised the importance. We Scots salute you."

"Thank you, your lordship. Thank you."

She stepped out into the smog of London and coughed, but not because she suspected an illness was coming on. She had never felt stronger nor more completed in a task. She spotted a mercantile with children's toys in the window and went inside the musty establishment, where she purchased a music box and a toy boat. On second thought, she bought a harmonica. All for Charles. She would return to Scotland and cajole and charm the supporters into finding a better place for the boy until the duke could make good on his promise. Great transformations took time, but the care of each little one could not wait. She would intervene as she could, as she had her entire life, sometimes winning, sometimes failing, but doing what she was called to do. She would relieve the suffering of others and thus relieve her own. She would do that one Charles at a time.

That night she wrote to Anne: "I shall see their chains off. I shall take them into the green fields and show them the lovely little flowers and the blue sky, and they shall play with the lambs and listen to the song of the birds and 'a little child shall lead them.' "

Epilogue

1869

"I think I have everything essential, though what one takes to the West I hardly know for certain." Dorothea surveyed her trunk in the middle of the living room in the Trenton apartment.

A nurse helped her pack and scanned the room

and her bookshelves. "You haven't taken every-thing," she laughed.

"No. I'll be back. This is home." She would leave behind mementos from her trips, the little boat returned to her when Charles the Scot died in his sleep at the asylum he had been moved into as a boy. If only Charles had had more time in safety. Dorothea sighed. The commission to oversee all aspects of Scottish care, including those in home care, had made such a difference to many relieved of their reason. She had helped. A seashell graced the bookcase, smaller than her St. Croix one, from the Channel Islands where she had brought reform. A carved box from Germany. She wasn't sure where she had put the shawl she had bought in France, but the lace from Holland she planned to give as a gift. From Italy she had a coin as a remembrance of her audience with Pope Pius IX where she had said, "Six thousand priests, three hundred monks, three thousand nuns, and a spiritual sovereign with temporal power has not assured for the miserable insane a decent much less intelligent care." The pope had heard her. Things had changed in Italy; she had kept track. The same for Turkey and Russia. From England she had taken a cutting from a yew tree planted at the grave of her favorite poet, Thomas Gray. She had planted it outside the Trenton hospital. "Be sure that the yew tree gets watered."

"I will."

"Don't forget." Was she getting cranky in her old age? She softened her tone. "What should I bring back from California and the Oregon and Washington Territories?"

"You'll bring back good news. There's been so much progress since your early surveys before the war."

Yes. The war, the terrible war that banished slavery from the land and on both sides saw suffering beyond anyone's imagination. It would be good to be in the West without the ravages of great cities or daily seeing the veterans with their amputations and unseen wounds. She had served as head of nursing during the war but had not enjoyed it. Dealing with doctors who did not think women could relieve suffering was worse than working with legislators. She needed a new trip where she would visit with a former student in Oregon and see the Hawthorne hospital her student said was a model of moral treatment.

"I guess I'm ready," she said. "Have them come for my trunk." She took the leash hanging at the back of the writing desk chair and clipped it to her spaniel's collar. "Ready, Precious?" A benefit of not traveling quite so much was keeping a pet. What a joy the dog was. The patients loved her too.

Dorothea, cane in hand, and Precious walked down three levels of steps. Dorothea's sixty-seven years were beginning to wear on her knees. But she was invigorated by the idea of a journey across a vast continent. She would see new fields, new mountains, new towns, new rivers, and at the end, visit with old friends. These were her dowry, the one she never needed: the riches of the land, her students, this small dog, and improving the lives of those who needed her most.

"Just remember to open your arms, Dolly, and learn to receive as well as achieve," Elizabeth Rathbone had whispered in her ear when she had left England thirteen years before. "You are cherished by many and I believe by God Himself for all you've done in this world to speak for those without a voice. You have been enough."

She prayed that it was so.

"Now to see what is left to do, Precious." She lifted the dog, tossed her cane into the stage, then stepped up to begin yet another journey on her purposeful life.

Readers Guide

1. Dorothea Dix had great talent, which was demonstrated through her success as a writer, teacher, and reformer. What social norms of the time prevented her from using these talents in a more public way to bring about the changes she sought? Do any of these restrictions exist today?

2. The author suggests that Dorothea's mother was "unavailable" and that her father was abusive and unreliable. How did these parental responses to life's challenges affect Dorothea? Were there options she could have chosen to improve her life and the life of her brothers that she didn't choose?

3. Dorothea and her colleagues had a conversation about whether asylums kept society safe from the mentally ill or whether the mentally ill needed protection from society. What are your thoughts about this? Is treatment part of the social contract? Do we have to look after those less fortunate? How well are we addressing the needs of the mentally ill today?

4. The great novelist Willa Cather wrote that the "most basic material a writer works with is acquired before the age of fifteen." I think as readers we're attracted to stories that derive from that period of our own lives. Perhaps that's why children and young adult novels can be as compelling as adult works. Cather, a Pulitzer Prize winner, also suggested that the two great emotions that drive such stories are "passion and betrayal." I would add "acceptance and forgiveness," that those are the emotions we connect with inside stories. What betrayals did Dorothea experience? How did she respond to these betrayals? Were her responses healthy? What were her passions? What was her greatest ambition? Did she seek acceptance? forgiveness? How were those journeys portrayed?

5. What role did children play in the life of Dorothea Dix? How might Dorothea's life have been different if she had been able to adopt Marianna Cutter or live with her or have her brothers at Orange Court? Would you say Dorothea was a good steward of her pain? Why or why not?

6. Dorothea initially did not support the abolition of slavery and believed that women's suffrage was a waste of time. Does a social

reformer need to be so focused on one avenue only? What other true believers come to mind in bringing about social change? How would their personalities differ or be similar to Dorothea's?

7. The Rathbones were Quakers. Dorothea had friends that were pastors and Harvard Divinity School students. What role did faith play in Dorothea's life as an activist? Would you agree with Elizabeth Rathbone's view that Dorothea was much like the older brother in the story of the prodigal son who struggled with how to receive the love of the father? Why or why not?

8. Dorothea's land bill failed at a time of debate over the role of the federal government and states' rights. President Franklin Pierce vetoed the bill on the basis that the federal government only had a role in the states if the law enhanced economic development within the states. Did such an argument change after the Civil War? Does this argument resonate today? Could Dorothea get her national charity bill passed today? Why or why not?

9. Where was Dorothea most at home? Who was her family? Why do you think Dorothea resisted the social requirements related to

marriage? What choices did a woman of the 1830s have to be independent? Could she have married and still been an activist?

10. Were you ever called as Dorothea was to act courageously to make a difference in the lives of others? How did you respond? Is that door still open? What would it take for you to walk through it?

Author Interview

The tapestry of history has no point
in which you can cut it
and leave the design intelligible.
—DOROTHEA DIX

Question: What drew you to this story of reformer Dorothea Dix?

Answer: When I was seven I sat in a church pew in a rural Wisconsin town. While we waited for the service to start, a girl with a waddle walk and unusual facial features sauntered in with her mother and thumped onto the pew beside my mom. I'd never seen a child with such a broad forehead, with gums that seemed to swallow her teeth, and eyes narrow and darting from side to side. She swung her feet and wiggled and made grunting sounds that her mother shushed to no avail. Her arms danced without music. As the choir sang, the girl calmed and stared, but when the pastor spoke in our Methodist church, she again kicked and wiggled. My mom put her arm around the girl and pulled her to her side. She patted her shoulder and gave the girl a pad and pencils. She scribbled and entertained herself throughout the rest of the service, with my mom—a nurse—holding her in comfort to her side. Later, when the girl's mother thanked my mom, I could see relief in the mother's eyes that they had sat beside someone who took the girl in rather than moved farther away. I asked what was wrong with her, and my mom said she had seizures and other problems and hadn't been able to go to school. She'd been in an institution, but her parents had wanted to bring her home, despite people's saying they should just leave her where she had been since she was a baby. She didn't talk. When I learned a few years later that she had died, I remember feeling great sadness though I didn't really know her; I never had. That encounter drew me later into my profession and this story.

Q: You're a mental health professional, right, with a master's degree in psychiatric social work? What has been your experience in mental health treatment?

A: My undergraduate degree is in communications and public address. Later, I worked in public welfare with families and realized I needed more training to help those who were mentally ill. After graduate school I came to Oregon and worked in the disabilities field, eventually becoming the director of a mental health clinic. Still later I worked with young children as an educational and mental health consultant on the Warm Springs Indian Reservation, where my work was a blend of administration and direct treatment. I did that for seventeen years before turning my healing hopes to stories. The lives of those I met in institutions and in their homes were with me in the writing of this book, as were those who came into our clinic day-treatment facilities seeking help to manage their lives of mental and emotional confusion and the suffering of friends and families that often resulted from the mental illness of those they loved. Law enforcement, hospital emergency rooms, jailers, and mental health workers are all a part of my experience and this story.

Q: What resources were most helpful in your research for *One Glorious Ambition*?

A: Biographers David Gollaher *(Voice for the Mad: The Life of Dorothea Dix)*, Margaret Muckenhoupt *(Dorothea Dix: Advocate for Mental Health Care)*, and Thomas J. Brown *(Dorothea Dix: New England Reformer)* led me to know Dorothea as more than a reformer. She struggled with her social role in a time when women were not allowed a place in public life without risking their reputation and possible loss of their femininity. Her fractured relationships recounted through letters kept by her many correspondents also brought insights about her work and her faith. Conversations with award-winning film director and screenwriter Charles Kiselyak helped crystallize those qualities of her character that I most wanted to emphasize: her passion and devotion, and her longing for family. Dwight Sweezy, retired chaplain at the Trenton Psychiatric Hospital in New Jersey, provided the buttonhook story as well as an awareness of the role of the many women in Dorothea's life and how they challenged and supported her. The real inspiration goes to Dr. Dean Brooks, former superintendent of the Oregon State Hospital, who many years ago told me that I needed to novelize Dorothea's story to bring to light that more than one hundred fifty years later we still struggle as a nation with the care of the mentally ill. Now in his nineties, Dr. Brooks continues to work out his passion for the mentally ill. He has transferred this legacy to his family members. Dennie (a social worker), India (a community health advocate), Ulista (a psychiatrist), and their families carry light into the next generation that we might find a way to truly make a difference in the lives of others. Dr. Brooks continues to promote changes in the system of care and to bring the stories of the mentally ill to the public in compassionate ways. He was a primary influence in the filming of *One Flew over the Cuckoo's Nest* at the Oregon State Hospital. I'm grateful that he also encouraged award-winning filmmaker

Charles Kiselyak to write a screenplay blending both Dorothea's past and the current challenges for those needing mental health services. Dr. Brooks and his children were instrumental in creating a mental health museum in Salem, Oregon, as part of the state mental hospital where Dorothea's work as both a mental health reformer and a teacher are honored. A bust of her by renowned sculptor John Houser of Santa Fe is there honoring Dorothea's life as well.

Q: What happened in Dorothea's later life? You allude to her work during the Civil War. What did she do there?

A: After her successes in Scotland and Europe, Dorothea returned to the United States in 1856 and involved herself in the construction of two new asylums and then spent time in Pennsylvania, raising funds for a school for mentally impaired children. With the outbreak of the Civil War, Dorothea turned her desire to relieve suffering to those with battlefield injuries. While she was named the head of nurses and had a military pass from President Lincoln directing "all persons in official charge of Hospitals, to render at all times every facility to Miss D. L. Dix," her tendency to strong opinions got in her way. I found one notation in which Dorothea cared for a volunteer nurse named Louisa May Alcott, and then she insisted the young nurse get away from the sicknesses that pervaded army hospitals. Fortunately for readers, Miss Alcott did. Historians note that Dorothea was never accepted nor appreciated by military physicians—or nurses—for her efforts as a supervising nurse.

At the close of the war, Dorothea again surveyed the asylums in the South to attest to the damages done to their facilities. It's reported that she was well received in the South, and as a result, she learned of and helped thwart an assassination attempt on Lincoln's life. After his election and before his inauguration, Dorothea shared what she knew with a railroad president about a Southern plan to cut off railroad access by Union soldiers in Washington DC, to take Lincoln's life and name the new Confederacy as the federal government. The administration was sufficiently alarmed by the details Dorothea confided that Alan Pinkerton was dispatched to determine the strength of the conspiracy. Upon his recommendation, the planned route for Lincoln to arrive into Washington for his inauguration was changed. She refused any public recognition for this effort, but perhaps she redeemed herself, as she pursued justice for the mentally ill, within her circle of abolitionist friends who thought she had closed her eyes to slavery. Dorothea also offered nursing support when she learned of the illnesses of the Lincolns' children. The offer was declined, but following

Willie's death, the Lincolns did request her recommendation for young Tad that he might not succumb to the same illness as Willie. Dorothea readily complied. One wonders, too, if she did not have a special affinity to Mary Todd Lincoln's emotional state as there is evidence that Dorothea's mother and Mrs. Lincoln suffered from similar severe emotional distresses. Her relationships with the Lincolns could be a novel by itself!

In the late 1860s, while in her sixties, Dorothea initiated yet another tour of facilities, these in Washington, Oregon, and California. She visited a former student in Oregon (whose name we do not know but who was identified in this novel as Shelley Mason). Dorothea sent books ahead "to a former student." While in the Northwest, she visited the private hospital for the insane operated by James Hawthorne, who had also contracted with the state of Oregon to provide care. She proclaimed it a worthy hospital. It appears she never stopped working, never stopped caring about those less fortunate than herself, never stopped relieving the suffering of many.

Q: Were Dorothea's family relationships as estranged as you have portrayed them here?

A: Her biographers refer to her mother as "unavailable." I wondered if this distance was possibly a result of postpartum depression or mental illness. Whatever the reason, Dorothea referred to herself in her letters as an orphan even while both her parents still lived. Her efforts to adopt Marianna Cutter were thwarted much as I conveyed in this story. Her close friendship with Anne Heath, which eventually became estranged, was an important relationship in her life. She was closer to her brother Charles than to her brother Joseph, who indeed never paid back any of his loans. She adored William Ellery Channing and George Emerson and saw them as father figures. She did have a close relationship with Millard Fillmore as well and his family, and letters kept by him from her suggest that there might have been a promise of more than friendship. But Fillmore married a wealthy young widow in 1858, and Dorothea appears to have rejoiced with him. Her former students were her closest allies, as were Elizabeth and William Rathbone, who truly rescued her from what appears to be depression and likely death by tuberculosis when she first came to them at Greenbank. Dorothea maintained correspondence with more than seven hundred individuals, so she had an active writing life, yet none of those did she claim as family. I think the mentally ill were her family.

Q: Dorothea was a successful teacher at fifteen and a royalty-earning author at twenty. Why wasn't that enough?

A: You'd think it would be! She attributes her calling to the day at East Cambridge prison. That she was able to bring heat into those cells, she wrote, was one of her greatest accomplishments. She also wrote that convincing Cyrus Butler to establish the fund for the hospital named for him (which still stands in Rhode Island) was one of the great successes of her life. She sought a life of purpose, and I think she didn't find it until that day in East Cambridge. She was rarely ill after that, despite long hours, difficult travel, and persevering in the halls of Congress, nor even later when she worked as a nurse during the Civil War.

Q: What surprised you about Dorothea during your research?

A: Her generosity. She performed all the state surveys at her own expense, for example. She funded a rescue fleet for the Sable Islands of Nova Scotia. She had a water fountain for horses commissioned for the city of Boston. When she died, she left five hundred dollars to the Humane Society, yet we have no evidence that she ever owned a pet. She did indeed buy a life insurance policy with the New Jersey State Hospital at Trenton as the beneficiary. She gave hundreds of music boxes to jails and asylums and really did find prints that she had framed and sent to asylums for patients' rooms. She spent hundreds of dollars on bandages and medicines during the Civil War. Her royalties and frugal life, along with what her grandmother left her from the sale of Orange Court, sustained her. She gave much of it away.

I was also surprised to learn that she spent the latter part of her life as a resident in the apartment in the Trenton hospital. A small museum is maintained in her honor there, and a yew tree she planted to commemorate the poet Thomas Gray still flourishes. She died in that third-floor apartment on July 17, 1887, at the age of eighty-two. She is buried in Mount Auburn Cemetery in Cambridge, Massachusetts.

It also surprised me that she spurned public attention, though she shouldn't have, given the limitations placed on women of her time. She turned down possible book reviews and articles that might have expanded her cause because the articles would be about her as well. She rejected a bronze bust planned by supporters in Tennessee. She started but never finished an autobiography. I think she never accepted herself as worthy, still the young child who ran away from home, hoping to protect her brother and failing. As with many passionate true believers, her failures weighed more heavily on her than all her successes.

Q: What's happening in mental health today? Would Dorothea recognize the system of care?

A: According to the World Health Organization, 450 million people suffer from mental disorders; many more have mental problems that interfere with their daily lives. Mental health is defined as "a state of well-being in which an individual realizes his or her own abilities, can cope with the normal stresses of life, can work productively and is able to make a contribution to his or her community. In this positive sense, mental health is the foundation for individual well-being and the effective functioning of a community."

In 2008, the most recent year for which comprehensive statistics are available from the Centers for Disease Control and Prevention, it's estimated that 58.7 percent of adults in the United States received mental health treatment, mostly in outpatient settings with medication. A smaller percentage was served in institutional settings. The most recent Department of Justice's Survey of Inmates in State and Federal Correctional Facilities and Survey of Inmates in Local Jails also indicate that fewer than half of inmates who have mental health issues have ever received treatment for their problem. A third or fewer received mental health treatment after admission. Currently it's estimated that one-quarter to one-third of those without insurance suffer from mental or substance abuse disorders. A fractured care system leaves many people needing treatment but unable to find it. Many of these people make poor choices that result in their incarceration. Dorothea located mentally ill persons in the debtors' prisons or almshouses. Today, we don't have such institutions, but we do incarcerate people at a significant rate, and many of those people desperately need mental health services. Today, most services are provided in overburdened community mental health programs rather than public or private institutions.

Crazy: A Father's Search Through America's Mental Health Madness is a must read. Written by award-winning journalist Pete Earley, it not only looks at contemporary mental health–system needs but is also a compassionate account of a family's struggle with a son who is mentally ill. Dorothea would have loved to know that there is a National Alliance on Mental Illness (www.nami.org) where families support each other and work together with professionals to bring about needed changes within the mental health care system.

Dorothea hoped that by placing people in institutions, better treatment would reach them and they would be protected from the insults of society. She was not concerned with the *cause* but rather the *care*. Her work drew many from the cellars and back rooms out into a life richer than they had ever known. She was compelled to this work by her faith and her belief that what we do for the least of these, we do for our Lord.

Her concerns about how to fund and sustain institutions continue in our contemporary world. Privacy and rights laws often affect access to treatment for individuals, unless they are dangerous to themselves or others. Medication can improve functioning, but it can also lead patients to feel no need for treatment, and without good follow-up support, individuals often stop taking medication. This aspect of treatment creates chronic chaos for patients, their families, and treatment providers, as well as for law enforcement. These issues continue to dominate the discussion among mental health and correctional programs today. New voices, new reformers like Dorothea Dix, are needed, as are volunteers across all settings. Dorothea, I think, would urge people to contact a local mental health clinic and offer to volunteer or be willing to share with state and federal legislators their own experiences of when they needed help and how they got it.

Q: What do you hope readers will take away from this story?

A: I hope readers will see how significant one person can be in relieving the suffering of many. I hope Dorothea's story inspires other present-day reformers. I also think Dorothea had a difficult time believing that she was enough. I know so many hard-working people who are compassionate.

They give to their community. They are motivated by family and faith. And I consider them all remarkable for all they do. Yet many of them do not see that in themselves. For them, I hope reading Dorothea's story will remind them to accept the open arms of those who cherish all they do, even when their grand idea or glorious ambition does not bring about their desired hopes. I also hope that readers might see the wisdom in Dorothea's belief that relieving the suffering of others helped to relieve her own.

Acknowledgments

My thanks to WaterBrook Multnomah Publishing Group from their president, Steve Cobb, to editorial and especially editors Shannon Marchese, Ed Curtis, and Laura Wright, to the marketing, publicity, and sales staff, for their professionalism and care in allowing me to tell these stories and place them in the hands of readers; agent Joyce Hart of Hartline Literary for standing beside me all these years; my family, especially Jerry who puts up with my angst; and my many friends, prayer partners. I also thank readers, who tell me they await my next book and the discovery of yet another fascinating story of remarkable women stepping from one generation to our own to teach us and touch us with their lives. And thanks to all the mental health mentors I've had in my life—professors, staff, and patients—who chose to make a difference and showed me how I might do that too. Thank you for being a part of this story.

Thank you for reading this story. If you care to leave a comment—and I would love to hear from you—go to:

www.jkbooks.com
www.facebook.com/theauthorjanekirkpatrick
www.twitter.com/janekirkpatrick
www.pinterest.com/janekirkpatrick.

You may also sign up for my monthly *Story Sparks* newsletter at www.jkbooks.com. If my schedule allows, I often meet with book groups by phone or Skype to discuss my books. I'd love to hear how you've made room in your lives for these stories.

Warmly,
Jane Kirkpatrick

Center Point Large Print

600 Brooks Road / PO Box 1
Thorndike ME 04986-0001 USA

(207) 568-3717

US & Canada:
1 800 929-9108
www.centerpointlargeprint.com